"What a gorgeous man,"

said Bolivia. "How about fixing me up with your client?"

Anne felt the tiniest bit of jealousy. "He's off-limits, Bolivia, at least until the trial's over."

Bolivia grinned at her. "And after the trial it's open season on Jack Quintana?"

"After the trial it's every woman for herself," retorted Anne, wondering where that had come from. It wasn't exactly that she was interested in him, but she sure as hell didn't want her friend to be. That didn't seem fair, but things never seemed fair when it came to men. Not that she would actually fight a friend over a man. Nor would it ever come down to that, because she wasn't the least bit interested in Jack Quintana.

But for the first time she admitted the possibility that she could be.

Dear Reader:

As usual, we've gathered the cream of the crop for you this month in Silhouette Intimate Moments. Start off with Beverly Sommers and the first book in a terrific new trilogy, "Friends for Life." In *Accused* she tells the story of Jack Quintana, a man accused of a murder he didn't commit. His defender is Anne Larkin, a woman whose memories of Jack are less than fond. As they work together to clear his name, however, they discover that love isn't necessarily the most logical of emotions. In the next two months, look for *Betrayed* and *Corrupted*, the stories of Anne's friends Bolivia and Sandy. These three really are *friends for life*.

Also this month, Heather Graham Pozzessere returns with *A Perilous Eden*, a story of terror on the high seas and passion under the hot Caribbean sun. It's an adventure not to be missed. Lee Magner brings you *Sutter's Wife*, the story of a make-believe marriage that quickly becomes the real thing. Finish the month with new author Dee Holmes and *Black Horse Island*, a stunning debut performance from a writer to watch.

In coming months, look for new books by Emilie Richards, Barbara Faith, Marilyn Pappano and Jennifer Greene, not to mention fall treats from, among others, Linda Howard, Kathleen Korbel and Patricia Gardner Evans. Something great is always happening at Silhouette Intimate Moments.

Leslie J. Wainger
Senior Editor

Accused

BEVERLY SOMMERS

Silhouette Intimate Moments

Published by Silhouette Books New York

America's Publisher of Contemporary Romance

 SILHOUETTE BOOKS
300 East 42nd St., New York, N.Y. 10017

ISBN: 0-373-07325-9

First Silhouette Books printing March 1990

Printed in the U.S.A.

Books by Beverly Sommers

Silhouette Intimate Moments

Reason to Believe #164
Accused #325

BEVERLY SOMMERS

grew up in Evanston, Illinois, and went on to college in California, graduating with a degree in English. Subsequently she has studied law, taught fifth grade, been a counselor in Juvenile Hall and owned an art gallery. She has lived in Spain and Greece and currently makes her home in California.

Chapter 1

Jack Quintana's first reaction when Marissa disappeared was one of relief.

But that was before reality set in.

At first he didn't even know she was gone. He got home from the university late in the afternoon on Wednesday. He pulled into the driveway in front of the two-story pink stucco house with the red-tile roof, and left the motor running while he got out of the car. When he lifted the garage door to put his car away he saw that her car was there, but when he entered the house through the door that connected the garage to the laundry room, calling out to her and getting no answer, he assumed she was out. Since their house was in walking distance of the shops in Coral Gables, and since Marissa liked to shop, he put two and two together and then didn't give it a second thought. To Marissa, a credit card that hadn't been used to its limit was a wasted opportunity.

It was spring, and the good weather was still holding, so instead of shutting himself up in his den to work on an article he was preparing for the *Harvard Law Review*, he disposed of his jacket and tie before carrying his work out to the patio, along with a cold bottle of lager. He had put on the radio and tuned to a classical music station before he came out, and now the sounds of the London Philharmonic escaped through the French doors and paused briefly before being carried away by the wind.

The setting was peaceful and always pleased him. Beyond the brick patio were a stretch of lawn leading to a retaining wall and steps that went down to a private dock on a wide canal that led to the bay. Most of his neighbors had boats moored at their docks, but Quintana didn't have a boat. Marissa didn't like boats, and Quintana's salary and the royalties from his hornbook and casebook, while covering the rather inflated mortgage payment on the house, didn't quite extend to yachts. While Marissa liked living by the water, she refused to go into it or even onto it. While not wont to daydream, there had been occasions since Marissa moved in with him when Quintana had pictured himself out on the water in a small boat and away from her constant quarreling.

One day he'd have a boat. Not yet, but one day.

The article he was writing was on Maritime Law, one of his particular interests, concerning oil tankers and spills, and he became so engrossed in it that it was only when the light had faded to the point where he couldn't see to write that he finally put down the pencil and legal pad and looked toward the house. No light showed from within.

A better indication that she wasn't home yet was the music. It was a spirited tune, something by Ravel, and the very sound of it seemed to lighten the air. Turning off the radio would have been Marissa's first action upon returning home. She claimed music gave her a headache.

Quintana moved inside to work, not minding a delayed dinner. Dinners with Marissa were usually difficult. Innocuous statements on his part, misinterpreted by her and blown out of proportion, often resulted in heated arguments.

He didn't mind a good argument. He actually thrived on good arguments, and when he found the rare student who could hold his own in an argument with him, that student usually ended up with an A for the course. Arguing with Marissa, however, was arguing with someone who not only consistently failed in logical polemic, but who, moreover, took everything, despite the subject, personally. And then grew shrill and yelled and often cried for no discernible reason. And since Quintana kept his own emotions very far below the surface, he didn't quite know how to handle someone whose emotions always hovered right on the surface and threatened to explode without warning.

Last night was a good example. He could hardly remember what had started the altercation. In fact, when he did conjecture about their arguments, it seemed to him that very often they were manufactured out of thin air and held no special relevance to anything he'd actually said. But whatever the premise of their disagreement of the night before, it had soon escalated into an out-and-out verbal assault, leading up to and culminating in Marissa's throwing a good portion of their dinnerware onto the terra-cotta dining room floor, resulting in the kind of mess usually associated with *tavernas* in Athens.

Perhaps that was what had precipitated her shopping expedition. Right now she was no doubt picking out new dinnerware, and while he knew she wouldn't buy plastic—in fact, it was unlikely the Coral Gables stores even carried plastic dinnerware—he hoped the new set wasn't quite as breakable as the previous one, whose pieces had seemed to implode when coming into contact with tile. Conversely, she could be buying a rug for the dining-room floor, which would serve to soften the concussion when china met tile.

Quintana worked for another couple of hours on his paper, then straightened up his desk and went out to the kitchen. It was now close to eight-thirty and rather late for her to prepare a meal, even if she did arrive soon. He got out the ingredients for an omelet, but even after he'd prepared and eaten it, she still hadn't returned.

It had been nice having a peaceful dinner. He had never been one who minded eating alone, preferring the company of a book or a newspaper and the sound of good music to contrived dinner-table conversation. He was aware of these reclusive tendencies, and had made concerted efforts in the past to change, even while knowing he was the happiest when left to himself.

He cleaned up the kitchen and went to his study, turning on a few lights along the way. He felt rather good, but not quite at peace, because he knew this calm was not going to last. Any minute she would walk in the front door and, no matter if he apologized for the previous night, no matter if he put renewed effort into saving their pretext of a love affair, something, anything, would set her off. It was rather like living with the kind of time bomb that was impossible to defuse.

It was only when he looked up from his writing several hours later and saw that it was after midnight that he felt the first frisson of unease. They lived in a relatively safe area, but she was, after all, on foot, and crime was ever on the rise in Miami.

Feeling a bit foolish, he called the local police station. They were more helpful than he had expected, probably because it was a quiet night and rather an affluent area. They said they would check on accidents and get back to him. When they called him back the sergeant informed him that there had been no accidents in the area and no incidents involving anyone of Marissa's description.

When the sergeant asked Quintana if Marissa frequented bars Quintana's immediate answer was no, although, on consideration, he had little idea how Marissa occupied herself during the day. He doubted she would hang out in bars, though, if for no other reason than she never took a drink. She would not even partake of a friendly lager with him on occasion, or drink wine with a meal. The sergeant said that it was likely she'd turn up any minute, but if she was still missing after twenty-four hours, Quintana could come into the police station and file a missing person's report.

Missing. The word evoked a sense of relief. A sense that perhaps she would leave his life with the same quick unexpectedness as she had entered it. It was a feeling he had gotten on occasion when transferring his writing to his word processor: that if he were able to delete her from his life as easily and with as little fuss as he could delete a word from the screen, he would certainly be tempted to exercise that option.

He admitted to himself that if she was indeed missing, he didn't want her found. He would be quite content to return to his old way of life: his solitary evenings at work in his study, the occasional dinner out with friends and colleagues, his sporadic tennis games with his friend, Guy, at the club.

Granted, Marissa had brought excitement to his life but the quality, as well as the content of that excitement, had changed almost the moment she moved in with him. The emotionally charged, often romantic period had quickly evolved into the highly volatile, practically sexless period of constant quarrels and, just lately, separate bedrooms. He put a good portion of the blame on himself. He must have unknowingly become the type of bachelor too set in his ways to change. And because he blamed himself, it never occurred to him to ask her to move out. He kept thinking that, given time, things would get better.

Before retiring for the night he did take a walk down to the commercial section of town, looking in on the few bars and restaurants that were still open.

He had the idea that the police sergeant had thought Marissa was having an affair. It was a natural assumption, but one that didn't seem logical to Quintana. Why would she be having an affair when she was already having one with him? Why not just move out, if that was what she wanted?

Furthermore, there had been no hint of another man. There had been no mysterious phone calls, no hang-ups when he answered the phone. This had been the first evening Marissa's whereabouts had been unaccounted for. Not that affairs couldn't be conducted during the day, but surely an affair would, at the very least, have improved her temper around him. The men he knew who conducted affairs always joked about being extra nice to their wives in order to allay any suspicions, which probably, in turn, induced suspicions. In his experience most people didn't think things through to their logical conclusion.

Nor would he have cared if Marissa *were* having an affair. He might even have encouraged her in it, hoping that it would culminate in her leaving him and moving in with someone else.

No, he didn't think Marissa was out with a man. He didn't know what exactly he did think, but when he fell asleep that night, alone in his antique, four-poster bed, it was with the certainty that his hopes were not going to be fulfilled and that Marissa would once again be there in the morning.

When Anne's boss took the call he said to her, "This will just take a minute."

Anne Larkin got up and moved across his office to stand by the windows in order to give him privacy. She looked down at the sporadic traffic on Brickell Avenue, hoping the sounds of the traffic would drown out Guy Talbot's voice. They didn't, and she could tell that it was a personal call. She didn't know exactly *how* she could tell, because Guy wasn't doing much talking. He was mostly listening, interjecting an occasional, "Yes," or "I see," or something equally innocuous, but it wasn't the tone of voice you used with a client; it was the tone you used with a friend.

Anne heard a screech of tires and looked down in time to see a very old lady with a walker attempting to cross Brickell in the middle of the block, while cars were braking and swerving to avoid her. The woman, looking neither to her right nor her left, continued maneuvering through the traffic and eventually arrived safely on the other side.

Anne heard Guy say, "I'd advise you to go to the police." And then, "Yes, in person. Definitely. That's what I'd do."

She wondered why whoever it was had called Guy rather than a lawyer who dealt in criminal matters. Surely a law firm that specialized in corporate takeovers and mergers would be of no help to someone in need of the police.

She heard the phone being hung up and walked back to his desk. She took a seat in the chair again, and bent down to find her place in the proposed merger she had brought to his office for his approval. "There's one slight legality we might have to watch out for," she said to him, sliding the papers around on his desk and pointing out a note she had made.

"That was an old friend of mine on the phone," said Guy, ignoring the note and gazing over her head toward the windows.

He seemed lost in thought for a moment while she wondered what she was to say to that. As the newest associate in the firm, she didn't feel it was her place to question him about a personal phone call, or even to show an interest. The senior partners, of which Guy was one of the most senior, rarely opened themselves up to talk of a personal nature. In fact, now that she thought of it, she couldn't remember a single incident.

"His, uh, lady friend appears to be missing."

Anne found herself saying, "Lady friend?" without thinking. The term seemed such an anachronism, though, and Guy Talbot couldn't be more than thirty-six or thirty-seven. He might even be younger.

"His 'live-in,' or whatever you call it these days. What *do* you call it, Anne?"

Was there a hint in his voice that she was no doubt living with a man and should know the correct phraseology? "Live-in sounds right," said Anne, "presuming it's more than a roommate situation."

"Maybe I should have let you talk to him. You know more about those things." She must have looked shocked, because he quickly added, "I meant police matters."

"If you'd like me to talk to him..."

"No, I don't think that's necessary...well, maybe it wouldn't be a bad idea. I don't think Jack's had much contact with the police, certainly none of a personal nature."

"If you think it would help," she said, hoping he'd change his mind and say no. Giving advice to her boss's friend didn't seem like such a good idea. There was always the chance she might give the wrong advice.

"Actually, you might know him," said Guy. "I forgot you went to law school here."

"I went to the University of Miami," said Anne.

"Yes. He teaches torts there."

Anne felt a sinking sensation in her stomach. "Torts?"

"Yes. He's quite well-known in his field."

"Surely he wouldn't need any advice from me."

"Well, you know how it is. You get one criminal law course in school, and then it's theory mostly, nothing practical. But you have practical experience."

"This wouldn't be . . . you're not talking about Professor Quintana, are you?"

Guy's face lit up with a smile. "You did have Jack for torts, then."

"Yes."

"Then you won't mind talking to him."

Before Anne could protest, he lifted the phone and dialed an outside number.

The last time Anne had spoken Quintana's name, it had been with intent to kill. If memory served, the exact words had been, "I'd like to take that bastard's casebook and shove it down his throat."

And now it seemed those words were coming back to haunt her. Almost seven years from the day Anne had spoken those words with passion, Quintana had been relegated to the far reaches of her memory. She couldn't even say he was the furthest thing from her mind. He was even farther than that; he was almost forgotten. And not only had she survived Quintana, she had prospered.

Anne found herself holding her breath while she waited, but after a few moments Guy hung up the phone.

"He must have left," he said. "I think he's on his way to the police station to file a missing person report."

Anne expelled her breath in relief. "That's exactly what I would have suggested he do."

Guy shrugged expansively. "Then I guess that's it."

Feeling as if she'd just been pardoned by the governor only moments before going to her death, Anne returned his smile and pointed, once again, to the merger agreement she had set before him.

Marissa hadn't been there in the morning when Quintana got up, nor was she there during the day when he intermittently called home between classes. So when his last class was over he called Guy for advice, then drove to the Coral Gables police station and perfunctorily filled out the necessary form to set a missing person investigation in motion.

He wasn't distraught and made no attempt to throw any weight he might have around, and as a result the policeman taking down the information was businesslike and didn't make any attempt to hide his disinterest. Still, doing something official about it lessened any guilt he might be harboring over his relief that Marissa was no longer around.

Her disappearance was made simple for him in that there was no one to notify; for the same reason, it would be difficult for the police to investigate. She was an only child; her father had died during her childhood, and her mother had died shortly before Marissa came to Miami. He had never heard her speak of any relatives and, as far as he knew, she had no friends. She didn't work, didn't even attend a class. Unless there was a man somewhere, he was probably the only one to notice she was missing. Of course, if there was a man, he was probably with Marissa.

Quintana was the kind of man who would have felt more at ease telling the police his wife was missing than having to couch it in words such as "the woman I'm living with." It seemed somehow unprofessional. Being married sounded legal, a sign of maturity. Living together, conversely, sounded sloppy, immature, the sort of thing his students would be more apt to be doing than their professor. The officer hadn't appeared to think anything of it, but just having to use those words seemed to have diminished Quintana in his own estimation.

In any case he had been to the police; he had done his duty, and now there wasn't anything he could do except sit at home and wait. It annoyed him, though, that she had put him in this situation. At the very least she could have shown him the common courtesy of leaving a note.

As soon as that thought came to him he realized he hadn't looked for a note. Of course, the point of leaving a note was so that someone would find it, and if she had left a note she wanted found, he surely would have seen it by now.

If he were going to leave a note, he would leave it in a place where she'd be sure to see it. The front door might be a good place, or the door to the refrigerator. A sure place would be the mirror over her bathroom sink. He knew she would see it there, as she was wont to spend hours applying makeup in front of that mirror.

He started with the downstairs, looking in all the spots where he could reasonably expect a note to be placed. It was in none of them. The thought occurred to him that she might have mailed him a note. Perhaps she hadn't decided to stay away until she actually got somewhere, in which case, the mail service being what it was, it might not arrive for another couple of days.

He went upstairs and gave a quick look into her bedroom and bath, although those would be the most unlikely places for her to leave a note for him. He already knew there wasn't one in his bedroom or bath, or he would have seen it.

When he was finished looking he wasn't really surprised that he hadn't found anything. In the time he'd known her, he'd never known Marissa to leave him a note. Of course, in that time he'd never known her to disappear, either.

The fact that there were loose ends began to bother him. He was the sort of person who liked everything brought to its logical conclusion and then tied up neatly.

Pete had asked her to meet him for a drink after work at the Carlyle in South Beach. He was already sitting at one of the tables on the front porch overlooking the beach when Anne arrived and climbed the steps. It was only a few doors from where she lived, and she had stopped home first to change from her linen suit to shorts and a T-shirt. Now she saw that Pete was dressed in a sport coat and slacks, which was unlike him.

She leaned down to give him a kiss, his beard tickling her face. He was not only dressed up, he smelled good, too, and it looked as though his beard had been freshly trimmed. Something was definitely brewing for Peter McKenna to be suddenly looking like a new man.

"What do you want to drink?" he asked her.

"I'll have one of those," she said, nodding in the direction of his vodka tonic with a slice of lime. She leaned back in the chair and stretched out her legs under the table. He seemed different, a little tense. Even his blue eyes lacked their usual sparkle. She waited while he placed her order, then said, "You off tonight? What's the occasion?"

Pete was a jazz musician who played in a basement club down the street. Generally she only saw him on the nights he was off or during the day on weekends, when they were both free.

"I thought I'd buy you dinner," said Pete.

Something was definitely wrong if Pete was offering to buy her dinner. A drink maybe, but she could never remember him buying her a meal. Not even offering. He knew she made more money than he did and seemed quite content to go dutch on their dates. If she had been watching this scene in a movie—an old movie—she would have thought maybe he was going to reach into his jacket pocket and pull out a small box, which meant a proposal. But they weren't having the kind of romance that would call for a proposal, and Pete wasn't the type to propose.

"Something happened," she said.

"You're really suspicious, aren't you? Can't a guy buy you dinner?"

"What's the occasion, Pete?"

"At least have your drink first," he said, calling one of the waiters over and ordering two more.

"You guys get fired?"

He smiled and shook his head, his long blond hair swaying around his shoulders with the movement.

"Is it your birthday? If it is, let me buy."

"My birthday's not for another month."

And he'd be twenty-four on his next birthday, and she'd be thirty-one on hers, but the age difference really didn't matter, because he was good-natured and fun and she got all the mental stimulation she needed at work. Anyway, there was nothing serious between them. If she ever got serious about a man, then maybe she'd start thinking about things like differences in age and intellectual parity.

In the meantime, he was also very cute, and there was something sexy about trumpet players, the way they pursed their mouths and pointed their instruments to the ceiling and made incredible, plaintive sounds come out. A good trumpet player could get to her every time.

"Where are we going to eat?" she asked him, wondering if she'd have to change her clothes once again. There were still some restaurants in Miami Beach that frowned on shorts.

"I thought we'd eat here."

"It's expensive here."

He shook his head again, then looked across the street to the ocean. "Remember when we met over there?"

She followed his glance. Without her noticing, storm clouds appeared to have gathered in the east. The way the weather had been lately, they could be caught in flash flood conditions without warning. She remembered that she had opened her living room windows to let some air in. Not that it would matter if it rained in, as there wasn't any furniture in the living room.

She had been jogging on the beach one morning, very early, and Pete had been sitting on one of the benches. She had just gotten up, and he hadn't been to bed yet. It was as good a way to meet as any, she supposed.

It was beginning to sound as if he was ending whatever there was between them. That "remember when" stuff sounded as though she were already becoming a memory. She'd heard that kind of talk before. In fact, she'd precipitated it a few times herself.

"You're leaving, aren't you?"

He nodded. "Miami's dead in the summer, and this gig's ending. We've got some dates lined up in New England, and we got offered a couple of weeks in New York in between." He gave her his half smile, the crooked one she liked so much.

"When do you leave?"

"Tomorrow morning."

And that was that, she guessed. Another young musician gone from her life. She wondered if she'd even remember his name six months from now. There had been several musicians in the years since college: three trumpet players, a couple of drummers, one who was talented on bass. They tended to blend together in her memory, forming one group. Each had given her the illusion of having a man in her life, while at the same time leaving ninety percent of her emotions free to pursue her career.

She looked at him in the same moment the first crash of thunder struck. It looked as though the elements were going to conspire to make their ending more dramatic than the romance had warranted.

That night there was a violent electrical storm that whipped up the canal into something resembling surf and caused a power outage of several hours' duration. The absence of electricity was frustrating to Quintana, because he had been in the middle of revising his article on his word processor when the power failed, and not only couldn't he work without electricity, he was afraid he might have lost most of the work he had done that night.

And without electricity there wasn't very much else he could do, either. He finally took a Coleman lantern up to bed with him, along with a colleague's book that he had agreed to review. The book turned out to be as long-winded and boring as the colleague, and several hours into the storm he grew restless and went back downstairs.

He couldn't even see outside; the windows appeared to be immersed in Niagara Falls. He went out to the kitchen for a bottle of lager, thinking it would help him get to sleep, and realized, once he opened the refrigerator, that all of his food was in danger of going bad.

He moved into the laundry room adjoining the kitchen, where they kept a well-stocked freezer, and opened the lid. It was filled with meat and vegetables, and he thought maybe he should do something about them. Without Marissa around—and by this time he was beginning to think of that as a permanent life-style—there was no way he would ever consume any of that food. He didn't like to cook and would no doubt revert to his old habit of eating all his meals out.

He thought of dumping everything in a trash bag and hauling it out to the garbage can in the garage. Then he thought of the stench of rotting food that would surely occur before the next garbage collection. Well, if he wasn't going to enjoy it, why not feed it to the fish? He could remove the wrappings and cartons, dump everything biodegradable into a trash bag, then dump the contents of the bag into the canal. The fish would enjoy a veritable feast. And if Marissa did return, it wasn't as though she was going to pick up where they left off, cooking his meals and keeping his house. If she did return he was now determined to ask her to move out. He would continue to support her until she found work and was able to support herself, but nothing she said at this point would effect a reconciliation as far as he was concerned. He knew that legally he wasn't required to support her for even that period of time, but his guilt over wanting to see the end of her would require it of him in order to ease his conscience.

It took him a good couple of hours to pry the contents of the packages away from the cardboard and into the heavy duty trash bag. It was after three in the morning by the time he had finished. The rain had abated, but the electricity was still off. He'd be surprised if they got it back any time soon. He added a few items from the refrigerator, and then, barefoot and pajama-clad, he dragged the heavy bag out the back door, across the patio and lawn, and then down the steps to his dock.

He held the bag open as the contents slid into the water with satisfying splashes. He wished he could see into the depths, where the fish must be ecstatic over their find. It was a feast to tempt an alligator. For a few years there, alligators had gotten to be a rare occurrence in the canals, but lately they were coming back again. In fact, they had proliferated to the degree where hunting them was once again allowed.

Exhausted and with a feeling of accomplishment, Quintana changed into dry pajama bottoms, then went to bed and slept soundly.

That night Anne had a recurring nightmare, and it scared her so badly that she woke up in the middle of the night, shaking, her body covered with sweat, firmly believing for about five minutes that she was still back in law school.

What was odd about it was that she hadn't had the dream since her first year in law school, but in those days she had it almost every night.

She'd dreamed she showed up for Jack Quintana's torts class unprepared. It ranked second amongst the most terrifying nightmares she had ever had in her life, right behind the one where she overslept on finals days. Or maybe it was third; the one where her typewriter failed to work during the bar exam was even worse.

In the dream Professor Quintana called on her to recite a case, and when she looked down at the casebook, there were no familiar yellow markings that would tell her what to say. She quickly began scanning the case in an effort to fake it, but the case went on and on, and when it was simply not possible for it to go on any further, it went on anyway. The class was dead silent, and Quintana was waiting, a smile on his face worthy of a shark. In reality, it had been worse when he stopped waiting, when he finally began to demolish her in front of the class, but in the dream nothing seemed worse than the waiting and the quiet and the case going on and on.

Still shaken, even when she realized it was only a dream and law school was in the past, she was too upset to get back to sleep and finally turned on the reading lamp and sat up in bed. The light from the lamp spotlighted her corner of the bed, leaving the rest of the room in shadow. The room was empty except for a mattress and box spring and a low table placed beside her. She had only recently bought the place and hadn't found the time or the energy to furnish it yet.

She lived on the top floor of the building, and she could hear the rain still pounding down and see it driving so hard against the windows that it looked as though someone were standing outside and throwing buckets of water against the glass. Normally she liked thunderstorms, but tonight the storm, combined with the nightmare, seemed almost gothic.

She suddenly couldn't remember whether she had closed the living-room windows when she came home, although she must have, because it had been pouring even then. Nevertheless, she thought she'd better get out of bed to check. She reached for the T-shirt she had discarded on the floor and pulled it over her head. Sleeping naked was nice; walking by windows at night in the nude wasn't so nice.

The windows were closed. She stared out, trying to see past the rain, but couldn't even see the beach across the street. As long as she was up, she got herself a glass of wine and took it back to bed with her in the hope that it might calm her down enough to sleep.

The scariest thing about her nightmares was that, in actual fact, most of her law school nightmares had come true. She *was* called upon by Professor Quintana when she was unprepared. She didn't oversleep on the days when they had finals, but the one about her typewriter not working was even worse than she could have imagined. Those typing the bar exam were in a separate room, and for forty minutes in the middle of the exam there was a power failure and they all sat there in terror, never thinking that they could take up a pen and write by hand.

When Anne got out of law school and started practicing law, she thought the nightmares would end, except then she dreamed that she overslept on the first day of an important trial, or that she was facing the jury and forgot her closing argument. The law was a nightmarish profession. One thing she liked about working on corporate mergers and takeovers was that the work didn't give her nightmares. There might still be stress involved, but it was a much milder kind that didn't play havoc with her nerves or with her sleep.

One time she and her friends had been sitting around a bar discussing dreams, and Anne had told them about her legal nightmares. She had just completed a very harrowing court case, and now that it was over, lost, and her client incarcerated, the nightmares had changed from losing the case in court to being threatened by her client.

Bolivia had looked at her in astonishment. "I didn't know you ever had bad dreams, Anne."

"Constantly," Anne assured her.

Bolivia nodded. "I know just what you mean. I have this one where I hear about the best exclusive of my career and then I don't get it in in time to make the deadline and I'm fired."

"I never thought you worried about stuff like that," Anne told her.

"I wouldn't have thought so, either," said Bolivia, "but I guess I must, or I wouldn't have nightmares. I guess it goes with the job, though—paranoia during the day and nightmares at night."

"Everyone worries," said Sandy. "My nightmare is worse, though. I always dream my revolver gets stuck and the perpetrator levels his gun at me."

"Do you get killed?" Anne asked her.

"I don't know. I always wake up at that point, and I'm always sweating. Sometimes I'm shaking so badly that if I didn't know better, I'd think Florida was experiencing its first earthquake."

"I guess there are worse things than not meeting a deadline," said Bolivia, and Anne had to agree.

After that Anne never complained about her own nightmares to her friends. And yet, if it hadn't been almost dawn, she thought she would have called one of them right now for a little aid and comfort.

In lieu of that she turned on her bedside radio to a local rock station. If there was one thing guaranteed to cheer her up, it was good rock played nice and loud. Only the hour and the proximity of her neighbors induced her to turn down the volume.

It was vintage rock, something ancient that she could remember her parents dancing to when she was a child. That gave it a homey feeling, a sentimental quality that might do the trick in soothing her back to sleep. Many were the nights she'd been lulled to sleep by her parents' music in the bedroom next to hers.

She took a sip of the red wine and then reached for the draft of the latest merger she was working on, work guaranteed to put her to sleep if the music and the wine didn't work.

Right before drifting off, Anne had the spiteful thought that she hoped Professor Quintana was having his own particular nightmares. It would serve him right for still having the power to disturb her sleep after so many years.

Chapter 2

It was two days later and still no word from Marissa when Quintana was visited at the university by two detectives. His last class had ended, and they were waiting for him in his office when he stopped by to drop off his textbooks.

They introduced themselves as Detectives Betancourt and Soffer. Betancourt was older, maybe early forties, dark, closely cropped hair, thin mustache, well dressed, almost elegant if one could forget about the gold chains weighted down by charms of different kinds that hung around his neck. Quintana couldn't. Gold chains in abundance were routinely worn by every drug dealer in Miami, and why the entire community had to emulate this tasteless display was beyond Quintana. Soffer was younger by a good ten years, prematurely balding and a bit of a slob. In typical redneck style, he wore his pants slung low with the beginnings of a beer belly already starting to fold over his belt buckle. The slob had intelligent, faded blue eyes, however, and Quintana was seldom deceived by appearances.

"Is this about Marissa?" asked Quintana.

The detectives exchanged looks, and Quintana was sure he caught a look of surprise on Betancourt's face.

"A neighbor has reported her missing," said Betancourt, watching Quintana closely for his reaction.

Quintana frowned. "A neighbor? I reported her missing myself. Has she been found?"

There was clear consternation in the glances the two officers exchanged. "You say you reported her?" asked Soffer, and when Quintana nodded he said, "May I use your phone?"

Quintana gave permission and then listened as the detective sought information from someone at the police station.

"We weren't aware of that," said Soffer, after hanging up the phone. "We should have cross-checked, of course."

"Then what was the purpose of your visit?"

Betancourt spoke. "Your neighbor brought forth certain allegations concerning your treatment of the young woman you were living with."

"My treatment?"

"The fact that you were abusive."

"Abusive?" He knew he was being annoyingly repetitive, but it was almost as though he were listening to a foreign language he didn't understand.

"She said you often beat the young woman," said Soffer, "and that she was worried about her, since she hadn't seen her in days, and she didn't answer the phone when she called."

"I didn't even know Marissa knew the neighbors."

"Then the allegations are true?" asked Soffer.

"You mean beating her? No, of course I never beat her. Believe me, if I had, Marissa would have told *you* about it, not a neighbor."

"Your neighbor reports that the young woman feared for her life."

"Since there is no basis in reality for any of this, I see no point in endlessly protesting my innocence," said Quintana, at a loss to explain why any of this was happening. "Could you give me the name of the neighbor?"

"A Mrs. Lasko. She lives next door to you on the north."

Quintana tried to form a picture of Mrs. Lasko, but all he could come up with was a man with a large gut whom he had occasionally seen sailing off in his boat. He couldn't even recall a wife.

"I understand you're a law professor," said Betancourt.

Quintana nodded.

"Criminal law?"

"Torts."

Betancourt seemed to become more expansive. "Well, who knows, it wouldn't be the first time a neighbor tried to cause mischief. She had never actually seen any bruises on the young lady but said that she often came to her in tears, telling her how you knocked her around. She also said shouting could often be heard from your house."

Quintana gave them a rueful smile. "The shouting I confess to. Even the breaking of crockery on one occasion. It was a stormy relationship at times, but never a physically abusive one."

The last thing Quintana would ever think of doing was "knocking around" a woman, although he knew that to protest too much would only make him sound guilty.

The detectives seemed satisfied when they left and promised him that they'd speed up the missing person investigation.

When Quintana drove into his street that day he passed the house to the north of him and slowed down, wondering if he'd get a look at the interfering neighbor. He didn't see her, but he did see a white Corvette in the driveway, and now he seemed to recall a very thin woman with frosted blond hair behind the wheel of that car. He had a feeling she was considerably younger—or at least better preserved—than the yachting husband with the beer belly.

It was the classic situation: bottom of the ninth, two outs, her team behind by two runs, a base runner on second and Anne up to bat.

Unfortunately, she didn't score the winning run. Instead she popped an infield fly, and the other team didn't even have to make a double play. And it wasn't because her mind was on her work instead of the game, either, although that had been known to happen. It was the doing of South Kendall's pitcher, Anne's particular nemesis, who invariably managed to get Anne with her curve ball.

Anne headed for the bench, where a row of glum faces avoided hers. The opposing team was acting obnoxious and squealing like a bunch of schoolgirls at a rock concert. Anne felt like personally kicking each one of them where it would do the most good. A childish urge, to be sure, but baseball always brought out the child in her.

Finally Bolivia and Sandy came over to her, and Bolivia patted her on the shoulder. "Cheer up, Annie, it could've been worse."

Bolivia only used "Annie" when she was being sarcastic.

"Come on, we'll buy you a drink," said Sandy, leading the way to the parking lot.

Sandy was driving tonight, which meant that Anne had to stuff herself into the back seat of Sandy's Subaru, because Bolivia, at five feet ten inches, claimed there wasn't enough leg space in the back to accommodate her. Anne was five feet five, and there wasn't enough leg space for her, either, but the only one who *could* fit into the back was

Sandy, at an even five feet, and since it was her car, she naturally insisted on driving. From her vantage point in the back, Anne couldn't even see Sandy's head over the seat, so it looked as if they were being driven by an invisible person. Not for the first time, Anne thought that the Motor Vehicle Department ought to have minimum height requirements for those wishing to drive. For one thing, it helped to be able to see over the steering wheel.

Sandy was about the size Anne had been at eleven. She weighed under a hundred pounds, had long bangs and straight brown hair in a short blunt cut, and with her innocent brown eyes and small features looked more like an aging adolescent than the thirty-year-old cop she was.

Conversely, Bolivia looked like *exactly* what she was, which was an investigative reporter with ambitions to be a foreign correspondent, preferably in a war zone. Except on occasions like tonight, when she was in her baseball uniform, she would be found in men's khakis astride her motorcycle, her short, dark hair not even showing beneath her helmet.

Anne always felt she looked blatantly feminine when she was with them, but she couldn't help it if she had curves where they were straight and the added blight of blond curly hair that she'd long since given up on straightening, particularly since the humidity in Florida was guaranteed to curl it back up the moment she walked out of her air-conditioned apartment. She supposed she could starve herself into anorexia nervosa and cut her hair short, but even then she had a feeling she wouldn't look boyish in her baseball suit. It wasn't fair, it really wasn't, because she was the best coordinated of the three, but coaches always took one look at her and then stopped taking her seriously.

The team's local watering hole was full of gloom by the time they arrived. Anne couldn't help comparing the atmosphere to what it would have been if she had won the game for them. She'd done just that on more than one occasion, but were they going to remember that tonight? No. No chance.

Their pitcher, Diane, who had given up more runs than she should have, was the only one feeling as bad as Anne. They consoled each other over a beer, and then most of the group broke up and headed home. Bolivia, Sandy and Anne headed for their customary end of the bar away from the TV set. Bolivia and Anne stood, letting Sandy have the bar stool, which made them all the same height and made it easier to converse.

"What's the matter with you tonight?" Bolivia asked her. "You're not your usual perky self."

"Perky?" questioned Sandy. "When is Anne ever perky?"

"I merely substituted 'perky' for 'big mouthed,'" said Bolivia. "I was trying for subtlety."

"My past came back briefly to haunt me," Anne said to Bolivia, "and I'm not sleeping well as a result."

"Past? What past? If you had a past I'd know about it," said Bolivia.

"You ever remember me talking about Jack Quintana a few years back?" Anne asked Bolivia.

"The name doesn't sound familiar," said Bolivia.

Sandy choked, spitting beer out all over herself and part of the bar. "Oh, God, the shark! You're talking about the shark! I'd forgotten all about that man."

"Hey, take it easy," said Anne, patting Sandy on the back. "He's my nightmare, not yours."

"You think he didn't give me nightmares?" asked Sandy. "He was half the reason I dropped out of law school."

"You dropped out right before you flunked out," Anne reminded her.

"You *hated* law school, as I recall," said Bolivia.

"I hated law school, but I hated him more. He scared the hell out of me. He scared the hell out of all of us, but I would've died to get him alone," said Sandy, a gleam coming into her eyes.

"It was a schizophrenic situation, all right," agreed Anne. "We were all afraid of him, but we all had a crush on him, at least the female law students."

"Whom, exactly, are we discussing?" asked Bolivia.

"Professor Quintana, our torts professor in law school," Anne told her.

Bolivia looked from Anne to Sandy and back again. "Is there some reason for your bringing him up, or are you just reminiscing?"

"It's nothing important," said Anne. "It's just that the guy used to give me nightmares back in law school, and my boss mentioned his name the other day, and it brought all those memories back again."

"I wish you hadn't mentioned him," said Sandy. "I've got goose bumps just thinking about him."

"I thought you were sleeping well since you got out of criminal law?" said Bolivia.

"It's just lately. It'll go away."

"If I had a cute guy like Pete," said Sandy, "I wouldn't be having any nightmares."

Anne swallowed. "Well, about Pete . . ."

"No, don't even tell us," said Bolivia.

"Not Pete," said Sandy.

Anne nodded. "I'm afraid so. He's off to bigger and better gigs."

"I thought he was at the Carlyle permanently," said Bolivia.

"Nothing in life is permanent," said Anne.

"Now we're going to get philosophy from her," said Sandy, "in which case, I need another beer."

"Me, too," said Bolivia.

"No philosophy," said Anne. "He was fun, but come on, guys, it was never anything serious."

"Where are they?" asked Bolivia, putting her arms around her friends' shoulders. "Where are the guys you could get serious about?"

"I don't know," said Sandy, "but they sure as hell aren't in Miami."

"You want serious men?" asked Anne. "Allow me to fix you up with some of the men from my law firm. You don't know the meaning of serious until you meet a corporate attorney."

"I wasn't talking *that* serious," said Bolivia.

"Semiserious would do," said Sandy.

"Forget serious, I'm free at last," said Anne. "What do you say we hit Key West for the weekend? We can do a little snorkeling, pig out at the Pier House—"

"Pick up a few musicians," said Sandy, giving her a blatantly suspicious look.

Anne held up her hands. "No more musicians, I swear. May I drop dead if I ever go for another musician."

"Oh, sure," said Bolivia.

"We've heard that before," said Sandy.

"I'm serious," said Anne. "In fact, I think I'm going to lay off drinking for a while, too. No men, no booze—I'm going to clean up my act."

"I'll believe that when I see it," said Sandy.

"I'll never believe it," said Bolivia.

"I don't mean forever," said Anne. "Just for a while. I really need a rest."

"Sounds like your New Year's resolutions, which lasted about a week," said Sandy.

"More like a day," said Bolivia.

"I'm serious," said Anne. "No drinking and no musicians for three months."

"Not even a lead singer?" asked Bolivia.

"I don't go for lead singers," said Anne.

"You did last time we went to the Keys," said Bolivia, amusing herself so much with the remark that she choked on her drink.

"In fact, no men of any kind," said Anne. "I mean it, guys—I need a rest." She could stand to lose a few pounds, too, which was never going to happen with all the beer she consumed. "And with all the extra time I'll have, I might even get my apartment furnished."

"I'll believe that when I see it," said Sandy.

"I like the way her place looks," said Bolivia. "Minimalistic, I think it's called. I aspire to owning nothing."

"Then you've already succeeded in your aspirations," said Sandy. "You could get everything you own in one bag."

"That's the point," said Bolivia. "Foreign correspondents travel light."

"You're not a foreign correspondent," said Anne.

"Yeah, but that's another of my aspirations," said Bolivia. She finished off her beer, and then said, "A hundred bucks."

"What?"

"A hundred bucks says you'll never do it for three months. The men *or* the drinking."

"You're on," said Anne, shaking hands on the bet.

"Me, too," said Sandy. "I'll bet you another hundred. Although it's hard to take you seriously for a hundred bucks. A hundred means nothing with the kind of money you make."

"She'd take a dime seriously," said Bolivia. "It's not the money, it's that competitive urge of hers. She can't stand losing."

"I don't intend to lose," said Anne. "You going to go a hundred?" she asked Sandy.

"Absolutely," said Sandy, holding out her hand.

"So, are we on?" asked Anne. "Two sun-filled days and one wild and crazy night in the Keys?"

"I have nothing better to do," said Sandy.

"There's something wrong with the world when three dynamite women like us have to go away together for the weekend," said Bolivia. "But yeah, why not? Who knows, maybe three Prince Charmings are at this very moment planning on cruising the Keys this weekend. Forget that, I meant two Prince Charmings. Annie, of course, is off men."

The next thing that happened—and Quintana hadn't even been aware of it, since he hadn't read a newspaper or seen the news that day—was that the body of a woman was found in the canal behind his house. His first awareness came when the two detectives again showed up, this time on Saturday morning.

When they broke the news to him, he felt the first stirrings of loss. He hadn't wanted to live with her any longer, but he certainly didn't want to see her dead. He still had feelings for Marissa, even if they weren't of the romantic variety.

"Are you certain it's Marissa?" he asked them.

"Not at all," said Soffer. "In fact, it's going to be very difficult to make any identification of the body."

"Then why do you think it may be Marissa?"

"Only the fact that you reported her missing and the body was found less than a mile from here."

"Do you want me to identify her?"

Betancourt shook his head. "I don't think you'd be able to. About all we can determine without an autopsy is that it's female and has dark hair. The fish have gotten to it, and there's not much left of the face or extremities."

Quintana felt his stomach plummet at the mention of fish. Perhaps at the moment he'd been feeding the fish, other fish had been feeding on Marissa. He felt nausea welling up and tried to control it.

"I wouldn't be surprised if it was an alligator," Betancourt continued, watching for Quintana's reaction. "The hands are completely gone."

Quintana made a run for the bathroom and got there just in time to lose his breakfast in the toilet. He forced the thoughts of alligators from his mind as he gargled with some mouthwash, then slowly made his way back to the door.

"I'm sorry," said Soffer. "It's very probable it's not your girlfriend at all. On the off chance, though, we were hoping to get the name of her dentist."

Quintana felt at a loss. "I'm afraid I have no idea. I've only known her five months, and in that time she never mentioned going to a dentist."

"Perhaps you could look over her checkbook and appointment book, and if you come up with a name..."

"Of course," said Quintana. "I'll get onto it right away."

It was beginning to sound to him like one of those television shows he never watched: a missing woman, neighbors' tales of beatings, a body in a canal... Certainly things like that didn't happen to someone who led as law-abiding and uneventful a life as he did. Of course, things had become more eventful since he met Marissa, but still...

He looked through the dresser drawers in her bedroom that night. He found her checkbook, but except for a few checks to dress shops, there was nothing. The absence of an appointment calendar didn't surprise him; as far as he knew, she never had any appointments.

He opened the shuttered doors to her closet and gazed inside. It was full of clothes, and he was unable to say whether anything was missing or not. On several hooks on the closet wall he found her array of handbags. He felt distaste at rummaging in her personal belongings, but with a dead body that could conceivably be Marissa and a neighbor who obviously thought he'd done away with her, he felt the invasion of privacy was justified.

In one handbag he found an ostrich skin wallet she had insisted on having, even though he deplored the destruction of animals for such purposes. A look inside revealed all her credit cards and eighty-seven dollars and change. Also in the handbag was her set of keys to the house and the car. Her disappearance instantly took on more serious proportions.

He berated himself for not having looked before. If he had looked the first night he would have known immediately that she hadn't gone shopping. In fact, from the looks of it, she hadn't gone anywhere. Even if she were running off with someone, what would be the point of leaving all her money and identification behind?

And yet, if she were the woman they'd found in the canal, how had she gotten there? She certainly hadn't gone in for a swim, not with her loathing of water. She had never for an instant struck him as suicidal, but even if she had, it would have been far more in character for her to use pills as her method. He didn't see it as an accident, because it would be fairly difficult to accidentally fall into the canal. As for murder—if it was murder—he was the only person he could think of who knew her well enough to have a motive, and since he hadn't killed her, that shot that theory.

Since the police didn't know he didn't have a motive, however, he thought it was about time he got some serious legal advice. Right after he mixed himself a serious drink. For the first time in memory, he saw that his hands were shaking.

They got back from snorkeling around noon, dumped their equipment in their hotel room, then headed for the small stretch of sand that the Pier House called a beach. The big advantage of this particular beach, aside from the fact that it was just a few feet from their room, was that the management provided longue chairs and pink towels, and waitresses came by to take orders for drinks.

Anne tied a scarf around her hair to prevent it from becoming a lighter shade of blond and piled on double digit sunscreen to prevent freckles. She put turquoise zinc on her nose, donned oversize sunglasses, adjusted her Walkman radio to the local rock station and opened a fashion magazine she had brought along.

Bolivia, who was chronically unable to sit still for five minutes, was already heading for the water, her long, muscular, bronzed legs flashing in the sun. Anne watched as she dived under a wave, then didn't emerge until she got to the raft, where she pulled herself up with an effortless motion. Anne saw that she wasn't the only one who had watched Bolivia's journey to the raft: three young men were now following her out there.

Sandy, clad in a pink and orange striped bikini she bought in the pre-teen department, was already engrossed in a recent police procedural. She wasn't as deeply tanned as Bolivia, but she was already four shades darker than Anne ever got.

Anne was feeling more relaxed than she had in weeks. Usually she took work home with her on weekends; this time she'd left it there and promised herself two days without even thinking about anything to do with the law.

A shadow moved over her, and at first she thought it was from the sun moving behind the palm tree beside her. When she realized it was a person, she looked up and recognized his face, his name coming to her a couple of seconds later.

"I thought that was you, Anne."

She took off her Walkman and smiled up at him. "Hi, Sean, what're you doing down here?"

"We're playing at Rick's for the month. You going to come by and see us?"

Anne saw Sandy looking over and introduced them.

"I imagine you're a musician," said Sandy.

"You can tell just by looking at me?" asked Sean.

"His group is playing over at Rick's," said Anne. "Maybe we could go by there tonight."

"I thought we were going to a movie?"

"Well, after the movie," said Anne. She didn't know what Sandy was so worried about. It wasn't as if she was going to start up anything with Sean. That had been over with for years, and anyway, they were only going to be here for the weekend.

Quintana got to the bar a few minutes early and ordered a lager. He had half downed it when Guy arrived. Quintana waved him over, then asked if he would mind drinking in one of the more private booths.

"Feeling a little alienated tonight, Jack?" asked Guy.

"Worse than alienated," said Quintana, heading for one of the booths. He barely allowed Guy time to order a drink before saying, "The strangest things have been happening to me."

"To you? Come on, nothing strange ever happens to Jack Quintana. Except maybe finally living with a member of the opposite sex."

Quintana, who didn't see any humor in the remark, asked, "Did that strike you as strange at the time?"

"I don't know whether 'strange' is the correct word. I was speechless for a few days, though. If we hadn't been roommates once upon a time, I would've begun to wonder about your sexual preference."

"I've dated women over the years."

Guy gave a short bark of laughter. "You date women the way some of us speak Spanish—just enough to get along but never with any real enthusiasm."

"She hasn't come back yet."

"Marissa?"

Quintana nodded.

"Why didn't you tell me on the phone? I figured since I hadn't heard from you she had shown up. What exactly happened?"

Quintana shrugged. "I came home one night and she wasn't there."

"Was that like her?"

"I don't know, but it was the first time it happened since she moved in with me."

"I confess to not knowing Marissa very well. How many times have I seen her? Two? No, New Year's would make it three. Three times, and we barely spoke. Beautiful woman, though. Full of life, was my impression."

And those three times Quintana had practically needed to drag her out of the house. Marissa was bored to death with "lawyer talk" and professed to find his friends dead bores.

Quintana related what had happened, ending up with, "Now that I've found her wallet, I'm afraid the police are going to figure the body belongs to Marissa and I'm the logical suspect. Hell, *I'd* think that—anyone would.''

''Not anyone who knows you,'' said Guy.

''You don't think I'm capable of murder? Come on, I remember those discussions we used to have in college. I thought we all agreed that, given the right circumstances, anyone is capable of murder.''

''Maybe, but not the murder of a girlfriend. What would be the point? If you wanted to get rid of her, all you had to do was ask her to move out.''

''How about in the heat of passion? Marissa and I did have some pretty strong arguments.''

''I've been in strong arguments with you, Jack. You get deadly cold and logical and destroy everyone with your decisive mind. I've never known you to get physical. I don't think you've ever even punched a guy out, have you?''

''Not since I was about ten years old, and then only once. I got a tooth knocked out, and my mother gave me hell when I got home. I don't know, Guy—none of this is making any sense to me. A missing woman, a convenient body in the canal...''

''They're always finding bodies in the canals, and they usually turn out to be drug related.''

''And usually men.''

''There have been a number of women's bodies found,'' said Guy. ''I hope you've talked to a criminal lawyer.''

''The only criminal lawyers I know are ex-students, most of whom hated my guts.''

''You haven't talked to a lawyer?''

''I'm talking to you.''

''What about this neighbor, the one who claims Marissa said you beat her, have you talked to her?''

''I don't even know the woman. And Marissa never once mentioned talking to any of the neighbors. In fact, she remarked on more than one occasion what an unfriendly lot they were.''

''Have you thought of hiring a private investigator?''

''No, Guy, and I'm not about to. I have a certain amount of confidence in our law enforcement agencies, and even more confidence that our system of justice isn't going to convict an innocent man. And I have an absolute loathing of people poking and prying in my business.''

''All right,'' said Guy, ''what do you want from me?''

''I think I just needed to talk to someone, get some feedback. I keep going over and over the circumstances in my mind, and nothing makes any sense.''

''Have you told the police about the wallet yet?''

''I thought I'd call them in the morning.''

''Don't. It's one thing going to them for help and another thing doing their work for them. You'd be handing them more circumstantial evidence that's going to look bad for you.''

''Well, I'll tell you, Guy, if I'd killed her, I wouldn't. But since I didn't, I'd like to help them in any way I can.''

''I've had about as much experience in criminal law as you, Jack—meaning none at all—but I still know enough that I wouldn't help the police drive nails in my coffin.''

''All they really have, Guy, is a missing woman and a neighbor who's a troublemaker. The body sounds pretty much unidentifiable, and I know Marissa wouldn't have gone near a canal. I'm not worried about the circumstantial evidence. I'm just eager to solve the mystery and get back to normal.''

''Normal meaning with Marissa?''

Quintana hesitated a moment before speaking. ''No. Not quite. I'd say that's over.''

''I'm sorry to hear that, Jack.''

''Like you said, I'm not very good with women.''

"That's because you don't try."

"I don't meet that many women. Oh, there are plenty of law students who come on to me, but all they want is an improved grade or a little extracurricular help. And anyway, I've never approved of professors who carry on with their students."

"There were enough women after you at Harvard."

"Yes, and you also remember how much time we had for them. Virtually none, as I recall."

"It's strange the way you suddenly met a woman and she moved in with you almost immediately, and now, just as suddenly, she's disappeared."

"It struck me the same way. But all that might mean is that it's in character for her. Maybe Marissa has a habit of meeting men and moving in with them and then disappearing. Maybe it's a career choice with her."

"A career assumes compensation. Did she abscond with your funds?"

"Didn't even take her credit cards."

"Then it's not a scam of any kind."

"I never thought it was."

"Sorry, Jack, you knew her a lot better than I did."

"Maybe not. Maybe I didn't know her at all."

Guy reached over and plucked a menu from behind the napkin dispenser. "What do you say, you want to order some food?"

"Why don't we just drink ourselves into oblivion?"

"Because we're law abiding citizens and we have to drive ourselves home. Come on, they've got pretty good steaks here."

"Life has to go on, right?"

"I've been thinking, Jack. We've got a sharp new associate at the firm, formerly with the Public Defender's office."

"Thanks, Guy, but I really don't think I need a lawyer yet any more than I need dinner. Let's just drink and forget about it."

"She not only had a good track record, I heard she was dynamite with a jury."

"She?"

"Never let it be said that our firm isn't an equal opportunity employer."

"A woman?"

"Wasn't it you who once told me that most of your best students were female?"

"That doesn't mean I want one defending me, if I even need defending. And I don't want to hear about juries. It isn't conceivable that this would go that far."

"In the rare event it should come to that, I just thought I'd throw it out. I'd highly recommend her."

"Since when are you hiring from the Public Defender's office?"

"She was also straight As, *Law Review*, and we needed a boost in our litigation department. And she's got an unbelievable body."

"Real professional, Guy."

"Hey, I was just kidding. She's got a fine mind, one of the best."

"Oh, right. I can remember how you always went for minds."

"When I'm hiring, I do."

"I'll keep her in mind, Guy, and I want you to know I appreciate your meeting me here tonight."

"You *appreciate* it? How many times have I called you and suggested we get together?"

"I won't let this much time go by again."

"How about tennis at the club tomorrow? If we're in any shape by then, that is."

"If they haven't locked me up by then, you're on."

Which, at the time, Quintana had meant as a joke. That, however, was before life played a couple of additional little jokes on him.

He had just finished shaving and was still in his pajamas when the police arrived on Sunday morning. He and Guy had stayed out late drinking, and he had punched the alarm clock when it went off for the tennis game and gone back to sleep. Knowing his friend's tendency toward hangovers, he figured Guy was probably doing the same thing.

"Sorry to disturb you, Mr. Quintana, but it's after ten," said Detective Betancourt.

Still not wide-awake and feeling at a distinct disadvantage in his blue-striped pajamas, Quintana said, "Could you come back a little later? Maybe an hour?"

"I'm afraid not, sir. We have a search warrant for these premises."

That woke him up fast enough. Now, looking past the detectives, he noticed for the first time that two squad cars were parked in the street. "A search warrant? May I take a look at it?"

Betancourt handed it over, and Quintana quickly perused it. "Does that mean the woman in the canal was identified as Marissa?"

"No, sir," said Betancourt.

"Well, then?"

"It was another neighbor, sir. He claims to have seen you dumping something heavy in the canal in the middle of the night about the time of her disappearance."

It took a moment for Quintana's mind to shift gears. "That was food. Food out of my freezer. The power was off that night, and I was afraid it would go bad."

"Yes, sir."

He could see they didn't believe him. And how did you prove something like that? Unless the fish were more particular than he thought they were, there wouldn't be any food still residing at the bottom of the canal.

"Come in," said Quintana. "Search wherever you want. Am I allowed to get dressed?"

"Certainly, sir," said Detective Soffer. "I'll just go with you, if you don't mind."

"Incidentally," said Quintana, "I was going to call you this morning. I didn't find an appointment book, but I found Marissa's wallet in one of her handbags. All her credit cards were in it."

Which they would have found anyway in their search, but now it sounded as though that were the only reason he was telling them.

When he finished dressing and went down to the kitchen to fix himself some coffee, the house appeared to be swarming with uniformed police, all busily making a shambles of the place.

He was sitting at the kitchen table with his cup of coffee and a rather stale doughnut when one of the uniformed cops emerged from the laundry room with the announcement that he had found a knife.

Quintana watched while Betancourt, being careful not to get his fingerprints on it, placed the knife in a clear plastic bag, then showed the bag to him. The knife had traces of what appeared to be dried blood.

"Do you recognize this knife?" Betancourt asked him.

Quintana looked over at the knife rack in the kitchen. The handles looked the same and one of the knives was missing from its place. "It looks like it belongs to that set."

At that point they read him his rights.

Chapter 3

Betancourt and Soffer led a handcuffed Jack Quintana out of the house.

Nothing seemed real to him, not the handcuffs, not the cops walking on either side of him, not the perfect spring day with the cumulus clouds hanging individually in the sky and looking primitively one-dimensional, or his front lawn that badly needed mowing.

He saw something move out of the corner of his eye and looked to the left to see his neighbors to the north come out of the house and stand by the front door to watch. The man was dressed only in pajama bottoms, hanging low beneath his stomach, the cuffs dragging on the ground. The woman was in white shorts and a halter top, and her hair looked perfectly sculpted, as though she had gotten out of bed and immediately put on a wig. He met their eyes for a moment, and their looks were rapacious. It stunned him that such looks were coming from people he didn't even know.

The police car was hot, and the cops rolled down the windows in lieu of air-conditioning. Quintana sat alone in the back seat. He rested his handcuffed wrists on his lap and tried to keep his back away from the blistering hot upholstery. Soffer was driving, and he burned a little rubber as he pulled away from the curb, but then he slowed down so that they could easily have been out for a Sunday drive.

Quintana couldn't seem to think. He couldn't get his thoughts together in order to make a plan of what to do. He was sure the police had it all planned out for him in any case, but it made him feel helpless not to have his own plan. He couldn't remember ever feeling so totally out of control of his own life. He tried to form questions to ask the two officers, but only sentence fragments came to him, and none of them made any sense.

Betancourt smoked while Soffer drove slowly through the quiet streets of Coral Gables and then more quickly into downtown Miami. The city was deserted on a Sunday. In the front seat the cops began discussing where they would go for lunch. Quintana hung on to the word "lunch" in his mind for a moment, but no image seemed to form, and the word finally broke up into individual letters that drifted away.

The jail seemed to be doing a brisker business than the rest of downtown Miami. Here cars lined the streets and people were going in and out of the glass doors. Betancourt parked the car and then opened the back door to allow Quintana to get out.

Quintana saw two men in shirtsleeves running in their direction, and the cops quickly moved to each side of him. Quintana first thought that friends had heard about his plight and come to his aid. As the men drew closer, however, he saw that he didn't recognize them.

The cops started to propel him up the steps, and it was then that one of the men shouted, "Hey, Jack, did you kill your lover?"

Quintana met the man's eyes. They had the cold, unfeeling look of a reptile's. It wasn't the eyes that bothered him, though, it was the way the man felt free to call him Jack, as though he were an old friend or a colleague.

Now the other man said something about a statement, but by this time Quintana had blanked his mind to what was happening around him, and it wasn't until he was in the booking room that he again allowed himself access to his surroundings.

The humiliation of being addressed so freely by a total stranger had in no way prepared him for the further humiliations he was to suffer.

"I guess we can at least take the cuffs off, Professor," said Soffer, looking over at Betancourt for his nod of agreement.

Quintana hardly noticed that the cuffs were being removed. His eyes were going around the room, separating the criminals from the cops; his ears were tuned to a preponderance of Spanish being spoken; his sense of smell was assailed from all sides by things he didn't want to give names to. It was a side of Miami as different from the university campus as it was possible to be. He was feeling something he didn't recognize at first. And then it came to him that what he felt was guilt. Knowing his innocence, he yet felt extreme guilt. It had started the moment the handcuffs were put on his wrists and come to fruition inside the station.

"You sure you don't want a lawyer?" asked Betancourt. He had first asked the question back at the house.

Quintana shook his head. A lawyer meant a colleague. He wanted to be alone with his humiliation. Anyway, he was a lawyer himself, wasn't he?

"The judge'll appoint you one," said Soffer.

"I can plead not guilty all by myself," said Quintana in a low voice, then repeated it a little louder. He repeated the words *not guilty* to himself a few times, as though by doing so he would begin to feel innocent.

They were in a large room lit by fluorescent lighting, the windows, for some reason, having blinds that were closed. Not being able to look out and see the palm trees and the sky seemed to make the walls close in on him. Quintana took a deep breath and slowly expelled it.

"Hey, don't worry, this won't take long," said Soffer and Quintana was grateful for the man's solicitude. He found he was getting the urge to confess even though he had nothing to confess.

Betancourt lit a cigarette, looking around as though to defy anyone to ask him to put it out, then leaned in close to Quintana. "You really ought to call someone, sir. Surely, teaching law and all, you know some lawyers. It's gonna make it a lot easier on you if you have someone here who knows the procedure."

Quintana thought of Guy. He wondered if Guy would be at the club playing tennis. He thought of putting through a call and having him paged, and then Guy resuming his game with, "That was a friend of mine, they've arrested him for murder." He imagined the embarrassed laughter from his tennis partner.

No, that wasn't Guy. Guy would drop everything and come down to help him. He'd do the same for Guy with no questions asked. If Guy were here he wouldn't be feeling so out of it; he'd have someone on his side to talk to.

Quintana turned to Betancourt. "All right, I think I will call my lawyer."

Betancourt seemed to cheer up. "Right over there, sir," he told him, pointing out the rows of wall phones, most of them in use.

Quintana reached in his pocket for change, saw he had a quarter, and followed Betancourt over to the phones.

He tried Guy at home, and he picked up on the second ring.

"Guy? It's Jack."

"Hey, buddy, you change your mind about tennis?"

"I've been arrested. I'm calling you from the jail."

"Don't move, I'll be right there."

Quintana saw that some of the other men, all of them in handcuffs, were eyeing him. They seemed to be waiting in line for something, although the line was somewhat scattered. They mostly looked like vagrants, and Quintana was grateful he'd shaved that morning. At least he didn't look like a common criminal, or like the probably false picture he had of what the criminal element supposedly looked like. Since he was a part of the criminal element now—alleged, anyway—he realized he'd have to revise that picture.

When it was Quintana's turn, he was asked his name, address and a few other questions while the cop behind the desk slowly typed out the information on a form. Then he was asked to empty his pockets and hand over the contents.

Quintana pulled out his wallet, some change and a pocket comb and placed them on the desk while the cop described them out loud as he continued his two-fingered efforts at the typewriter. He wondered now why he had thought to slip the comb into his pocket before he left the house.

"Your watch, too," said Soffer, and Quintana slipped it off his wrist and dutifully handed it over. He didn't even glance at it, as though time had no more relevance for him.

"Okay, I'll need your belt and your shoelaces," said the cop behind the desk.

Quintana was wearing no belt with his chinos, and his Docksiders had no laces. He supposed he could at least feel grateful that he wasn't going to be subjected to the added humiliation of having his pants fall down or his shoes fall off.

"We'll be seeing you later when you're arraigned," said Betancourt. "You'll see your lawyer up there, too." Soffer gave him a pat on the shoulder before the two of them headed for the door. Another cop seemed to have taken their place and was now taking his arm, so that Quintana found himself walking in the direction of a long corridor. He could hear the sound of cell doors being banged shut, but before they entered the corridor, the man steered him into a smaller room and handed him over to another cop.

Quintana stared at the new cop, this one a young Latino with a mustache half the size of his face. He took Quintana's picture, front view and then profile, and after that came the fingerprinting. Quintana no longer felt human; he felt like a cipher.

After that he was handcuffed again and put in the holding cell.

Quintana stood in a corner of the cell leaning against the wall and trying to appear invisible. He didn't ordinarily think of himself as a snob, but he didn't feel he had anything in common with the other occupants. For starters he noted that he was the only one who wasn't wearing flashily-striped running shoes. He had thought only joggers wore running shoes; now he was beginning to think they were normal criminal attire.

Everyone was speaking Spanish, and the fact that he was Cuban, and looked it, probably helped. God help him if he were the only Anglo in the cell.

One edgy little man with needle tracks down both arms sidled up to him and asked him for a cigarette.

"I don't smoke," said Quintana in Spanish.

The man shrugged and edged away to ask someone else. Quintana thought the cell was one of the few remaining places in Miami where they didn't segregate the smokers. Maybe the jail system was pure democracy at work.

He looked around at his fellow cell mates, taking care not to lock eyes with any of them. He supposed he should be feeling fear, but all he felt was despair. Despair for himself for ending up here when he was innocent; despair for them, whether they were innocent or not, for being treated as subhumans. And because they were treated as such, he was sure they began to act accordingly. He was already fighting an urge to grab hold of the bars and scream to be released.

A palmetto bug the size of a child's sneaker scuttled out from a corner of the cell, and one of the men stomped it to death. Quintana turned to the wall and rested his face against its cool surface. He felt as if he was going to be sick. Judging from the smell in the cell he wouldn't be the first one, but he forced himself not to be. Being sick all over himself would be the final humiliation and one, he felt, he might not recover from.

A cop carrying a clipboard stood outside the bars and read off a list of names, Quintana's included.

He fell into line behind three others, and they were led down a corridor and then up some stairs. He blinked when they were led into a brightly lit room. It held a judge's bench, some desks, seats for the spectators and a multitude of people milling around, seemingly with no purpose.

Out of the confusion and commotion Guy strode into view, approaching Quintana with a wry look and a shake of his head. Like Quintana, he was dressed in chinos and a pale blue oxford-cloth shirt with the sleeves rolled up twice. Harvard habits died hard.

"You holding up okay?" Guy asked him, putting an arm around his shoulders.

"Our criminal justice system is unbelievable," said Quintana.

"That's why neither of us went into criminal law."

"I appreciate your coming down, Guy."

"There's nothing to be appreciative about," said Guy. "If our circumstances were reversed, you'd do the same for me."

Quintana couldn't conceive of their circumstances ever being reversed. A well-ordered life, as Guy's was, didn't lend itself to appearances in criminal court. It came to him in a flash that the first break from his own pattern—living with a woman—had made a rent in the fabric of his life through which more and more bizarre incidents had slipped through. If he hadn't agreed to a live-in relationship with Marissa, then she wouldn't have lied to a neighbor and a body wouldn't have been found in the canal and he wouldn't be here today being charged as a criminal. Quintana didn't believe in coincidence, but he did believe in conspiracy, and only the notion of how paranoid it would make him sound prevented him from sharing his notion with Guy.

Quintana heard a number being called out, followed by his name, and Guy, taking him by the elbow, said, "That's us."

They approached the bench from behind a rail, and the judge asked Quintana if he was represented by counsel.

"I'm representing him, Your Honor," said Guy.

Separating himself from the crowd of people, a young man who looked as though he hadn't slept in days said, "We're asking bail be set at a hundred thousand dollars, Your Honor."

"Your Honor," said Guy, acting as though he were in criminal court every day of his life, "my client is a member of the law faculty at the University of Miami and a respected member of the community. He's never so much as gotten a parking ticket in his life. I see no reason why he shouldn't be released on his own recognizance while this error in justice is being sorted out."

"Where did you learn that stuff?" Quintana asked Guy under his breath.

"From watching television," whispered Guy.

In a surprising move, the young man with the district attorney's office said to Quintana, "I had you in law school, Professor."

Quintana managed a grim smile. He'd much prefer that the young man had never heard of him. Unlike some jolly professors, Quintana seldom had former students look him up to reminisce over old times. Old times in Quintana's class didn't make for sentimentality, which was all right with him. It was his difficult profs at Harvard who he recalled with appreciation, not the ones who were easy under some misguided desire to be friends with their students.

The judge, looking harassed and overworked, said, "The court releases defendant, Jack Quintana, under a bond in the amount of twenty-five-thousand, pending presentation of this complaint to the grand jury."

"What happens now?" Quintana asked Guy.

Guy gave a shrug. "I'm not quite sure."

The former student made himself helpful. "What you do is go to a bail bondsman—you'll find several in the neighborhood. As soon as you make bail, they'll release the professor.'' Then the young man turned to Quintana. ''Good luck, sir. I'm sorry about asking for that amount of bail, but, you know, I'm just told what to do.''

''Don't worry about it,'' said Quintana.

A cop was already taking him by the arm when Guy said, ''Hang in there, Jack. I'll be back with the bail as quick as I can.''

When this was all over—and Quintana had to believe that it would be, and very soon—he vowed he'd get Guy the best tennis racket money could buy and even let him beat him for at least a set. For a man who liked his solitude, he'd never been so glad to see anyone in his life.

A worse ordeal than the court appearance took place on the steps outside the building, when Quintana was duly released on bail. It must have been a slow Sunday for news, because a gaggle of reporters were lying in wait for him, yelling out the familiar ''Jack'' again and shouting out questions that even his friends would feel were too personal to ask.

''We're going to be on the six o'clock news,'' Guy warned him as they ran for the parking lot where Guy had left his car.

''I'm really sorry to have put you through this,'' said Quintana.

''Will you stop it, Jack? The whole city should be feeling guilty at putting you through this. All I'm getting is my picture on TV, which my kids are going to get a big charge out of.''

Guy drove out of the parking lot, narrowly avoiding hitting one of the reporters who had sprinted after them. ''Have you eaten, or is that a stupid question?''

''I had breakfast before they arrived.''

''Well, come on home with me and we'll have some lunch.''

"I don't want to put you to any more trouble, Guy."

"I swear to God, if you don't stop it with the gratitude, I'm going to throw you out of the car and leave you to the mercy of the press. Anyway, if you go home now, you'll probably have reporters camping on your front porch."

"Thanks. Lunch sounds good. Oh, and Guy, did you know you lied back there in court?"

Guy took his eyes off the road and looked at Quintana. "Lied? What're you talking about?"

"About my never having gotten a parking ticket. I've had several."

"That's all right," said Guy. "I wasn't under oath."

Halfway back from the Keys, Anne said, "So what do you say we stop for a . . . hamburger."

"You were going to say drink," said Sandy.

"Old habits die hard."

"I could use a burger," said Bolivia.

"Why don't you take me home first?" said Sandy.

"You don't want to eat with us?" asked Anne. "You can't wait to get rid of our company?"

"I have a dinner date," mumbled Sandy.

Anne almost had a traffic accident on I-95 from pure shock. "Did you say *date*?"

"Date? What's a date?" asked Bolivia.

"You remember," said Sandy, "it's when a man asks you out."

"It's hard to remember that far back," said Bolivia.

"Who is it?" said Anne.

Sandy seemed to suddenly find the view out the side window totally enthralling. "I don't want to talk about it."

"Wrong," said Anne. "You can't say something like that and then not talk about it. Come on, we'll have a burger and you can tell us all about it. What time's your date?"

"Not for a couple of hours."

"Perfect," said Anne, pulling off the highway and driving down two blocks to a Burger King.

Sandy refused to talk until they were at the table with their food, and then didn't make it easy for them.

"What's the big mystery here?" asked Bolivia. "You dating a married man or something?"

"I hope not," said Sandy.

"Where'd you meet him, when did you meet him and why haven't we heard about him?" Bolivia had the reporter's knack for asking questions.

"I haven't exactly met him," Sandy admitted.

"A blind date?" asked Anne. "I thought women didn't do that kind of thing anymore."

"It's not a blind date," said Sandy.

"Well, what exactly is it?"

"You're going to kill me," said Sandy.

"Don't tell me you're dating a musician," said Anne.

"I put a personal ad in the paper."

There was dead silence for about five seconds. "That's disgusting," said Bolivia.

"I know," said Sandy. "But what am I supposed to do? The only men I ever meet are criminals."

"I wish I'd thought of that," said Bolivia. "What'd you say in the ad?"

"I don't remember."

"Don't give us that," said Anne. "I'll bet you spent hours composing that ad. It's inconceivable that you wouldn't remember every word."

"I said, 'Female law enforcement officer, thirty—'"

"You advertised the fact you're a cop?" asked Bolivia.

"Well, that's what I am."

"You're asking for it," said Bolivia. "Every nut who likes to be tied up and handcuffed is going to answer that ad."

"That might be fun," said Anne, trying not to laugh.

Sandy wasn't amused. "I said I was looking for a man between twenty-five and forty—"

"*Twenty-five?*" asked Bolivia. "You're beginning to sound like Anne."

"There's nothing wrong with twenty-five-year-olds," said Anne. "In fact, there's nothing wrong with twenty-one-year-olds."

"Anyway," said Sandy, "you should see all the letters I got. And they don't sound like nuts, either." She reached into her straw bag, took out her wallet and extracted a picture from it. She handed it to Bolivia. "This one is the one I'm going out with tonight."

"Not bad," said Bolivia after a moment, "if you like blonds."

"I like blonds," said Sandy.

"That good-looking, you wonder why he has to answer an ad."

"Let me see," said Anne, grabbing the picture. The guy was cute—nice teeth, strong chin, muscular shoulders. "Of course you don't know what he looks like from the waist down."

"He doesn't know what I look like at all," said Sandy. "All we've done is talk on the phone once."

"He'll be pleasantly surprised," Bolivia assured her. "You're probably the best-looking woman who's ever placed an ad."

"But I'm short."

"Men like short women," said Bolivia. "Take my word for it."

"You know something?" said Anne. "Here I am, I've given up men, and I'm not even jealous."

"Big deal," said Bolivia. "You've given up men for two whole days. I'm jealous. I'm ready to meet a good man."

"And settle down?" asked Anne.

"Hell no! Let's not get ridiculous here."

Anne wasn't ready to meet a man. She was actually looking forward to a sabbatical from men.

It was after ten when Guy dropped Jack off at the house. If there had been reporters there earlier, they weren't in evidence now.

"Thanks," said Quintana. "For everything."

"Despite the circumstances, Jack, I really enjoyed seeing you today."

"Your kids are funny."

"They're at a great age."

"Barbara's pretty funny, too."

"Yeah, we're a regular family sitcom. You ought to visit more often."

"Maybe you guys will all visit me in prison."

"Very funny."

"This attorney of yours, you really think I ought to talk to her?"

"You ought to talk to some attorney. All that law school, and neither one of us knows a damn thing about criminal law. Ironic, huh?"

"She's really good?"

"Don't take my word for it, ask around. She made quite a reputation for herself at the Public Defender's office."

"I'll take your word for it."

"Just don't fall in love with her and steal her away from me. She's got a real future with us."

"Fall in *love* with her? I'm in this mess because of one woman, you think I'd be that stupid?"

"Only joking. I doubt she'd allow that kind of unprofessional behavior from you anyway. But wait'll you see her. You're not going to believe your eyes."

"You'll set it up?"

"Be glad to."

A woman? Did he really want to talk to a female attorney? "What's her name?"

"Anne Larkin."

"Sounds like a Vassar girl."

"As a matter of fact, she was a student of yours."

He gave Guy a look of disbelief. "And you're just telling me now?"

"I didn't think it was pertinent."

"Just what I want, to be at the mercy of one of my former students. That's like one of my nightmares coming true."

"Maybe that'll teach you to be nicer to your students in the future."

"I probably flunked her."

"No way," said Guy. "She got straight As in law school."

"That's a relief," said Quintana. "She might not have liked me, but at least she can't grouse about getting a bad grade."

"I'll talk to you in the morning and confirm, then set it up with her. Wait'll you see her," he repeated. "You won't believe me until you've actually seen her. If I were on a jury I'd give her anything she wants."

"You got something going with her I should know about?"

Guy widened his eyes. "Me? Hey, I'm in love with my wife."

"I was beginning to wonder."

"That doesn't mean I can't look, though. I'm not dead yet."

Quintana reached for the door handle. "Well, thanks again, and I'll talk to you in the morning."

He waited until Guy drove off then turned toward his house. He saw movement from his neighbors' lighted window and looked in that direction. The neighbor who was partially responsible for him being in this mess was standing in the window staring out at him. She was probably worried that the murderer was on the loose.

Quintana gave her a big smile and a wave and saw the curtain quickly fall back into place. Women. They seemed to be the cause of all of his problems.

Chapter 4

Anne was hard at work trying to save a client from a possible corporate takeover when her secretary buzzed her to say that Guy Talbot wanted to see her in his office.

"Did he call personally?" Anne asked her.

"His secretary called," said Jeri.

This procedure was unusual enough that Anne felt instant trepidation. Usually the senior partners dropped by the associates' offices if they wanted to talk. More often they sent interoffice memos. If Anne needed to get Guy's approval on something, she called his office and asked his secretary if she could get in to see him. But invitations to come to senior partners' offices usually meant something serious like a raise or getting fired, and since Anne wasn't due for a raise, the other possibility had to leap to mind. The problem with working for a large law firm was that they fired someone just often enough to keep everyone else slightly paranoid.

Something in her mind flashed the words *Professor Quintana*, but she ignored it. That was another subject she seemed to be becoming paranoid about; he might invade her dreams, but she'd be damned if she'd let him encroach on her daylight hours.

She picked up her dictation in the middle of the sentence, completed her thought, then headed for Talbot's office. This necessitated taking the elevator, since senior partners were on the penthouse floor and only secretaries and law clerks were supposed to use the stairs. It was supposedly beneath the dignity of the associates, although Anne never found anything very dignified about waiting for the slowest, most unreliable elevator in creation.

Guy Talbot didn't look as if he was going to fire her when she walked in. He looked serious, but he didn't look that serious, and he was seated in his Eames chair rather than behind his desk. Anne began to relax a little and took a seat on his leather couch while he had his secretary bring them both coffee. Her choice of seating turned out to be a mistake. The couch was deceptively soft, and Anne sank way down, putting her knees at eye level and herself at an immediate disadvantage. She tried to be surreptitious about yanking at her skirt to get it past her knees, but from her vantage point she couldn't tell how successful she was.

Thank God Talbot was too much of a gentleman to have his eyes anywhere near her legs. Or anywhere else they shouldn't be. If he even noticed things like that, which she doubted. She had always regarded him as something of a stuffed shirt in that respect. Some of the senior partners actually acted human at times and could even be seen flirting with the secretaries on occasion, but not Guy Talbot. Guy Talbot was Mr. Spotless.

"So how's it going with Centricon?" he asked her, the kind of thing that passed for social banter in their office.

"It looks good," said Anne. "I'll probably have to fly to Delaware on it next week."

That seemed to be the extent of his interest in Centricon. He waited while his secretary served the coffee, at which point Anne managed to get up off the couch and take a chair next to a small table, knowing she would never be able to manage both her skirt and the coffee otherwise.

"We don't want to be disturbed, Janet," he told his secretary as the woman left his office.

Quintana flashed again, but she was sure she was being paranoid. Lightning didn't strike twice in the same place.

Still, things were taking a mysterious turn when a senior partner didn't want to be disturbed while talking to a lowly associate. Formerly *the* lowest, but recently two more associates had been added to the firm, so she was no longer the new girl in town. Not that anyone at Hutchinson, Talbot, Withers, et al, would dare breathe the word *girl* when referring to a female attorney.

"I have a favor to ask of you, Anne," he said, getting down to business.

It was something associates prayed for—a chance to do a favor for one of the partners. "Certainly," she said, trying to hide her eagerness.

"A very close friend of mine was arrested yesterday for murder."

What could she say to something like that? If he'd said an old friend had died, then she would offer condolences; if he'd said his kid had flunked out of law school, she would commiserate. But what did you say to someone whose friend had been accused of murder? Since the chances were good that she'd say exactly the wrong thing, Anne didn't say anything. Relief swept through her, though, that it wasn't anything to do with Professor Quintana. She did, however, begin to wonder about Guy's taste in friends.

"It's Jack Quintana. He called when you were in my office last week."

Anne sat very still in a near state of shock. Why, after years of never even thinking about him, was this now happening to her? And Professor Quintana a murderer? She was sure he was capable of it, but she could more easily imagine him having been murdered.

"He's an old friend of mine. We went to Harvard Law together."

She tried to picture Guy Talbot and Jack Quintana back in their Harvard Law School days. They must have been that young once; they must have laughed and joked around and complained about their classes. They must have—but no picture would come to mind. It was easier to imagine that they were both fully grown and serious.

"He needs counsel, Anne, and I recommended you."

"I don't imagine he would remember me out of all the thousands of students he's had."

He shook his head. "At least he didn't mention it. I said you were the only one in the firm with any criminal experience. I told him we all thought highly of you."

She risked speaking her mind. "Do I have a choice?"

"Of course you do. But he's an old friend, and I want him to have the best defense we can give him."

"Why doesn't he go to a firm that specializes in criminal law? After all, a law professor must know dozens of criminal lawyers."

"I would guess he trusts my judgment. And, in my judgment, you're a fine criminal lawyer. Actually, that was the deciding factor when we hired you. We'd never hired anyone out of the Public Defender's office before, and it was just this kind of contingency we had in mind. That and experience in litigation, of course."

Anne thought of walking out right then and having her secretary type up her resignation. She thought of calling her old boss at the Public Defender's office and begging for her job back, pleading with him to give her the scum of the earth to defend rather than having to defend the number one man on her most hated list. But then she thought of her new co-op and her Jaguar and her charge cards and the investment portfolio she was quickly acquiring and, most importantly, the fact that she truly loved her job.

That left her no choice but to say, "It will be a privilege." Meaning it would be a privilege to defend a senior partner's friend, thus assuring her of a few points when they next selected a partner.

Then came another low blow. "I told him, as a favor to an old friend, that you'd stop by his office on campus this afternoon and get acquainted."

"He's out on bail?"

"The bail appearance was yesterday." He stood up and walked over to his desk.

Anne set down her coffee cup. The interview appeared to be over. She got up, nodded to her boss and tried to maintain her smile all the way out of his office.

Jack Quintana was still lean and dark and sexy, and Anne still felt the same trepidation on walking into his office that she used to feel upon entering his Torts class.

He stood up when she entered, as befitted a proper Harvard gentleman, and held out his hand.

She took it for the split second that was necessary, saying, "I'm Anne Larkin," and then fought the urge to wipe her palm off on her skirt. Damn it, he still made her sweat.

"Sit down," he said, moving a stack of papers off a chair, then resuming his seat behind the desk. "Guy speaks highly of you."

Was there a twinkle in his eye when he said that? No, it wasn't possible. People like Professor Quintana didn't twinkle. Nevertheless, she didn't return the compliment. "I understand from Mr. Talbot that you've been arrested for murder."

When he merely nodded, she said, "He didn't tell me any of the details."

"I've been accused of murdering the woman I was living with."

"When did this happen?"

"The police arrested me at home yesterday, and I'm currently out on bail. Today the dean has asked that I take a leave of absence from the university until the matter is cleared up. As it seems certain that will take at least until the end of the semester, I was just about to clean out my office."

He sounded disappointed and resigned, but she was sure he understood that a law school couldn't have a suspected felon teaching their innocent students.

He stood again and seemed to measure, with his eyes, the shelves full of books against the few cartons on the floor. "Do you mind if I work while we talk?"

If he had been anyone else, she would have offered to help him, but aside from the fact that the only help he was going to get from her was under duress, she didn't wear a four-hundred-dollar white linen suit to clean her own place, so she didn't know why she should risk ruining it for his.

"Go right ahead," Anne told him, "but this shouldn't take long. I'd like you to come into my office tomorrow so that I can record the details. For today I thought I'd give you a chance to meet me and turn me down, if you wish. And if you decide to engage me, I'd like to hear what precipitated the arrest."

His eyes narrowed as he surveyed her for about the third time, and she knew he was balancing her youthful appearance against his friend's recommendation. "Are you good at swaying a jury?"

"Oh, yes." Much too good on a couple of occasions, when the defendants should have been sent up for life.

"The thing is," he said, now staring off into the distance, "none of it seems quite real. I've never knowingly committed a crime in my life, and I keep thinking the police will be by any minute to apologize."

He sounded sincere, but criminals had a way of sounding sincere, and it was the rare criminal who ever admitted to doing anything wrong. And as far as she was concerned, he'd done worse than commit a crime. Murdering a woman was probably a piece of cake for him after demolishing countless law students.

"Why don't you just tell me about it while you pack up?" She wanted to hear it and get out of there.

He nodded a couple of times, then began to pace around his office. He was wearing tan cotton pants and a light blue dress shirt with a button-down collar. He was still dressing for Harvard Square even in the tropics of Miami. His narrow black knit tie, several years out of date, was already loosened, but now he rolled up his sleeves, took a quick look at his conservative, tasteful tank watch and then began to pull books out of the bookcases and put them in liquor store cartons and some shopping bags bearing a local grocery store logo on the sides.

The sight of the advertising on the cartons made her long for a drink. If it hadn't been for her wager with her friends, she would have fortified herself with a stiff one before coming to see the professor.

He paused for a moment, looking unsure; then he straightened up and reached for more books. She could see he wasn't used to explaining himself; that was something he left to his students. She could vividly remember explaining herself to him one morning in class while all the time his frosty brown eyes bore into her and his sarcasm boiled up inside him, impatient to spill out and demolish her. And that had been on a day when she had been extremely well prepared, to the point where she couldn't possibly slip up, and still he had scared her to death.

He had aged since she had seen him last. His thick dark hair still swept straight back from his forehead, but his forehead was a little higher now, which seemed to throw his cheekbones into relief, making them even more prominent, and there were some gray hairs mixed in with the black. Except for a few lines at the corners of his eyes, his skin was still as smooth as ever. He had the kind of satiny skin that looked as though he never needed to shave. The kind of skin that must feel like pure silk against a naked body, which was not the kind of thought that ought to be coming to mind at the moment, and she wondered at herself for even thinking it. Naked bodies, indeed. She would have preferred to be wearing a suit of armor when she was within shouting distance of him.

Not that she hadn't had some fantasies along those lines in law school, but at the time he had been the most compelling man she had ever met. She'd found in the interim that musicians were easier on the nerves.

Again, it must be the wager that was getting to her. It was twenty-four hours since she'd given up drinking and men, and naturally she was already starting to crave exactly what she couldn't have. It was part of her perverse nature, something she was well acquainted with after thirty years.

Anne made an attempt to wait him out but finally grew impatient. He was suddenly turning into the reticent type, which was not how she remembered him. Still, in her experience defending criminals, people with something to hide often became reticent.

"The police don't make a habit of arresting people for no reason, Mr. Quintana," she said, hoping to prod him out of his silence.

He nodded in agreement. And then he told her the story, slowly, concisely, as though he were teaching a point of law to one of his classes. He ended up with, "And then they searched my house and found a kitchen knife hidden away in the laundry room bearing traces of blood, which, the way things have been going, no doubt also bears my finger-prints and her blood type."

She nodded. If she were the prosecutor, she could win the case easily with that amount of evidence. Except she didn't for a minute believe a law professor would have been stu-pid enough to leave the knife around where the police could find it. Unless that was what he would assume people would believe. Still, if he had been anyone but Jack Quintana, she would have begun to have the slightest glimmer of belief in his innocence. She asked, "Does anyone hate you enough to murder your girlfriend and rig the evidence to make it look as though you did it?"

She was gratified when he winced at her use of *girl-friend.* "Several hundred law students I've failed over the course of my teaching career."

He didn't mean this in jest. The rate of suicide in law schools showed the level of tension the students were un-der. At one time she could have killed him or worse, and she had ended up with an A in his course.

"Do you believe she's dead?" she asked him.

"I'm sure she isn't."

"How can you be so sure?"

He gave her a lofty look. The kind of look he would give a student who asked a stupid question. "By looking at the evidence myself. I seriously doubt the body was Marissa's because I know I didn't throw her in the water. Since I didn't cut her with a knife, it had to be Marissa who cut herself and then planted the knife in a place where I wouldn't look. And, I for damn sure never beat her.''

"It would appear someone, perhaps your girlfriend, is out to get you," she said, but she let the doubt show in her voice.

"I agree, but I simply cannot think of a logical reason. If she wanted to leave, all she had to do was walk out the door. There's no way she could reach my assets if she's presumed dead, even if she had any legal recourse to them. The ironic thing is, if I had beaten her, then maybe I could reason it was revenge on her part, but I didn't.''

"Maybe someone else was in on it. Someone who either wants to see you in prison or wanted to see her dead."

He shook his head. "I think she's alive. If someone wanted to kill her and blame me, that person could have arranged for her body to be found in recognizable condition. She could even have been killed in the house, so I would have been the obvious suspect.''

Anne looked at her watch. She was expected at Sandy's for dinner, and Sandy always had a fit if they were late and the food was overcooked. Plus she couldn't wait to hear the details of Sandy's date.

She said, "I wouldn't take it personally if you wished to find your own attorney, perhaps one who specializes in criminal law.'' She gave him a hopeful smile.

He smiled back, but there was no humor in it. "I'll rely on Guy's judgment.''

So, that was that. She stood up and didn't hold out her hand this time. Not out of pure animosity, but because his hands were quite filthy by now. "Can you be in my office tomorrow morning at ten?''

He nodded. "Is there anything you want me to bring?"

"Not at this stage. Well, yes, maybe a picture of the girl-friend."

He reached down into one of the shopping bags and pulled out a silver frame. When he handed it to her, she saw an absolutely stunning young woman. She had short, dark curls framing the face of an angel, a teenager's body, and she was laughing at the camera in a way that made Anne want to smile. She found herself wondering what such an appealing young woman had seen in Jack Quintana.

"May I take the picture?" asked Anne.

He slid it out of the frame and handed it to her. She looked at it for a moment before putting it in her briefcase.

"Thank you for making an exception and coming here to see me," he said. She could tell by the way he said it that he wasn't used to thanking people for doing him favors.

It hurt her in a way to see this once arrogant professor humbling himself to thank her. At the same time, another part of her was reveling in it.

"Guy?"

"Yes, Jack, how'd it go?"

"She just left."

"Don't judge her by her looks, Jack. She's extremely in-telligent and highly qualified."

"How old is she?"

"You know we're not allowed to ask that question of employees. Age discrimination and all that. But judging by when she graduated from law school, I'd say twenty-nine, thirty, somewhere around there. Well preserved, wouldn't you say?"

"Tell me something, Guy, and I want the truth. Did you order her to defend me?"

"Don't be ridiculous."

"Was she given a choice in the matter?"

"Of course she was given a choice, Jack. In fact, she asked me that very question herself. When you're a new associate in a firm, however, and one of the senior partners asks a favor of you . . ."

"I thought there was a distinct coolness in the office, and it wasn't from the air conditioner, because I didn't have it on."

"Jack, she agreed to take you on, and she'll do her best for you. And believe me, her best is about as good as it gets."

"She seemed a bit nervous."

"Serves you right for scaring the hell out of your students."

"We got the hell scared out of us, didn't we? Did she remember me?"

"Oh, yes."

"I don't remember her. I even looked up her records, but all they did was confirm what you said about her grades. I have no recollection of her at all."

"That confirms my view that there's something wrong with you, Jack. A woman with her looks and you don't remember her?"

"You're the one who's always had an eye for the women, Guy."

"A man would have to be blind not to notice her. I'll tell you, she's added some glamour to this law firm. Was she wearing one of her hats?"

"Yes, she was."

"The secretaries are all trying to emulate her, but we don't pay them enough that they can afford those kinds of clothes. How about those legs of hers? When she was in my office earlier, I almost fell out of my chair when she crossed them."

"Look, Guy, I'm really not interested in her looks or her clothes. Is she as good as you say she is?"

"Probably better. She piled up the best record at the Public Defender's office since Crafty Cruz, back in the sixties. They were playing funeral dirges at the going-away party they threw for her."

"Well, let's hope I don't need someone that good."

"Want to come by the house tonight, Jack? Have dinner with us?"

"Thanks, Guy, but I have some work I have to do here."

He hung up the phone and then took it off the hook. He didn't want to hear from any more colleagues, their hushed tones suggesting he had already been convicted.

He thought of Anne Larkin. If he had passed her on the street, he never would have taken her for a lawyer. He would have thought her the spoiled young wife of a rich man, with nothing more on her mind than a shopping spree. He had thought Marissa dressed well, and she'd certainly shopped extensively, but she'd never looked as exquisitely put together as Ms. Larkin. Her large straw hat in a soft shade of brown had perfectly matched the tailored silk shirt that dipped and swayed over the rounded breasts hidden beneath it. Her white linen suit was impeccable, and when she sat and crossed her legs he'd seen a flash of lace. Her slender feet had been encased in the highest of heels made of some endangered species, the shoes a shade or two lighter than the hat and blouse. On one wrist were three chunky silver watches, and dangling silver earrings hung from her ears. Even her briefcase looked expensive. Her wide, hazel eyes had been skillfully made up, and her full lips had just a hint of pink applied to them. The only thing that saved her from the cold, impersonal look of a high-fashion model was the riotously curly hair in several shades of blond that hung to her shoulders and looked unmanageable. That and the fact that her nose appeared to be sunburned.

He was drawn by beauty: the beauty of words on a page; the sounds of a Bach cantata; sunset over the Keys. He had been drawn to Marissa's beauty, not finding until too late that her beauty was not backed up by anything of substance. But her beauty had been the familiar beauty of small, dark Cuban women; she could have passed for his sister or a cousin. Anne Larkin had the cool, remote Anglo beauty he had always considered untouchable. When he was growing up in Miami, the Cubanos and the Anglos didn't mix; even now, when most of his colleagues and friends were Anglo, he was still intimidated to a degree by their women.

Intimidated, but also intrigued. As he was intrigued by this Anne Larkin who, according to Guy, had a mind to rival her looks. Intrigued but not attracted. He was too wary of women now to fall into that particular pit again.

Bolivia's Kawasaki was already parked on the lawn when Anne pulled up in her Jaguar and parked in front of Sandy's house. It was a small cottage, really, surrounded by huge old trees whose branches met across the roof and kept the house cool and rather dark. Under the trees, thick tropical plants grew wild and gave the appearance of jungle.

She put the top up on the car and locked it. Sandy lived right off the main drag in Coconut Grove, and Anne didn't much like the neighborhood. It attracted a lot of teenagers looking for trouble and tourists looking for a good time, and tampering with her Jaguar might appeal to either group.

Anne pushed open a screen door that did very little in the way of keeping insects out as Sandy's dog had jumped against it so many times that the screening was torn loose and now the cat could go in and out at will. She hoped the cat would stay off her car this time. Last time she had been at Sandy's for dinner she had found muddy paw prints crisscrossing her hood when she left.

Anne walked through the small, crowded living room, filled with overstuffed furniture and the evidence of several discarded hobbies, the latest of which, needlepoint, was verified by several new pillows scattered around and a homily now framed over the fireplace.

She found Sandy in the kitchen. Through the open French doors, she could see Bolivia swinging in the hammock.

"Sorry I'm late," said Anne.

"No problem, I'm making crab salad."

"Need any help?" She asked this knowing that Sandy would, of course, refuse. Anne and Bolivia tended to be of no help whatsoever in a kitchen.

"Make yourself a drink and go talk to Bolivia," said Sandy, looking like a child playing house in her apron.

"Well? How was the date?"

"Could we please leave that subject until after dinner? I don't want to lose my appetite."

"That bad, huh?"

Sandy groaned in response.

Anne found a pitcher of margaritas in the refrigerator and poured herself one, then managed to evade the dog, who was trying to jump up and paw her white skirt.

Bolivia caught sight of her from the hammock and said, "Hey, let me have that. You're not drinking, remember?"

"I forgot," yelled Sandy from inside the house. "Don't you dare touch that drink!"

Anne grudgingly handed Bolivia the margarita and went back into the kitchen. "Do you mind if I get rid of these shoes and stockings?" she asked Sandy.

"I don't care if you eat stark naked," said Sandy. "What did you do, come straight from work?"

"Not exactly."

"Well, if you want to put on something of mine, help yourself."

"Nothing of yours would fit me."

"There's a pair of sweatpants in the bathroom that would fit you."

Anne changed into the sweatpants and found an oversize T-shirt, leaving her clothes hanging up in Sandy's bedroom. She got a charge out of Sandy's bedroom. She still slept in the twin-size canopy bed she'd had as a child, and the yellow ruffled bedspread was piled high with her collection of stuffed animals.

She poured herself a glass of boring ginger ale and went outside. She was glad she had changed when she saw how dirty the metal chairs were, covered with leaves and other treelike droppings. "What's up?" she asked Bolivia. "Still working on that exposé of the corrupt Miami cops?"

"Lower your voice when you say that," said Bolivia. "Talk of police corruption makes Sandy nervous, and we don't want her screwing up the dinner."

"Sandy knows what's going on."

"What about you? You don't look so happy tonight. Is corporate law finally getting to you? Is making all that money giving you a guilt complex?"

"Corporate law will never get to me," said Anne. "Corporate law is sane and wonderful. And it's incredibly satisfying to be making more money than I can spend. What's getting to me is the fact that I've been handed a criminal case."

"I thought they didn't handle criminal cases."

"This is a favor for my boss's friend. You remember me mentioning my old professor the other night, Jack Quintana?"

"I could hardly forget."

"Well, it looks as though he's still going to give me nightmares. He's been accused of murdering his lady friend."

"Wait a minute, yes, the one who threw his girlfriend into the canal," said Bolivia. "It was in the papers this morning."

"I didn't see that," said Anne, trying to remember if she'd even read a paper that day. She couldn't recall reading one, so she probably hadn't. "Hey, Sandy," she called out, "do you have this morning's paper?"

Sandy came out carrying the paper, saying, "What's this all about?"

"Your old professor made the papers today," said Bolivia. "Accused of killing his live-in lover."

"Male?" asked Sandy.

"Female," said Bolivia.

"You don't mean . . . ?" asked Sandy, turning to Bolivia.

"Right. Old Shark himself."

Anne took a look at the front page. There, in large type was "U of M Law Professor Accused of Dumping Lover's Body in Canal." There was a blurred picture of Quintana in handcuffs, but at least he had the dignity to face the camera and not shield his face. For some reason suspects who shielded their faces always looked guilty to her.

Something else would happen to shove the story off the front page, but that knowledge had probably been no consolation to her client. No wonder the university had asked him to take a leave of absence.

Sandy was reading over her shoulder. "He looks terrible."

Anne said, "He looked better in person."

"I don't remember seeing a police report on this. Is this something I should know about?"

Anne said, "All you need to know about it is that I'm defending him, albeit against my better judgment."

"Good," said Bolivia. "At least you'll have something to talk about besides your latest corporate takeover."

"Why would you be taking on a criminal case?" asked Sandy. "I thought you went with that firm so you wouldn't have to defend criminals anymore."

"He's a friend of one of the partners. They went to law school together. I really didn't have a choice in the matter."

Bolivia said, "It'll be like the old days, when we were all involved in crime."

"I hadn't realized you missed that," Anne said.

"We never know what you're talking about anymore," said Sandy. "So how's the murderer, still as sexy as ever?"

"He hasn't been found guilty yet," Anne reminded her. "But to answer your question, he's exactly like he was in law school: sexy as hell and still scary."

"So tell the truth now, Annie," said Bolivia. "Are you still attracted to him?"

"In case you've already forgotten, I've given up men for the duration."

"I haven't forgotten," said Bolivia. "I was just wondering if *you* had."

"Okay, so I'm still attracted," said Anne. "It's not like I can do anything about it. He's a client. Anyway, I never trusted that man by half."

"Oh, goody," said Sandy, "we're going to have great dinner conversation for a change. Help me bring the food out, Anne. I can't wait to hear about this."

"Hold it just a minute," said Anne. "I'll tell you all about it, but not until I hear about your date last night with the blond bombshell."

"That says it all," said Sandy. "He bombed."

"What was he, just a cute face?" asked Bolivia.

"Nothing wrong with a cute face," said Anne.

"Shall I put it succinctly?" asked Sandy.

"No, we want to hear all the details," said Anne.

"Well, he picked me up, came in the house, and five minutes later he was having a severe asthma attack. It seems he's allergic to animals."

"Well, you can hardly blame him for that," said Bolivia.

"I don't blame him for that," said Sandy. "I blame him for taking me to a hamburger stand for a $2.99 dinner special and griping about his ex-wife all through dinner. I blame him for asking for a receipt for the dinner so he could write it off as a business expense. And I blame him for ending up this thrilling evening by telling me he doesn't like short women and asking me if I have any friends I'd fix him up with."

"What a loser," said Anne.

"I hope you didn't mention me," said Bolivia.

"I gave him your phone number."

Bolivia was already rising from the table in anger when Sandy raised her hands, yelling, "I'm kidding, I'm kidding!"

"Well, so much for personal ads," said Anne.

"Not at all," said Sandy. "I'm trying out another one tomorrow night. This time I made sure he isn't allergic to animals, and I said I'd cook dinner."

"Did you tell him how short you are?" asked Bolivia.

"It's okay, he's short, too."

"With your luck," said Bolivia, "he'll probably turn out to be a dwarf."

That subject taken care of, Bolivia and Sandy, both of them expert interrogators, turned their eyes on Anne and began asking questions.

Anne settled in for a long session.

* * *

Quintana felt at loose ends.

Usually, in the evenings, he had classes to prepare for. Tonight all he had to do was find space for his books, and since there wasn't any, he carried the cartons of books into his den and left them piled against one wall. He thought of putting up extra shelves, but he was sure he'd be back at the university as soon as the police cleared up this mess, so there was no reason to act precipitously.

He found himself wandering around the house and finally sat down in the living room and turned on the television set. He wasn't a television viewer. Luckily, Marissa had been, which had meant he could go to his den and work on his class preparation, and she would be entertained.

All he could find were silly comedies about family life and a baseball game, which he also found silly. He wasn't entertained. He found his mind wandering, just the way his feet had done. He loved teaching. He was going to miss his classes. They gave a structure and a purpose to his life that he needed, and now he didn't have any purpose at all. He wouldn't have any life at all, either, if he didn't start trying to solve the mystery of Marissa's disappearance with the same concentration he used to solve points of law. He needed a plan. He needed to start making notes. He should have learned more about her when she was living with him; now it was going to be much more difficult.

He turned off the TV, went to his den and took out a new legal pad and a pencil and began to make a list.

Marissa

Height—5'1''
Weight—approximately 105 lbs.
Hair—dark brown, short, curly

Eyes—dark brown

Skin—olive

Identifying marks—three moles on her left shoulder, long fingernails.

Manner of dress—short dresses, high heels, lots of costume jewelry and a gold chain around her neck. Always well groomed. Lots of makeup.

Voice—high pitched, sometimes shrill, spoke very fast. Nice laugh, though.

Walk—distinctive, very bouncy

Hobbies—shopping? Poor but enthusiastic tennis player. Reads fashion magazines. Good cook. Good dancer, but then he was such a bad dancer maybe she wasn't as good as he thought.

Personal traits—Neat. Maybe excessively so, but he was neat himself, so he wasn't sure where it became excessive. Afraid of water. Afraid of thunder and lightning . . .

He paused, trying to think of more to write down, but nothing came to mind. It was ridiculous that he could have lived with a woman and known so little about her.

He had met her quite by accident. He had been at the tennis club and was heading off the court, his racket held low, and she had tripped over it and gone sprawling on the concrete. Horrified at what he'd done, he helped her up and found himself looking into a lovely face with large, brown, tear-filled eyes looking plaintively into his, the lower lip of a sweet mouth trembling. He could feel the trembling of her body as he held her by the arms. She was tiny, delicate, and so fragile looking he was afraid she'd fall apart.

"I'm so sorry," he had said to her.

"I'm so clumsy," she'd murmured, looking down at her now bloody knees and the tear in the skirt of her white tennis outfit.

"I feel totally responsible," said Quintana.

"I should have watched where I was going."

"Would you like to sit down? Can I buy you a drink?"

She seemed to hesitate at first; then she gave him a tremulous smile and let him lead her into the clubhouse bar.

Two drinks later she told of being new in the city, of having found a furnished studio apartment but not having found a job yet, of knowing no one at all.

All of which immediately brought out every protective instinct he had and some he hadn't even known about. And when he drove her home and walked her to the door of her apartment, where she immediately melted into his arms, he supposed he was a goner.

Now, going over the details in his mind, when he looked at it logically, none of it added up. No job. A studio apartment in a shoddy area of Miami. And yet she showed up at a private tennis club in a new tennis outfit? He supposed it was possible. In fact, after getting to know her better, it seemed in character for her to blow money on a tennis outfit rather than on rent.

Oh, hell, maybe it was all possible. Maybe it was love at first sight, the way she had claimed, but then, why had that love changed so radically as soon as she moved in with him? And why did he always get the feeling that she never enjoyed their lovemaking? And where was she now, when he was being charged with her murder?

The phone rang, startling him. His first thought was that it was Marissa. His first reaction was not to pick it up. She would be stuck somewhere, wanting him to pick her up. He almost decided he would rather be accused of murder than have her suddenly show up. Which was absolute nonsense, and he knew it.

On the fifth ring he picked up the phone and found it was one of his colleagues offering sympathy.

Two hours later, they finally wound down. The consensus was this: Sandy, with her cop's mind, thought he was guilty as hell and that he'd hidden the knife in his own house, rather than get rid of it, just so that his attorney could point out to the jury that he was too smart to do such a thing. Bolivia, who saw intrigue in the most ordinary circumstances, thought it was a plot of some kind to get revenge on Jack Quintana, possibly by one of his students. And Anne refused to give an opinion until she had more facts at her disposal.

Anne remembered the picture of his girlfriend that she had put in her handbag and took it out to show them.

"What a doll," said Sandy.

Bolivia studied the picture for a moment. "Well, I guess you can't fault his taste in women."

"Yes, but what I can't understand," said Anne, "is what she saw in him."

"You mean besides his good looks?" asked Bolivia.

"Yes, besides that."

"And you know he's sexy," said Sandy.

"Okay, so he's good-looking and sexy, so what?" asked Anne. "I still don't see what she saw in him."

"And his brilliant mind," said Bolivia. "Don't forget about that."

"So he's got a brilliant legal mind," said Anne. "That doesn't mean he can talk about anything else."

"And didn't you say he was well-known in his field?" asked Sandy.

"Okay," said Anne, "so he's good-looking, sexy, brilliant and well-known. He's not rich."

"I'd settle for four out of five," said Bolivia.

"I'll second that," said Sandy.

Anne shook her head. "You two are no help at all."

"Any digging you want me to do for you?" Bolivia asked her.

"Not yet," Anne said. "I'm seeing him tomorrow, and I'll get more details."

"Remember," said Bolivia, "the guy deserves a good defense no matter what he did to you in law school."

"I just hope, though, that he's feeling some of the terror he used to make us feel. Just so he knows what it's like."

"That's not even worthy of you, Annie."

"So who ever said I was perfect?"

Chapter 5

Despite Anne's wish of the night before, Jack Quintana didn't look terrorized when he showed up at her office the next day. He looked tired, and he seemed a bit depressed, but he didn't look afraid. He was dressed the same as he had been the day before, although the shirt and pants looked freshly laundered and pressed. She wondered if tan pants and a blue shirt were a uniform with him, or whether his mind was so muddled with what was happening that he couldn't think about anything else. If so, Professor Quintana with a muddled mind would be a new experience for her.

Her secretary showed him in, and Anne saw him glance around the office. It was six times the size of his and had a view of downtown Miami and the river.

His eyes took in the view outside the window, her degrees framed and hanging over a pecan credenza, the law books neatly lined up in the bookshelves, and even the David Hockney print of a swimming pool.

She let him get a good look before asking him to sit down. He approached her desk and removed the lightweight sport jacket he was wearing, hanging it neatly from the back of a wooden chair and taking a seat in the more comfortable leather chair that faced her desk.

"Good morning, Mr. Quintana." She couldn't bring herself to address him as "Professor." That appellation belonged to a time when he held all the power. Surprisingly, she no longer felt intimidated by him. She still found him as sexy and compelling as he'd been when he was teaching her torts, but now that she was behind the desk it put them on more equal terms. In fact, the balance of power was leaning in her direction.

"Good morning, Ms. Larkin." His voice was low, polite, as indifferent as if he were a senior partner stopping by for a progress report and not a man charged with murder.

"Are you ready to get to work?"

He nodded, his eyes seeming to linger on the silver alligator pin she had fastened to the lapel of her tan gaberdine suit. Judging by his lack of adornment he probably thought it frivolous.

She set up her cassette recorder, looked over at him for permission, and when he nodded she turned it on, speaking a few words into it and then playing it back before beginning.

"Please start, Mr. Quintana, by telling me everything you know about Marissa Jarlan."

His dark eyes lightened for a moment. "Everything, Ms. Larkin?"

Anne was in no mood for games. "Everything that you know, yes."

He seemed to draw into himself. She got the feeling he was a private person, the kind who didn't take to answering personal questions. Well, that privacy had now been irrevocably invaded, and he'd have to learn to deal with questions quickly or fall apart under cross-examination.

He sat thinking for a few moments, then said, "Actually, I don't know a great deal. I mean, I'm aware of her personal habits, things like that, but if you mean factual information..."

Anne nodded.

"I went over this last night, even made up a list. It's surprising how little I actually know about her. We've only been living together for about three months, and I hadn't known her long before that. I do know she's from Austin, Texas."

Anne noted that he used the present tense. He was either truly convinced she was still alive or he was devious as hell. She didn't rule out either option. She was surprised to learn of the whirlwind romance. She would have thought Quintana to be the type to move cautiously.

"Where did you meet?"

"It was purely accidental. We met at my tennis club. She tripped over my racket, sprawled on the cement, and I helped her up. She had bloody knees and elbows, and after she washed herself off, I bought her a drink at the bar."

It sounded contrived to Anne. It sounded like one of the stunts a fan might use to meet a media star. The only thing wrong with that theory was that the professor didn't put out albums or star in his own series. "Did the accident seem planned?"

He looked up from the floor he had been staring at and met her eyes. His eyes had the kind of look he rarely gave a student, and then only when the student had perfectly recited a case law. "Very good. I hadn't thought of that myself until last night. But to answer you, no, not at the time. And in retrospect, any accident can be made to seem planned."

"But it could have been planned?"

"Of course. She really did take a nasty fall, though, and if it had been planned, I would think she could have faked it a little better. Just bumping into me would have accomplished the same thing."

"Would it?"

"If you're pursuing this line of questioning because you think her purpose was to meet me, then yes, it could have."

"Would you have bought her a drink if she'd only bumped into you?"

He was silent for a moment. "No, probably not. I would have said 'Excuse me,' and that would have been it. But, since she didn't know me, she wouldn't have known that. She might have presumed I'd be quite willing to buy a drink for any pretty female I bumped into. The tennis club has become quite a meeting place for singles, and pickups have been negotiated over less than that."

Anne deduced they were wasting time on pure speculation. Somewhere, if they dug deeply enough, there must be some facts that would help them. "Had you ever seen her at the tennis club before?"

"No, and I would have remembered. I think I know all the members by sight and most of them to speak to."

Anne thought of the beautiful Marissa and didn't doubt him. "So what happened after that? Did you begin to date?"

He looked a little uncomfortable at the word "date." "What happened was that we were inseparable after that. It was Christmas break, which meant I wasn't teaching, and Marissa had just come to Miami and hadn't found a job yet. She was living on her savings, and we just had a good time. I took her to Sanibel Island, up to St. Augustine—we pretty much covered the state. And shortly after school resumed, she moved in with me."

That was more than whirlwind; that was almost instan- taneous. "Whose idea was it?"

"It was mutual."

"But who actually suggested it?"

"I think I did the actual suggesting, but not until she had dropped several hints."

"Can you recall the hints?"

"She was living in a rather nastily furnished studio. She was embarrassed to have me there and was usually loath to have me take her home. And she remarked on several oc- casions how lucky I was to have a big house all to myself. By the time I did suggest it, she was practically living at my house anyway."

"Where did she attend college?"

He seemed thrown for a moment by the change of sub- ject. "She mentioned taking courses at the university, by which I assumed she meant the University of Texas at Aus- tin. I didn't get the feeling she had gotten a degree."

Anne gave him a disbelieving look, letting her doubt show on her face. "Excuse me, Mr. Quintana, but I find it hard to believe a professor would take so little interest in his girl- friend's educational background."

He surprised her by smiling. "I'll wager, Ms. Larkin, that if you had met me in a social situation, such as over a game of tennis, that wouldn't be the first thing I would have asked. I was interested in Marissa as a woman, not as a stu- dent or a coworker."

"Weren't you interested in her educational back- ground?"

"Why should I be?"

"It seems perfectly natural to me."

"I assure you, a degree was not a prerequisite to my being interested in her."

"What did interest you, her game of tennis?"

"I don't recall our ever playing tennis."

"Even though you met her at a tennis club?"

"She was afraid she'd be no competition for me."

"What was it that did interest you?"

His dark eyes narrowed. "I don't find this line of questioning pertinent, Ms. Larkin."

She was about to tell him that she would decide what was or wasn't pertinent, but then she realized he was right. She was merely being nosy, wanting all the private details.

"What about her family?"

"Only child, parents deceased."

"Any living relatives?"

"Possible, but none that I heard about."

"I'd like to hear about your relationship. Where you went, what you did, the people you saw."

"I find this entire line of questioning distasteful," he told Anne. "Your time would be better served in discrediting the witnesses and finding out the identity of the body that was found."

"You don't understand, Mr. Quintana. Of course I'll try to do that, but if I could find your lover—alive—the charges against you would be dropped."

There was the slightest glint in his eyes at the word "lover," but he hadn't winced. "She has no friends in Miami that I'm aware of. There could, of course, be another man, but if there is, I'm also not aware of him."

"Did she show an interest in other men?"

"No. And if she had been interested in another man, she would have been free to leave."

Switching gears, she asked, "Did the police take anything when they searched besides the knife?"

"Not that I'm aware of. I suppose they could have, though, because they were still there when I was taken to the police station. I haven't noticed anything missing, though."

"Mr. Quintana, you don't seem curious about what happened to her."

"I reported her missing."

Anne felt that if he was this calm and cool and this unfeeling on the stand, there wasn't a jury in the world that wouldn't convict him.

She turned off the tape recorder and leaned back in her chair. Someone professional could find out the answers to her questions in a lot less time than it was going to take to get them out of Quintana.

"I'll explain to you how I'm going to work," Anne said to him. "The firm keeps investigators on retainer for just such contingencies as this and I'm going to make you an appointment to talk to one of them—"

"No," he said, interrupting her, and she was a student once again, freezing in her chair the way she had done in class when he used that particular tone of voice. "No investigators," he reiterated.

"Mr. Quintana, I have neither the time nor the skill to run around looking for a woman you think is missing and whom the police believe you murdered."

"I have the time," he said. "I don't want people poking into my private life."

"You may not like it, but you'd better get used to it," Anne said, thinking that an innocent man would welcome it.

"I believe you were with the Public Defender's office."

She nodded.

"I don't believe they employ investigators. Surely you must have gotten a good deal of experience investigating when you worked there."

"Mr. Quintana, although I will give you the best defense in my power, I am currently working seventy to eighty hour weeks. And we don't get school holidays off, either. And while we were forced to do our own investigating at the Public Defender's office, a trained investigator would do a much better job of it.''

His eyes seemed to darken. "I'll speak to Guy."

Great, he was going to run to her boss and complain about her attitude. "I apologize for being sarcastic."

He said, "You can be as sarcastic as you like, it doesn't bother me. What will bother me is sitting at home doing nothing when I know more about Marissa than any investigator you could find. Just tell me what you want done and I'll do it."

"That's not the way it's done!"

"That's the way it's going to be done in this case, and you'd better get used to it!"

Quintana followed his friend into Cye's Rivergate, feeling only a brief twinge of jealousy that Guy could eat the best lunches in town and probably write them off as business expenses. In the next moment he realized that the lunch could very well be written off to him and added to his bill. He and Guy had yet to discuss the cost of his defense, and he supposed he'd better bring it up soon and hear the worst.

Quintana declined a drink, and Guy followed suit, ordering iced tea instead.

"So," said Guy, after the ordering was done, "did you have a productive meeting with Anne?"

"Ms. Larkin and I reached a rather abrupt impasse."

"Oh?"

"She doesn't appear to want me involved in the case."

"Well, it would be pretty hard not to involve you, Jack."

"It sounds as though she's busy, as though she wants to turn everything over to your investigators."

"We have some excellent investigators on the payroll. We might as well let them earn their money."

"I told her I'm perfectly capable of doing the investigating myself. I'm the one who knows Marissa best, and they'd only be asking me questions and coming to the same conclusions I would come to on my own."

"It's not just a matter of asking you questions, Jack. They'd be able to mount their own investigation along the same lines as the police."

"Guy, I've been told to take a leave of absence from the university. If I don't have something to do to fill the time before this goes to court, I'll go nuts. I can devote all my time to this, and, believe me, I have more of an incentive than your investigators, no matter what you pay them. Put yourself in my place, Guy. Wouldn't you want to do the same?"

"Did you suggest this to Anne?"

"She seems to want me out of the way."

"Oh, really? Well, I think I can do something about that, Jack."

"Thanks. I'd appreciate it."

"Other than that, what do you think of her?"

"Let's not start that again, Guy."

"Perhaps it's too soon after Marissa, but I would've thought—"

"Don't even say it, Guy. An attorney-client relationship is a professional one. Let's leave it at that."

"Quite so," agreed Guy, but he didn't sound convinced.

He was no longer calling her Anne, and he wasn't offering her coffee. She stood in front of Mr. Talbot's desk, not having been offered a seat, and concentrated on controlling her reaction to the words that were ticking her off as nothing had ticked her off since finding out everyone else in her law class was using illegal study aids and she hadn't even known about their existence. And to add insult to injury,

Professor Quintana was seated on the couch in Talbot's office, a witness to her embarrassment. Actually, he was probably more than a witness; he was no doubt the cause of it.

When her boss was finished, Anne said, "Mr. Talbot, I love my work here. I have established a good working relationship with Centricon, and I have four other takeovers, seven mergers, two bankruptcies and a score of incorporations I'm in the middle of."

He was adamant. "Follow through on Centricon, but I'm spreading the rest of the work around."

"But, Mr. Talbot—"

"Are you of the opinion you're indispensable, Ms. Larkin?"

"No, sir."

"And, Ms. Larkin?"

"Yes, sir?"

"Jack Quintana will be working with you."

Anne stole a glance at Quintana. He was now gazing out the window as though none of this was of any concern to him. She wished she had the guts to tell her boss that leaving it to a criminal to come up with his own defense made about as much sense as leaving grading to the students. "I don't think that's a very good idea, sir."

"You're talking about one of the finest legal minds in the country."

"Murder is not a tort."

He let her get away with that one, but she could hear a muffled snort from the vicinity of the couch.

Guy said, "Put yourself in his situation. That's what I'm doing. If you were accused of murdering someone, and you were innocent, wouldn't you want to do everything you could to clear yourself?"

She wanted to say, *Yes, but if I was guilty, I would sure as hell want to be the one investigating then, too*. She didn't say it, though. She had already said more than enough to get herself fired.

"I'll work with Mr. Quintana," she said, forcing the words out.

Then the smile broke out. "Splendid, Anne, I'm very glad to hear that."

Sure. *Splendid*. If she had wanted to continue defending criminals, she would have stayed with the Public Defender's office.

She saw the professor start to get up from the couch, and she tried to beat him to the door of Guy's office. Just as she was making her escape, Guy's voice stopped her.

"Oh, and Anne?"

"Yes, Mr. Talbot?"

"Use the rest of the afternoon to clear off your desk, but then I want you to devote all your time to Jack." He turned to his friend, "What do you think, maybe a dinner meeting between the two of you tonight? Or maybe just dinner, a chance to get to know each other better?"

Anne saw that Professor Quintana looked as uncomfortable with this suggestion as she was feeling. In fact, he began to edge toward the door to make his own escape.

"I'll leave that up to Ms. Larkin," he said.

"Oh, come now," said Guy, "I don't think we need to be so formal, do we? Let's make it Anne and Jack."

Anne could swear she saw a glimmer of mischief in Mr. Talbot's eyes, but she was sure he couldn't possibly be up to what she thought he was up to.

It looked as though the professor had the same idea, though. Edging closer to Anne at the door, he turned to Guy and said, "Let's just leave things as they are, Guy."

Mr. Talbot was now smiling broadly. "Oh, come now, let's stop this bristling at each other. You're going to be working very closely together, and it would make it much easier if the two of you were friendly."

With a shake of his head, the professor beat her out the door and was halfway to the elevators before Anne caught up with him.

"Mr. Quintana, would you mind stopping by my office for a minute?"

"Not at all."

"Would you mind taking the stairs?"

"Of course not."

Once in her office, Anne took one of her business cards out of the desk and wrote her home number and the number for the phone in her car on the back and handed it to him.

"You should be able to reach me at one of these numbers most of the time." She hesitated a moment and then said, "About dinner tonight . . ."

"I'm sorry about that. Just ignore Guy—he gets carried away at times."

"I would, however, like to see the scene of the 'alleged' crime, if that's possible."

"Well, why *don't* we have dinner, then? I don't cook, but I could get some food in."

Anne said, "I'm sorry, I can't—I have practice tonight. But I could come by at around eight-thirty, if that wouldn't inconvenience you, Mr. Quintana."

"Please don't worry about inconveniencing me, Ms. Larkin. I expect I'll be inconvenienced quite a bit from now on. Eight-thirty would be fine. Guy did have a point, though. It would make things much simpler if you'd just call me Jack."

"All right. As long as you're going to be doing the investigating, if you have some free time this afternoon—"

"I have nothing but free time, Anne."

"What I was going to suggest is that you get on the phone this afternoon and start checking out Marissa's background in Austin. Call the schools for any records, check out any relatives she might still have there."

"I thought I could also check with the neighbors, see if anyone saw her leaving the house that day on foot. Someone walking is pretty noticeable in our neighborhood."

"Good idea," said Anne. "And you could also check with the phone company and see if any calls were made from your house that day. If they give you any trouble about that, I'll get a subpoena."

"You might as well call me Jack and start getting used to it."

"Okay, fine."

"Go on, Anne."

"Yes, okay. Well, if you wouldn't mind getting out of here now, *Jack*, and letting me clear my desk so I can concentrate on your defense...."

When Anne mentioned having practice that night, the word immediately signaled music to Jack. He pictured her in a long black dress, a cello leaning against one knee. It made a graceful image, as did a further picture of her fingers moving back and forth across the strings of a harp. He tried a violin, but a picture wouldn't come to mind. She wasn't the violin type. He wondered if she played with a chamber music group. He had a fondness for chamber music.

Maybe Guy knew something he didn't know. Maybe he and Anne had a lot in common. There was the law, of course, and now there also appeared to be an interest in classical music, which would be two things more than he and Marissa had ever had in common. Of course, there were probably quite a few female attorneys with an interest in classical music. Probably not any who looked quite as good as Anne, however. He wasn't currently in the market for a woman, but he still had an eye for beauty. And she certainly was beautiful. He admired women who groomed and dressed themselves with as much elegance and style as Ms. Anne Larkin.

He tuned his car radio to a classical station, and all the way home he found himself picturing Anne at the cello.

Anne used an outside line to call the District Attorney's office and asked to speak to Margaret Gilford. When the familiar voice answered, Anne said, "Hey, Maggie, it's me, Anne. How're things going?"

"Annie? What's new? You back in the Public Defender's office?"

"Fat chance," said Anne.

"You don't miss the excitement, the challenge—"

"The long hours, the low pay... No, I'm afraid I don't."

"I hear it's gotten worse since you left."

"It couldn't get worse."

"One more year and then I'm quitting and getting a high-paying job like you."

"I've heard that before, Maggie. Listen, I need a favor from you."

"Shoot!"

"Who's prosecuting the Quintana case?"

"That one was so popular everyone was bidding on it. I think ninety percent of the lawyers here had him for Torts and want to see him hanged."

"So who was the lucky winner?"

"Get ready for this—Howie Leonard!"

"Howie the Sleaze?"

"None other. The one who was hot for you third year, as I recall."

"Howie was hot for anything he could get."

"Ain't it the truth. And he hasn't changed."

"So why's the D.A.'s office going after this one? The case looks purely circumstantial to me."

"I hear it looks pretty good."

"Really?"

There was a moment of silence from Maggie's end of the line. "Why the interest, Annie?"

"I'm defending him."

"Wait a minute, aren't you some big corporate attorney now, or am I talking to the wrong Anne Larkin?"

"It seems he's my boss's best friend, and I got hooked into it."

"Is he as obnoxious outside the classroom as he was inside?"

Anne laughed. "He's not my idea of a fun person."

"This is going to make you infamous, you know. I don't know anyone personally who'd defend that man."

"I wasn't really given a choice in the matter."

"Well, now that you're the enemy again, I probably shouldn't be talking to you."

"I wish you'd been assigned to the case. I was hoping I'd never have to run into Howie again as long as I lived."

"I can't wait to tell him he'll be facing you. He's still single, you know."

"I wonder why that doesn't surprise me."

"So listen, are we going to have lunch sometime, Annie, or what?"

"Probably 'or what' until this is over, but after that I'm buying."

"I'm going to hold you to that."

Anne hung up the phone and groaned at the thought of coming into contact with Howard Leonard again. Howie had been short and arrogant, with bad skin and an already balding head, when they had met in first-year law school. He had treated her like a blond bimbo until the grades came out and she had wound up with the higher grade point average. In their second year, Howie had pursued her with a single-minded determination exceeded only by his determination to become every teacher's pet. He didn't succeed in either endeavor. In their last year of law school, even Howie was worried enough about passing the bar to leave her alone, but later, when she was with the Public Defender's office and he was an assistant D.A., they often came into contact, and by then he had a thick chip on his shoulder, not helped by the fact that on several occasions he had seen her in clubs around town in the company of other men. She was sure it had looked to him as though she were willing to date anyone in Miami with the exception of him.

If it had been anyone but Howie going against her, she would have given the person a call.

Canvassing the neighborhood in an attempt to find someone who might have seen Marissa leaving the house on foot turned out to be fruitless. Jack hated to admit it, but an investigator would have had more luck.

Although he didn't know any of his neighbors by sight, they all seemed to know him. Several people wouldn't answer the door to him, although he knew they were home because he saw curtains move as the occupants checked him out. Two neighbors, both mild-looking women, slammed the door in his face. Only one woman answered his questions, and then only with whispered, "Noes." She appeared to believe herself in the presence of a murderer. Her white face, her frightened eyes, proved too much for Jack, and he returned to his house, unwilling to put the fear of God into any more of his neighbors.

He had no more success with his telephone calls to Austin, Texas. He spoke with elementary schools, high schools, colleges, the university, even parochial schools and a couple of private Christian schools. None had any record of a Marissa Jarlan. A check with the operator there revealed that there were no Jarlans living in Austin. Jack was beginning to wonder if Marissa had been nothing but a figment of his imagination. And yet, if that were the case, he could hardly have been charged with murder.

The woman at the phone company was rude and ignorant, and he finally, out of frustration, hung up on her.

With misgivings over his value as an investigator, he called Anne at her office.

"Any luck?" she asked him.

"It appears you were right."

"About what?"

"About my talent as a private investigator." He went on to tell her of his lack of progress.

"I should have warned you against talking to your neighbors. Next it'll be hate mail and burning crosses on your front lawn."

"Are you serious?"

"Well, maybe not burning crosses. Would you mind if I put an investigator on it?"

"Not at all," said Jack, thankful she wasn't saying, "I told you so."

"I think we'd better go through channels with the phone company, too. Not coming up with anything in Austin, though, is surprising. You sure you tried all the schools?"

"Every one listed in the phone book. Unlike here, the operators there were very helpful."

"I might want you to fly out there on that later on. Right now, though, it might help if you tried to remember every single detail about her that you can."

"Again?"

"Again. It's really all we have to go on."

Jack hung up with a sigh. There was something wrong with the fact that he was giving more thought to Marissa now than he ever had when she was living with him.

"Where are you rushing off to?" Bolivia asked her after practice.

Anne, sweaty, dirty, hoping to have time to go home and shower before going to Jack's house said, "Work."

"Work? What kind of work?"

"Come on, Annie, we're going to dinner," said Sandy. "You've got time."

"I don't have time. I'm supposed to be at Jack's house at eight-thirty."

"Jack's house?" asked Bolivia.

"Is that Jack as in Jack Quintana, the murderer?" asked Sandy.

"My boss ordered us to use first names."

"Oh, right," said Sandy.

"I'd like to meet this Jack," said Bolivia.

"Good," said Anne, "then why don't you come along? What we need to have is a real brainstorming session, and it would really help to have two more brains."

"So you admit we have brains," said Sandy.

"Strike the brains and make that a cop's instincts," said Anne. "And, of course, the talents of an investigative reporter."

"I'd like to get a look at him," said Bolivia.

"I just hope he doesn't remember me," said Sandy.

"He didn't remember me," said Anne.

"Then he sure as hell won't remember me."

"I don't know, Sandy," said Anne. "He might remember the way you used to turn white and freeze whenever he called on you."

"Thanks," said Sandy. "I needed that. You want to come in my car?"

"No, I'll ride behind Bolivia. I'm hoping the wind will dry my sweat before we get there."

"Hey, wait a minute," said Bolivia. "Does this mean we don't eat?"

"Stop for take-out and we can bring it along with us. I'm buying," said Anne.

"If you think you can buy our brain-trust that easily..."

Anne not only thought it, she knew it.

Chapter 6

By eight-thirty, Jack Quintana had straightened up the living room, set some wine to chill in the refrigerator and put Beethoven on the stereo. He saw no reason why a business meeting shouldn't be as pleasant as possible.

At eight thirty-five he heard the roar of a motorcycle in front of his house, and then a series of backfires. He went to the front window and looked out. As he watched, the outside lights from three houses across the street went on.

Directly in front of his house two guys were getting off a motorcycle. They stood there for a minute, still helmeted, and a small car drove up and parked behind the motorcycle. Out of the car stepped what looked like a child in a baseball uniform. Except a child shouldn't be operating a car.

Now the two helmets came off, and Quintana saw the three figures heading for his house. They all appeared to be in baseball uniforms. And as they walked into the light from his front porch, he saw that they weren't guys, which was a relief, because he'd been beginning to think this was when the cross was going to get burned on his lawn.

He went to the front door and opened it. There stood Anne. Or at least a reasonable facsimile of Anne. Her hair was tied in two pigtails, her face was dirty and her elegant attire was nowhere to be seen. Still, there was something appealing about seeing her without the protective armor of her usual impeccable appearance.

"You going to invite us in, Jack?" she asked him.

"Yes, of course," he said, holding the door wide and watching as they entered his house. Behind Anne was a tall woman with the rangy look of a ball player and two six-packs of beer in her arms. Behind her was the short one, now loaded down with bags that had burgers printed on the sides.

"Where can we eat?" asked Anne.

"The kitchen's straight in the back," he told her. "Or there's a dining room, if you'd prefer."

"We're not fit for your dining room," she said. "We had a hard practice, punishment for losing our last two games."

When the bags of food and six-packs were set on the table, Anne introduced him to Bolivia and Sandy. "Sandy's a cop," she told him, "and Bolivia's got a column in the morning paper that you might've read. I figured we could use their input."

Jack felt a little uneasy that a cop was now sitting at his kitchen table. Even a very small cop. Anne must have read his mind because she said, "They're my best friends. What we say here won't go any farther."

"Unless, of course, you're in the mood to give me an exclusive," said Bolivia, smiling at him.

"Or to give me a confession," said Sandy.

"I'm afraid the answer is no to both requests," said Quintana, "but I'd be glad to give you some plates and silverware."

Anne shook her head at him. "Please, Professor, don't you ever eat take-out burgers?"

"Not if I have a choice," said Quintana.

"Well, you eat them by hand. That's the beauty of it," Anne informed him. "Come on, sit down, we got you some, too."

Jack watched as Anne's friends tore off the tabs on their beer cans and drank. Anne, it seemed, was having a Coke. He hadn't eaten anyway, and he thought, What the hell? He grabbed himself a beer and then unwrapped the burger that was thrust in front of him.

He was just thinking, So much for chamber music, when Anne, as though reading his mind, said, "Would you mind turning that music down? It's hard to think with it so loud."

"That's Beethoven, isn't it?" asked Bolivia.

He was about to reply when Anne said, "What a show off," and Sandy said, "It's all those piano lessons she was forced to take as a child."

He got up and turned the music off, but when he got back to the kitchen, no one appeared to be doing any thinking. All that seemed to be happening was that a lot of food was being consumed in the shortest time possible. He found himself grabbing a package of fries before they were all gone. He briefly had a sense of déjà vu before he remembered what this reminded him of: life in the dorm when he was an undergraduate. It was a little like going back in time.

"So I hear we have a mystery woman on our hands," said Bolivia, fully able to talk and chew at the same time.

"So it would appear," said Quintana. "At least, it looks as though she lied to me about where she comes from. Or her last name got changed somewhere along the way."

"That's easily explained," said Sandy. "Perhaps she married after leaving Austin and kept her married name."

"She couldn't have been married before I met her," said Quintana, immediately regretting he'd said it as three pairs of inquisitive eyes turned toward him. "At least, it doesn't seem likely."

"How on earth did you come to that conclusion?" asked Anne.

"Unless it was some kind of a business arrangement and not a marriage at all," he said, ignoring the question.

"What is he implying?" asked Bolivia.

"Could it be? Today? In the 80s?" asked Sandy.

"It certainly sounds like it," said Anne. Then giving him a humorous look that already had him smiling she asked, "You're not trying to tell us, Jack, that the lady was a virgin, are you?"

"Yes, she was. I was surprised myself at the time," he said.

"Incredible," breathed Sandy, reverence in her tone.

"Unbelievable," said Bolivia.

"Wait a minute," said Anne, clearly doubtful. "Are you saying that this young woman, who conveniently tripped over your tennis racket and ended up in the bar with you, this young woman who almost immediately moved in with you, this rather fast little worker, was a virgin?"

"That was certainly my impression," said Quintana. "I'm not trying to stretch your credulity, I'm just making a case against the likelihood of her being married before she met me."

"No wonder there's no record of her," said Bolivia. "A virgin in her twenties? She must have been from another galaxy. What a great article this would make."

"Don't even think about it," said Anne.

"All right, let's get down to verifiable facts here," said Sandy, who didn't look like a cop but obviously thought like one. "I understand she left her wallet behind. What kind of identification did she have?"

"Actually, none," said Quintana. "Two credit cards, and they were both on my accounts."

"What about a driver's license?" asked Sandy.

"I don't know," he said. "I obviously assumed she had one, and she never led me to believe otherwise, or I wouldn't have bought her a car. She was certainly an experienced driver. So, either she took it with her, or she didn't have one. But, on the surface, at least, it didn't look as though she took anything with her."

"Checkbook? Social security card? Library card?" asked Bolivia.

"Nothing," said Quintana.

"Letters? Diary? Address book?" asked Sandy.

Quintana shrugged. "I never saw any of those things around, but the police might have searched and found them."

"Okay," said Anne, "now, for the sake of argument, we're going to assume that this young woman voluntarily disappeared. Is there anything absolutely essential that you would take along with you if you were going to disappear?" she asked her friends.

"How do you disappear on foot in Miami?" asked Bolivia.

"There are such things as buses," said Anne.

"I guess the most essential thing would be money," Bolivia offered.

"There was money in her wallet," said Quintana, "but of course, she could have had more."

"I would disguise myself," said Sandy. "If she was setting it up to look like Jack did away with her, then she couldn't let herself be seen leaving the house. Someone would be sure to see her."

"I hadn't thought of that," he said.

"No one expects you to think like a criminal," said Sandy. "But in my line of work it helps if you do."

Quintana was beginning to enjoy them and their humorous repartee. Guy would get a kick out of sitting in on something like this.

"I'll make a note of that for the investigator," said Anne. "Okay, she had to look different if she hoped to get out of the neighborhood unseen. So how does a small, dark woman disguise herself effectively? Just throwing on a blond wig wouldn't do it, because it would be too obvious."

"Perhaps as a child," said Jack, getting their attention. "I thought of that because when you arrived tonight—well, don't take offense, but I thought you were a young boy getting out of the car, Sandy. Your height, the clothes you were wearing..."

The three of them were nodding. Anne said, "Yes, she could've done it that way. Not as an obvious blonde, but as a young girl, maybe with braids, or even a boy. Nobody notices a child. Maybe someone saw a kid coming out of your house."

"I don't think she'd walk out the front door," said Quintana. "She could've gone out the back, ducked through the neighbors' yards unseen and surfaced farther down the block. I'd even suggest the canal, but she was afraid of water."

"Now that's interesting," said Bolivia. "She obviously lied to you about everything, but you're taking her word for it that she was afraid of water. Maybe she swam across the canal and made her escape that way, assuming that you'd think she was afraid of water."

"I don't know," said Quintana. "I'll certainly agree that she lied to me, but she seemed genuinely afraid of water. I thought I'd try to get her over that fear and tried to get her to go swimming in the ocean once, and she got within a few feet of the water and turned white and started to shake so badly I gave it up. I don't think she was faking it."

"Still, it's something to consider," said Sandy. "I think there's an easier way to find out who she was, though, than all this conjecturing. Let's get her prints, and I'll run them through the computer."

"I should've thought of that," said Quintana.

"What do you think, Sandy, something in the kitchen?" Bolivia asked.

"I have a better idea," said Quintana. "She had her own bathroom upstairs. If there are any prints in there, they'd definitely be hers, and I haven't touched anything in there since she left."

"Well, if we're through eating," said Sandy, "let's take a look at the bathroom. You got any baggies, Jack? Even a small trash bag would do."

Quintana found some plastic bags in one of the kitchen drawers and handed them to Sandy, then led the way upstairs.

"This is a beautiful house," Sandy told him, looking into the living room before following him up the stairs.

"Thank you," said Jack.

"I love these old Spanish houses," she said. "Did you have a decorator do it?"

"I did it myself," said Quintana.

"Well, it's charming."

Quintana walked into the bedroom Marissa used and stopped, waiting for them to come into the room. "This was her bedroom," he said. "Her bathroom's over there."

"Separate bedrooms?" murmured Bolivia.

"She really was a strange lady," said Sandy.

Anne merely laughed.

He felt as though his privacy was being invaded, which, of course, it was. He caught Anne's eye, and she gave him a look as though to say, "Don't worry, we all have weird things in our lives."

They were all heading for the bathroom when Sandy said, "No, let me do this. You two klutzes will probably get your own fingerprints on everything. Why don't you look in the closet and drawers?"

The bright, fluorescent light went on in the bathroom, and Quintana could hear the medicine cabinet being opened. In the bedroom Bolivia was opening drawers in the dresser and looking inside. Anne went to the closet and slid open the door.

"She had quite a wardrobe," Anne observed.

Quintana said, "Marissa likes clothes."

"A woman after Anne's heart," said Bolivia.

"Just because we can't all dress like African explorers at work," said Anne, and Bolivia burst out laughing.

"The underwear's incredible," said Bolivia, lifting out a pile of silk and lace undergarments. "Look at this, Annie."

Quintana thought "Annie" suited her in her present garb.

Anne was seated on the bed surrounded by Marissa's handbags, which she was searching. "Come on, Bolivia, we're probably embarrassing the professor."

"I suppose I'd better get used to being embarrassed," he said, still not liking it.

Sandy came out of the bathroom. "I think I'll get some good prints. I took the bathroom glass, a tube of toothpaste and a jar of moisturizer. You want a receipt for these, Jack?"

"I don't even want them back," Quintana told her.

"I noted something very interesting," said Sandy. "There's no makeup in the bathroom. Is this where she applied her makeup, Jack?"

"Actually, I don't think she wore any," he said. This got a laugh that confused him.

"I'm sure she wore some," said Anne.

"No, I mean it," he insisted. "She was the natural type."

"Tell me, Jack," said Anne. "That picture you gave me of her. Was that the way she usually looked?"

"Exactly," said Quintana.

"Then she wore makeup," said Anne. "In that photograph her eyes were lined, she had on several coats of mascara, a touch of brown eye shadow, a little blush and definitely some lip gloss. I don't know if she was wearing a base, but that's a possibility, too."

"She always looked natural," said Quintana.

"That's the point of makeup," said Anne.

Trying to be surreptitious about it, Quintana took a closer look at the three women. It didn't go unnoticed.

"No, we're not wearing any," Anne said, "but that's because it got sweated off playing baseball. And Bolivia never wears any, but she's the exception, and that's only because she's getting in practice for being a foreign correspondent in some remote jungle."

"She's right, Jack," said Sandy. "I saw that picture of Marissa, and she was very artfully made-up."

"So where's the makeup?" asked Bolivia.

"There had to be some," said Sandy, "so I'd guess she definitely took it with her."

"That proves it then," said Quintana. "If she took her makeup with her, then she wasn't killed. Couldn't we tell the police about this?"

"The police don't just take your word for things," said Anne. "They would just counter by saying that you probably threw it out to make it look as though she took it with her.''

"At least we'll get some prints out of this," said Sandy, "and maybe we'll find out who she really is."

"Other than to me, to satisfy my curiosity," Quintana asked, "does it matter who she really is?"

"It could," said Anne. "And it would at least cast some doubt on the charge. If they can't prove there was a Marissa, how can they prove you killed her?"

"Well, I was living with *someone*," said Quintana. "And someone complained to the neighbors that I was beating her. And someone's blood was on that knife."

This met with silence. "I have some wine chilling in the refrigerator," he said. "Would you care for a glass?"

"Not me," said Bolivia. "Thanks, but I'm driving."

"Me, too," said Sandy. "And Annie's on the wagon."

"You're making it sound as though I'm an alcoholic," said Anne.

Quintana waited to hear if this was the case, but her friends ignored her and started downstairs.

Sandy had cleaned up the kitchen by the time he and Anne went down, and Bolivia, looking impatient, was standing by the front door.

"I hope you didn't mind my bringing them along," Anne said, following him down the stairs.

"Not at all. I think they've been very helpful."

"The three of us work well together. We always have. I think they're pleased to see me back in criminal law, even if only for one case."

Sandy joined Bolivia at the front door, and Quintana said, "I want to thank both of you. It would have been a pleasure meeting you anyway, but this was really good of you."

"I'm sure we'll be seeing you again," said Bolivia, and Sandy nodded in agreement.

"I'll have one of our investigators get in touch with you tomorrow," Anne said to him. "Tell him what you've done and where you've run into trouble, and I think he'll be able to help. If you don't mind, that is."

"I don't mind," said Quintana.

"And, Jack—call me whenever you need to. We're going to solve this mystery for you and get you off, I promise."

"She's good," said Sandy. "You wouldn't believe all the criminals she got off. Sorry, I didn't mean that I think you're a criminal."

"I just had an idea," said Bolivia. "What if I write a column using Marissa's picture? The headline could be something like: Does Anyone Know This Woman?"

"Will the paper go for that?" asked Anne.

"They'd be delighted," said Bolivia. "So far no one has a picture of the victim, which would mean we'd have the scoop. Who knows, maybe someone will come forward who's seen her since she was supposedly killed." She was the same height as Quintana, and she threw a companionable arm around his shoulders. "Hey, don't worry about a thing, Jack—you're in good hands."

He had never had a woman throw her arm around his shoulders like that. It was more the kind of gesture Guy might make on the tennis court. Nevertheless, it pleased him.

"I guarantee it'll tick off the Department," said Sandy, grinning over at him.

"Go for it," said Anne, "unless you have any objections, Jack."

"It sounds good to me," he said. "I really appreciate it. I was beginning to feel like an outcast in the community after this afternoon. It's good to know there are three people on my side.''

"Good. I think we've made some progress," said Anne.

Quintana felt more optimistic after they left than he'd felt in days. He was beginning to believe he'd been fortunate in Guy's choice of an attorney for him, and equally fortunate in said attorney's choice of friends. He wondered if the three of them were as indomitable on the baseball field.

He liked Anne's friends. In fact, he liked Anne. She seemed far less formidable in a baseball uniform, and he realized he'd felt as at ease with the three of them as he did with his male friends. This was a relief after Marissa and, in fact, after all the women he'd known.

Maybe things weren't quite as hopeless as he'd envisioned.

"What a gorgeous house," said Sandy, turning around for a last look at it.

"What a gorgeous man," said Bolivia, strapping on her helmet. "No wonder the two of you went bonkers over him in law school. If I'd known there were professors like that, I might have gone to law school with you."

Sandy was still in raptures about the house. "Did you see the tile floors and all that woodwork? And the fireplace. I'd die for a fireplace like that."

"So trip over his tennis racket and you, too, can move in with him," said Bolivia.

"That wasn't nice," said Sandy.

"Hey, I was just joking," said Bolivia. "Hell, I might move in with him even without the house. That is one sexy man! Of course, Annie wouldn't notice that, because our Annie goes for emaciated musicians."

"I don't go for anyone at the moment," Anne reminded her. "I'm off men, remember?"

"Well, while you're off men," said Bolivia, "how about fixing me up with your client?"

Anne felt the tiniest bit of jealousy. "He's off limits, Bolivia, at least until the trial's over. If there is a trial, but it sure looks as though there's going to be."

Bolivia grinned at her. "And after the trial it's open season on Jack Quintana?"

"After the trial, it's every woman for herself," retorted Anne, wondering where that had come from. It wasn't exactly that she was interested in him, but she sure as hell didn't want Bolivia to be. That didn't seem fair, but things never seemed fair when it came to men. Not that she would actually fight a friend over a man, though, if it ever came down to it. And it wasn't going to come down to that, because she wasn't the least bit interested in Jack Quintana.

But for the first time she admitted the possibility that she could be.

Chapter 7

When he opened the door to find himself being served with two subpoenas, Quintana decided that first thing in the morning wasn't turning out to be a very good time for him. First the cops, now this.

The subpoenas were from the grand jury. One summoned him to testify before them, the other to produce physical evidence, namely a blood specimen. The second made no sense at all. If the police were assuming it was Marissa's blood on the knife, why did they want a sample of his? It was amazing how much he knew about torts and how little he knew about criminal law.

He made himself a cup of coffee and decided he had better call his lawyer. The problem was she was probably on her way to work. On the off chance that she might have gotten to the office early, he called there first. The switchboard operator informed him that Ms. Larkin wasn't in yet. Thinking maybe she was late leaving for work this morning, he tried her at home. He got an answering machine and didn't leave a message.

He tried the third number she had given him, and she picked up on the first ring. He could have sworn he heard traffic noises over the considerable static.

"What is this number, a phone booth?" he asked her.

"Is that you, Jack?"

"Yes. What's all that noise I hear."

"You got me on my car phone."

"You've got a phone in your *car*?"

"Yes."

"Why?"

"So people like you can reach me when you need to. What's up?"

He was still trying to picture a phone in a car. He knew there were such things, but he'd never ridden in a car that actually had one. "I got subpoenaed this morning by the grand jury."

"And?"

"Twice. They want me to testify, and they want a blood sample."

"I should've thought of that."

"Of what?"

"Maybe that was your blood on the knife. What type are you?"

"I can tell you for a fact it wasn't my blood on the knife. If I'd cut myself, I'd certainly remember. And I would have washed it, not hidden it away."

"Yes, but they can't prove that. And it might turn out to be your blood type. I don't suppose you know Marissa's type."

"It never occurred to me to ask."

"Ah, but I should've thought of this. I should've been the one demanding a blood test."

"So do I give them one?"

"Yes. Definitely. But you are not going to testify."

This seemed to be the kind of thing a lawyer would tell a client whom she was sure would be lousy on the witness stand. "I want to testify," he said.

"No way."

"I think we should talk about this, Anne."

"There's nothing to talk about. I'm telling you that you're not going to testify before the grand jury."

"Listen, I have a right to testify. Furthermore, I'm sure if they hear me, they won't indict."

"I don't believe I gave you a choice."

"I don't believe it's up to you. The law provides me with an opportunity to tell my side of the story, and I intend to tell it."

There was the sound of a car horn, then a muffled swear word and then Anne was saying, "You don't happen to have a side to the story. At least, not yet."

"I have no trouble speaking in public."

"You don't have to convince me of that. I was your student, remember?"

"Then you know I won't get up there and make an idiot of myself."

"Jack, I'm just going to say this once. If you insist on testifying, you can get yourself another lawyer."

"I'm not sure I heard you."

"You heard me. Either I'm in charge of the case, or you can find another lawyer, or damn well defend yourself. And keep in mind the old saying about a lawyer defending himself having a fool for a client, because it's still true."

Quintana slammed down the phone.

It took three more cups of coffee before he was willing to admit that she was right and he was wrong. He would have plenty of opportunity to testify later, if there was a trial. He had absolutely nothing of any value to say to the grand jury. And rather than the grand jury being impressed with a legal scholar of his stature testifying before them, they would more than likely find him an arrogant son of a bitch. It had been known to happen.

It took a further cup of coffee for him to admit to himself that he wanted Anne to remain as his attorney. She might be young, she might be female, but for some reason he felt confident in her.

This time he tried her at her office, and her secretary put him right through.

"Okay, I'm sorry. You were right and I was wrong."

"Apologizing?"

"Don't rub it in," he warned her.

"Well, as long as I've got you in a humble moment, I have a couple of other rules for you. First, I don't want you to talk to anyone about the charge. And second, I definitely don't want you talking to reporters."

"Does that latest stricture apply to Bolivia?"

"Absolutely. Unless she's with me, don't trust her an inch. Her journalistic instincts are deadly."

"I'll get a blood sample this afternoon."

"You'll get it this morning. I have you booked on an afternoon flight to Austin, with an hour layover in Dallas."

"Am I allowed to leave town?"

"I got permission from the D.A.'s office. Just don't escape over the border or my name will be mud."

"You knew I'd call you back, didn't you?"

"Of course."

"How could you be sure?"

"Because I'm a great lawyer, and because you're crazy about my friends."

"I *am* crazy about your friends."

"Good. They liked you, too."

"Is there some reason for your getting me out of town fast?"

"I don't want to wait until the grand jury brings in an indictment before we get moving on this."

"You sound pretty sure that they will."

"It wouldn't surprise me. They've been known to indict on less than this. And if and when they do, I'm going to try for as early a court date as possible. I'm assuming you want this over with quickly."

"Within reason."

"Of course within reason."

"What do you want me to do in Austin, the same as I tried to do over the phone?"

"Essentially. I think you'll find out more if you go in person. I was going to go with you, but I've got to fly to Delaware tomorrow on business. Take Marissa's picture with you and show it around. Check the Motor Vehicle Department, the County Clerk's office for records, anything you can think of. If she ever lived there, you should be able to find out."

"What time is my flight?"

"Three-thirty. I'll pick you up at two, and we can do some more talking at the airport. They've got a fruit bar there that I'm crazy about. Do you like milk shakes made with fruit?"

"You don't need to drive me. I can get a taxi to the airport, or just leave my car there while I'm gone."

"Hey, it's no problem. You're my client—I'm going to take very good care of you."

Quintana was smiling when he hung up.

His annoyance with her on the way to the airport had evaporated by the time his flight was called.

He hadn't thought he was jealous of lawyers who used their talents in the marketplace in order to amass large amounts of money until he had seen that sleek car pull up in front of his house and realized that this young woman, this former student of his, was driving a car he could never afford to own. He had always liked speed, but the lawful speed limits and his salary had always conspired to make sure he'd never gotten what he liked.

Since he lived only a short distance from the airport, she never did manage to get up much speed, but she certainly left every other car in the dust each time she took off from a stoplight.

The phone in her car was extremely annoying. Despite the fact that both phone calls she received during the short ride—the first from Bolivia, saying she had the go-ahead on the article about Marissa; the second from Sandy, saying that there was no record anywhere of the fingerprints she had taken from Marissa's bathroom—were directly concerned with him, he still didn't like the fact that he got interrupted midsentence both times and that Anne immediately picked up the phone, driving one-handed at that point, and seemed, for a few moments, to forget that he was even in the car. Even on good days the telephone was not one of his favorite instruments. With Anne it appeared to be an extension of her arm.

Once inside the airport, things got better. She led him to the fruit bar she was so crazy about, insisting that he have a pineapple-banana shake, which turned out to be every bit as delicious as she had promised. She had typed up a list of places he should visit in Austin, going over each point with him and offering some suggestions. She had also booked a suite for him at a downtown hotel on 6th Street, a charming neighborhood, she assured him, and a newly renovated hotel. The luxury appealed to him enormously. No doubt it would eventually be billed back to him, but still, he had pictured himself in some seedy motel, and he had never stayed anywhere in a suite. She even gave him a list of restaurants about which she had heard great things, although she didn't go so far as to tell him what to order. She had also made arrangements for a rental car to be waiting for him at the airport. He didn't ask what kind. At this point, anything less than a Jaguar would only be a letdown.

And then, before boarding his plane, she had dragged him into one of the many airport shops and bought him newspapers and magazines and candy bars, enough to last him to Australia had he been going there, which he pointed out to her, and which she countered with the fact that he could save some of them for later in the hotel.

Lastly she walked him as far as the metal detectors, which was as far as she was allowed to go, and then had reached up and given him a quick kiss, telling him to call her when he got there so that she'd know he arrived safely. Even his mother had never taken such good care of him.

It was beginning to seem almost like a vacation when he boarded his plane.

Three days later the Dade County Grand Jury brought in an indictment of murder in the first degree.

Anne had expected it. What she hadn't expected was the sudden blitz of media coverage, the kind of coverage one would expect if Elvis were indeed to be found alive, or if a UFO actually landed in the White House rose garden, but not what she would have expected from just another murder case in Miami. Murders in Miami had become ordinary everyday occurrences. She supposed the difference was that, for a change, this one wasn't in any way drug-related.

Unfortunately the picture of Marissa that had been featured with Bolivia's article was picked up by every other paper after the indictment, some of them answering the question of Marissa's whereabouts by suggesting strongly that she was indeed the very person whose body had been dragged out of the canal. Various pictures of Jack also appeared, and the papers appeared to be convicting him before the trial even began. The case had all the makings of a media circus.

Anne was on the way back to the office from lunch when she got a call from Bolivia.

"Hey, Annie, I finally got a bite from that article." There had already been several calls, but all of them from the kind of crazy people who confess to every murder and spot Nazi war criminals sunning themselves on Miami Beach.

"Tell me," said Anne.

"It's a hairdresser from Coral Gables. Claims he did Marissa's hair for her every week."

"Did he sound reliable?"

"I'd say so."

"So what do you think?"

"I think we should go by and see him. You busy right now?"

"Not really. I was just going back to the office to call Jack and tell him he can come home."

"Did he get anything there?"

"I don't think so. I never figured he would. I just wanted him out of town while the grand jury was in session."

"You just wanted to get rid of him?"

"Bolivia, I gave him a nice vacation. He'll come back rested and much less tense."

"A vacation in Austin, Texas?"

"Have you ever been to Austin?"

"I'm proud to be able to say no to that question."

"Well, you don't know what you're missing. I'm crazy about Austin. Great clubs, lots of musicians there—"

"Say no more, I'm getting the picture. Where are you now?"

"Not far from you."

"Good. Why don't you swing by my office and we'll check out Steve."

"Steve?"

"As in Steve's Unisex Salon."

"I hate going to beauty parlors," said Anne. "They always take one look at me and decide they can do something with my hair."

"Darling, I could really do something with that hair," said the aging beachboy with the brown mustache and blond ponytail.

"Are you Steve?" Anne asked him.

"You've heard of me."

"Not exactly," said Anne, nodding to Bolivia to take over the conversation.

"I'm from the paper," Bolivia told him. "You called me earlier about a picture..."

"Marissa, yes," said Steve, looking disappointed that they weren't customers. The only customer in the shop was a woman in a pink smock with a plastic cap over her head.

"You knew Marissa?" Bolivia prompted him.

"Sorry, sweetie," said Steve, "but the police were just here, and I'm not supposed to talk to anyone. I'm going to be a witness."

"I'm Mr. Quintana's lawyer," said Anne, "and—"

"Especially to you," said Steve. "Have you ever thought of doing your hair in a shag? With all that curl, it would be outrageous."

"I thought shags went out of style ten years ago," said Anne.

That didn't go over well with Steve. "Yes, but there's not much else you can do with frizz, now is there?"

"He was just being catty," said Bolivia, having pulled Anne bodily out of the shop.

"I hate hairdressers!"

"If you'd let him work on you he would have been raving about your hair. You have gorgeous hair."

"How the hell did the cops get on to him?"

"They searched the house, didn't they?"

"Yes."

"They probably found an appointment card. Or maybe he called them. Obviously, if he's a witness for them, he wouldn't have done you any good anyway."

"This is crazy. The whole thing is crazy. I'm defending a man who's accused of killing a woman who doesn't appear to exist. And I'm getting nowhere. The state might not have much of a case, but I have *no* defense."

"That never stopped you from winning when you were a public defender."

"You're right, it didn't. Keep reminding me of that, Bolivia, okay?"

Anne expected him to come off the plane dejected. When she had called him in Austin to tell him of the indictment, he had said, "I never actually believed it would happen." He had seemed somewhat cheered by the news that he could now come home, however.

In fact, there was a bounce in his stride as he caught sight of her in the crowd and headed in her direction. And—surprise! surprise!—instead of his usual chinos and blue shirt, he was wearing a T-shirt with a picture of a large cowboy boot and the word *Austin* printed beneath it. The staid, Ivy League professor suddenly looked endearing.

He put his arms out, and she found herself giving him a hug. It started out to be the kind of hug she would have given Sandy or Bolivia if she were meeting them at the airport, but it turned out to be a little friendlier than that. She was surprised by the hug. He seemed less formal than usual, as though a few days in Texas had served to loosen him up. She would make a human being out of him yet.

He was the first to pull away. "You know what? I loved Austin."

"I thought you might," said Anne.

"Did you? I never would have thought so. It's nice there, and the people are great."

"Texans are very friendly."

"The weather's good, too. Same temperature as here, but without the humidity. Have you ever seen the hill country in the spring? It's spectacular. All those wildflowers in bloom."

"I'm sure they'd hire you at the university there."

"I'm not thinking of moving. I wouldn't mind going back, though, maybe driving around and seeing the whole state. Hey, I bought you a T-shirt, too."

"Well, thank you."

She turned to leave the airport, but he was bending down now and opening his leather carryon. He pulled out a plastic bag and handed it to her.

"Thank you," she said.

"Go on, look inside. I wasn't sure of your size, so I got a large. Mine's extra large."

"Large is fine," she said, pulling a white T-shirt out of the bag. Instead of a cowboy boot, hers had a large cactus printed on it. It also said Austin. "This is great," she told him.

"You really like it?"

"Very much."

"I wasn't sure whether you wore T-shirts."

"Everyone wears T-shirts."

"I know my students do. I've never worn one with a picture on it before."

She began to think that all this chatter was an effort on his part to mask the fact that an indictment had been brought in. "Jack, you understand that we have to go to trial now?"

"I need a drink. You want to get a drink before we leave the airport?"

"No thanks."

"Well, I want one."

"Can't you wait until you get home?"

"I want one now."

"All right, I'll sit with you while you have it."

"Why won't you drink with me?"

"I don't drink."

His eyes narrowed. "What are you, AA?"

"No, I'm not AA." She was mentally cursing Sandy and Bolivia, because she could use a drink, too. His nervousness was transferring itself to her.

They went to one of the bars on the main level, and he ordered Scotch on the rocks. "You sure you won't have something?" he asked her.

"I really can't."

"Why not?"

"All right. One. But only if you promise not to tell my friends."

"What is this? They were both drinking at my house."

"We have a bet. They bet me I couldn't go three months without a drink."

"That sounds like a stupid bet."

It was sounding pretty stupid to her, too. She finally ordered a gin and tonic, but when it came she found she had scruples after all, or maybe it was a stubborn determination to show her friends up. In any case, she didn't touch it. And Jack didn't mention it again.

Anne finally got him out of the bar after two drinks. As they passed a newsstand on the way out of the airport, she saw him stop, then swear under his breath. She looked around and saw that he was seeing his name in the headlines for the first time.

"I meant to warn you," she said.

"My God, it looks like something the tabloids would print."

"Scratch any one of them and you'll find the tabloid mentality at work, but don't tell Bolivia I said that."

He bought a copy of each paper, ignoring the look of the cashier, who appeared to recognize him. Whatever the drinks had done to cheer him up was destroyed by that one look of recognition.

Anne reached into her handbag and handed him a pair of aviator sunglasses. "Here, put these on."

"I guess it's incognito time," he said, but he put the glasses on. They looked good on him, albeit not serving as much of a disguise.

Jack was quiet on the drive to his house. He read the newspapers, the phone didn't ring once for a change, and it wasn't until they were half a block from his house and he noticed the reporters camped out on his lawn that he said anything. And then it wasn't anything repeatable.

"I expect they'll be there from now on," Anne told him.

"Can't I do anything about it? Can't I get the police to chase them off?"

"You can get them off your lawn, but you can't forbid them access to the sidewalk."

"Could we go somewhere else? How about your place?"

"Jack, they're not going to go away. I think it's better if we deal with them now and get it over with."

"I'm not talking to them."

"Good. I'm glad to see you following my orders."

"Then what did you mean by 'deal with them'?"

"I'll talk to them. Now, as soon as I pull into your driveway, I want you to grab that carton in the back seat and carry it into the house. I'll be in in a few minutes."

"What's in the box?"

"I stopped by the County Building on the way to the airport and picked it up. It's stuff the prosecution has to make available to us, copies of documents, reports, witness statements—you'll see."

As she pulled the car into his driveway the reporters converged on them. "Go on, do as I said," said Anne, getting out of the car and holding up her hands to stop the reporters. She knew most of them from previous cases, and there were shouts of, "Anne, over here, Anne."

"Hi, Tommy," she said to one of her favorites, who had always given her good press. "Listen, my client isn't talking, but I'll make a statement."

"You're defending the professor?" asked Tommy.

"That's right."

"I thought you got out of criminal law."

"I'm making an exception for Professor Quintana. I had him in law school, and when I saw him being wrongly accused, I wanted to help him all I could." Forget that at the time she would have been glad to see him hang.

"Hey, Anne, did he kill his girlfriend?" someone yelled out. She saw Quintana make it inside his front door, and she relaxed a little. She had never minded talking to the press. She'd had drinks with a lot of them on more than one occasion.

"Did you kill yours?" she yelled back.

There was some laughter from the reporters, and then Anne saw something that wasn't funny at all. She saw Bolivia trying to hide behind someone else's broad back.

Anne plunged into the crowd and dragged Bolivia out from behind her cover. "What do you think you're doing?" she asked her, furious that her friend was stooping to this.

"I've been assigned to the case," said Bolivia.

"Since when?"

"Since I convinced my boss I had an inside track. Come on, Annie, this is my big chance."

"Why, you traitor!"

"Hey, whatever you've said to me before this is off-the-record. Anyway, I'd think you'd be glad to have one of us on your side."

She *was* glad to have someone on their side. She just wished Bolivia had informed her of it instead of surprising her.

"Hey, how about a statement?" someone yelled out.

Anne made it short and succinct.

Quintana set down the carton filled with papers, then lifted out the one lying on top. It was the indictment, and it looked ominous and official: THE PEOPLE OF THE STATE OF FLORIDA V. JACK QUINTANA. He didn't think he'd ever seen an indictment before, except perhaps for a facsimile they might have shown him in law school.

He had liked Austin, but he'd found that he missed Anne. He'd thought he missed her in her capacity as his attorney, that he would have missed his attorney equally if the attorney were a man. He couldn't be completely sure of that, however, as his reaction to her hug had definitely not been the reaction he would have had if she'd been a man. He felt very much within her authority and found he didn't mind that the way he had always minded authority figures. He thought he ought to begin to harden himself not to depend on her so completely, because there would come a time when the trial would be over and he'd be on his own once again.

He wondered when he had become someone who could depend on someone else. It was the circumstances, of course. He had never been in a situation like this before.

He walked over to the window and pulled aside the curtain. She was out there, facing a battalion of reporters. She appeared to be at ease, even enjoying it. He would never make it as an attorney who had to deal routinely with the press. He found it difficult enough dealing with students who were prone to ask idiotic questions; the press would be much worse.

"Did you kill your girlfriend, Jack?" How dare complete strangers ask questions like that? After this case, would he never again be afforded the privacy that every citizen had a right to? Convicted or not, was this going to haunt him for the rest of his life? If so, he knew he wouldn't be able to stay in Florida. At least he had one thing to be thankful for: while it might make the newspapers in Miami, it wasn't the kind of case that would attract national attention. He thought again of Austin. He had liked the city, but he was pretty sure he wouldn't like it if he had to live there because he was no longer welcome in Miami.

He heard the door open and then slam shut. He turned to see Anne looking energized by her encounter with the press.

"Did you take a look at the contents?" she asked him, looking toward the box.

"No. Just the indictment."

"Good, we'll go over it together. Can you believe Bolivia was out there with the rest of the hyenas? I can't believe she would do that to me."

"Does that mean we no longer trust her?"

"Privately we can still trust her. Just don't talk to her if she comes on to you like a reporter." She knelt down on the floor beside the carton and started to lift out its contents.

"Why don't we take that into the den?" Quintana asked her.

She looked up at him. "You have a den?"

"Of course I have a den."

"What a luxury," she said, getting to her feet and then lifting the box in her arms. Quintana thought of taking it from her but knew the gesture wouldn't be appreciated.

"I, however, don't have the luxury of a car phone," he said. Or the luxury of a Jaguar, for that matter.

"That phone's not a luxury," said Anne. "It's a necessity. Mostly all I get are business calls on it."

He led the way into the den and pulled the blinds open to let the sun in.

She looked around at the bookshelves, the large worktable, the computer terminal and the comfortable reading chair. "I could live in this room," she said.

"Where do you live?" he asked her, surprised that he didn't know very much about her at all.

"I just bought a condo in South Beach. Across from the ocean."

"Sounds nice," said Jack, although he personally hated the beach. He liked boats and open water, but sand and tourists turned him off.

As she stood there with the box still in her arms, he took it from her and set it down on the worktable. "What exactly is in here?"

"Essentially, the D.A.'s case." She pulled out a thick bunch of papers. "These are the witnesses' statements."

"Witnesses? How many were there?"

Anne started to look through the papers. She would glance through one, then wordlessly hand it to him to peruse. There was the testimony of his neighbor to the north, who told how Marissa was afraid for her life. There was another neighbor who saw him dump something heavy into the canal in the middle of the night. There were other neighbors willing to say they had heard loud arguments emanating from his house.

"A hairdresser?" he said. "I didn't even know she went to a hairdresser."

"That would be Steve," said Anne. "Bolivia and I met him after he called her paper in response to the article and picture. The police had just been there, though, and he wouldn't talk to us. He did offer to do something about my hair."

"I like your hair," said Jack without thinking.

She was silent for so long that he finally said, "You have beautiful hair."

"Thank you. I didn't think you noticed things like that."

"I notice lots of things you don't think I notice."

She gave him a serious look, and he went back to reading the reports. Next was some young man who worked in a service station. "Did you see this one?" he asked. "This gas station attendant who says Marissa was planning on leaving me?"

"That's rather damaging," said Anne.

"Why this one in particular?"

"Because it goes to motive. Maybe you killed her to prevent her from leaving you."

"What utter nonsense," said Jack. "I would've helped her pack. What it looks like to me is that she set this up very carefully. I'm sounding paranoid, aren't I?"

"Perhaps with good reason," said Anne.

He didn't much like that "perhaps." "Not the body, though, that must have been coincidence. She must have laughed herself silly when a female body was found. It was like icing on the cake."

There was testimony from the cops on the physical and scientific evidence. There were statements by Betancourt and Soffer. And there was the coroner's report.

"Do you understand this?" he asked, handing her the autopsy report.

"I understand from it that they can't prove anything yet, which, as I see it, is to their benefit, not ours."

"I don't see that."

"Well, it's not Marissa, is it? So they couldn't possibly prove it was her. But we can't prove it's not her. Damn fish, eating up the body like that!"

"Would you like a drink?" he asked her.

She nodded. "Something cold and nonalcoholic. Could we have it outside? I wouldn't mind getting some air."

He brought glasses of iced tea out to the patio for them. She was at the end of the yard looking out at the canal. He set the glasses down on the table and walked to where she was standing.

"This is a great place," she told him. "You could have your own boat, couldn't you?"

"Yes, that dock is mine."

"This place must be worth a fortune."

"Are you adjusting my bill upward?"

"I'm just impressed, that's all."

"It might be worth a fortune now, although I doubt it, with real estate the way it is right now. It was in total disrepair when I bought at a foreclosure sale. I got it for little more than back taxes."

"Did you do any of the work on it yourself?"

"All of it. During summer vacations and school holidays. It probably sounds strange to you, but I was tired of apartment living and wanted a real home."

"You're like Sandy."

"Sandy the cop?"

"Yes. She's not happy unless she's making a home for herself. She loved your house immediately. Unlike Bolivia, who lives in a cheap hotel room and can move out in five minutes."

"And you? You've bought yourself a home of sorts."

"Not really. I just go in for investments, and South Beach is currently the place to buy. I work such long hours that all I really need is a place to sleep."

She turned to him. "Listen, Jack, there's something I think we should talk about. I'm sure the D.A.'s office is willing to plea bargain on this. I haven't been in touch with them on it yet, but they're usually willing. We could maybe get it down to manslaughter."

"Forget it! I'm innocent."

"It's entirely up to you. I just felt I should set forth your options."

"You've never asked me if I killed her."

"It's not relevant."

"It's sure as hell relevant to me!"

She stood silent, gazing over the water.

Her silence began to infuriate him. "Do you think I'm guilty?"

"No," she said, but she sounded tentative.

"That sounded like a qualified no."

"I really don't think you did it. It's not that I don't think you're capable of it, but I think you lack the passion for this kind of murder. I think that if you wanted to get rid of her, you would have ordered her out."

He'd asked for it, but now that he was getting her opinion, he didn't like it. "You think I lack passion?"

She nodded. "Except maybe over points of law."

"You think you're any more passionate?"

"I'm not the one being accused of murder."

Acting totally out of character, he reached out and pulled her to him, closing his mouth over hers and suddenly feeling more passion than he could ever remember feeling. If a woman like this wanted to leave him, maybe he would be capable of murder to prevent that happening.

Her body, which had initially stiffened in his embrace, began to relax, and he realized, with a feeling of wonder, that she was starting to return his kiss. The gentlemanly thing to do would be to break it off and apologize. For once, however, he wasn't feeling all that gentlemanly.

He tightened his arms and felt, with a thrill, the softness of her breasts pushing against his chest. In fact, she was soft all over—even her lips, which had now parted, and her breath, warm in his mouth.

Her arms were slowly making their way around him as his tongue found hers. Up until now he had been able to keep the soft stirrings in his groin in check, but now something was set loose in him that he had no control over at all, something so alive, so powerful, that all his instincts were crying out for him to pick her up and carry her into the house and make her his. It came as a shock to someone used to being in total control over his emotions.

It was finally a movement from his neighbor's yard that made him end the kiss. It was the man with the gut, the one whose wife said he'd beaten Marissa. He supposed now he was giving the neighbors more ammunition.

He let go of Anne. She stepped back a step or two and eyed him somewhat warily. "Why'd you do that?" she asked him. "Did you feel like hitting me, but instead decided to assault me sexually?"

The logic of her conclusion escaped him. "I didn't feel like hitting you."

"Are you sure?"

"Very sure. I've never mistaken an urge to kiss for an urge to hit."

"Be that as it may, don't let it happen again or I'll have to disqualify myself from your case because of conflict of interest."

"Does that mean you're interested?"

"I'm serious, Jack. I don't fool around with clients. In fact, at the moment, I don't fool around at all."

"What's that supposed to mean."

"It means that bet I made with my friends also includes laying off men for three months."

"Men and booze?"

She nodded.

Quintana was absolutely delighted to hear it. At least by the time the trial was over she wouldn't be involved with anyone. What was happening to him anyway? Accused of murder and falling in love both at the same time? It seemed incredible. He should be swearing off women for life after Marissa, and instead a curly-headed blonde was playing dangerous games with his emotions.

"Just don't try to pretend it didn't happen," he told her. "Because I intend to resume as soon as you get me acquitted."

"And if I don't get you acquitted?"

"Then you can visit me in prison."

Anne laughed. "Where's that cold drink you promised me?"

Anne eyed him across the black iron table inlaid with hand-painted tiles. He was different. She had sent a staid law professor to Austin and he had come back a different man. And it wasn't just the T-shirt, although that helped. It was in the way he looked at her, in the way he was loosening up, showing some humor. As for his kiss, he was more talented than a trumpet player, and that was saying a lot, particularly since trumpet players had well-developed muscles in their lips.

"We need to talk," she said at last. "The arraignment is only a week away."

"And what do we do there?"

"You plead not guilty, and the judge sets a trial date. I'd like to ask for an early one, but we don't seem to be getting anywhere investigating Marissa. You didn't find anything out since I talked to you in Austin, did you?"

"I would've told you first thing. If she ever lived there, it wasn't under that name."

"I guess we can thank her for not telling you she was from Alaska. At least it saved on air fare."

Chapter 8

Anne knocked, and Jack opened the door immediately. "Good morning," he said, actually smiling at her. She had been afraid his mood would be down, since the arraignment was that morning.

"Good morning yourself," she said.

"Do you have time for a cup of coffee?"

Anne looked at her watch. "Sure, we can take five minutes."

She followed him back to the kitchen and took a seat at the table, while he carried a second cup over. He looked the same as usual. In fact, he looked exactly the same.

"Jack, are those the only clothes you own?"

He looked down at himself, as though he had forgotten what he was wearing. She found it inconceivable that he could be even momentarily at a loss when he appeared to wear the same outfit day after day.

"I usually dress like this," he told her. "Is anything wrong with it?"

"Everything," said Anne.

His eyes went to her gray linen suit and mauve silk blouse, lingering on the blouse for a moment. "I don't own a linen suit."

"Good," she said. "At best a linen suit would make you look like Sydney Greenstreet. At worst you'd look like a Colombian drug dealer."

"Then what's the problem?"

"Jack, if I'm already tired of seeing you in blue shirts and khaki pants, the jury's going to be gagging at the sight of you after the second day."

He shrugged. "It's about all I have."

"I don't believe that. Would you mind showing me your closet?"

"I'd be delighted to show you my entire bedroom."

"Just the closet will do." She finished off the coffee and stood. "Come on, I want to make an inspection."

On the way to the closet, she couldn't help seeing the bedroom anyway. It looked like something out of the magazine section of the Sunday paper. The walls were painted a dusty mustard color, and it was filled with massive, dark furniture, the kind that would be guaranteed to give her nightmares. But it had a fireplace and French doors that she was sure led out to a balcony. Throw out the furniture, paint it white and it would be livable.

The closet was something else. It was a gigantic walk-in closet, almost the size of a small boutique. Anne would kill for a closet that size, where half her things wouldn't have to be at the cleaners at any given moment so that the other half had room to breathe.

Further frustrating was the fact that two-thirds of the closet were empty. The other third held several pairs of pants, identical to the ones he was wearing, three corduroy sport jackets, the kind with leather elbow patches, and a black suit that looked suitable for the funeral of a poor relation. Neatly placed on a shoe rack were two more pairs of Topsiders, a pair of loafers, two pairs of tennis shoes and a pair of two-tone shoes she didn't even want to think about.

She closed the closet door and leaned back against it. "Are all your dress shirts blue, or should I check them out?"

He was trying not to smile. "They're all blue. I like blue."

"Jack, my friend, we're going shopping today."

"I hate shopping."

"That's pretty obvious."

"I've never shopped with a woman."

"That's also obvious. And I have no intention of standing here arguing about it. Come on, we've got an arraignment to make. And when we get there . . ."

"Yes?"

"Don't say a word. Just be quiet and look properly serious, do you understand?"

"Yes, ma'am!"

Hordes of press were lying in wait outside the courthouse. Anne spotted Bolivia in the crowd, probably because she was wearing her trademark safari hat, and tried to put a curse on her from a distance, but since Bolivia didn't disappear in a puff of smoke, she changed it to glaring at her. Bolivia grinned back.

"Don't say a word to them," she warned Jack.

"I have no intention of speaking to them. That guy over there, though—the one in the red shirt—I think I know him."

"You only think you know him because you probably see him on the news every night."

"Oh, right—yes, I have seen him on the news."

Anne hustled him inside, found the room number they needed, then hurried him upstairs. At the door to the courtroom, she looked in. They were appearing before the Honorable Edith Crenshaw. She was the oldest judge on the bench and had always seemed to like Anne. Anne couldn't be positive, but she thought the judge was partial to female attorneys. She kept her fingers crossed that they'd get her for the trial, too.

Anne drew Jack into the art deco courtroom and went straight to the front to take a seat in the first row. She thought that would make him feel at home. She was sure he had been the kind of student who always sat in the front row and always knew the answers. She had been that kind of student herself, the one exception being the morning she hadn't known the answer when Jack called on her. She wished she hadn't remembered that just when she was really starting to like him. She stole a glance at him and noted his solemn profile. For a moment he looked like the intimidating Professor Quintana of old, and then he turned his head slightly and winked at her, and she relaxed.

They had to wait almost an hour before the docket clerk called out Criminal Case 96-1433, which was their case. By then Anne was dead bored, but Jack actually seemed to be enjoying the proceedings.

Anne nodded for him to follow her, and they approached the bench. Judge Crenshaw, wearing a little too much blush on her cheeks this morning, smiled down at Anne.

Anne felt something move behind her and saw Howie Leonard coming up to stand beside her. "Annie," he said, and winked at her. She ignored him. He then looked past her at Jack and said, "Professor," with a deferential nod. Jack politely nodded back.

"Who is he? He looks familiar." Jack whispered to Anne.

"One of your former students," she whispered back.

She thought Jack turned a paler shade of off-white.

Judge Crenshaw said, "This is Criminal Case 96-1433. Let me ask counsel to identify themselves for the record."

Howie said, "Assistant District Attorney Howard Leonard on behalf of the people of the state."

"Anne Larkin, Hutchinson, Talbot, Withers, Carey and Smith, on behalf of the defendant, Jack Quintana. I would request leave, Your Honor, to file our appearance."

"Motion allowed," said the judge, "and the court records now officially indicate that Anne Larkin is the attorney for the defendant."

Howie looked ready to jump in, but Anne beat him to it. "Your Honor, defendant is present in court. We acknowledge receipt of Indictment 96-1433 and waive formal reading. On behalf of Mr. Quintana, Your Honor, we would ask the court to enter a plea of not guilty of the charge."

Howie was looking at her in consternation.

The judge nodded. "Plea of not guilty to the indictment. Is there a request from either party for a pretrial conference?"

This meant a plea-bargaining session, which was usually automatic, and Howie now seemed to be holding his breath. Well, he was about to get that breath knocked out of him.

Anne said, "Your Honor, we waive the conference and request the court set an immediate trial date."

Howie muttered something under his breath that Anne didn't catch.

The judge was perusing some paper, probably a court calendar giving dates when judges were available. She finally spoke. "Judge Silva's docket for motions and trial. Defendant's motions to be filed in fourteen days." She picked up the gavel, and Anne turned away.

She didn't know Judge Silva; he must have been appointed to the bench since she had gotten out of criminal law. The Hispanic name, though, might bode well for Quintana. Then again, the judge might be a sexist who resented female attorneys in his courtroom.

"That's it?" asked Jack by her side.

"Just a preview of what's to come," she told him.

"That wasn't so bad."

"Did I lead you to believe the arraignment was some kind of an ordeal?"

"Well, no."

"I'll let you know when it's going to get bad."

They were outside the courtroom when Howie grabbed her arm. "Hey, Annie, I need to talk to you."

Anne took the car keys out of her handbag and handed them to Jack. "You want to wait in the car for me? I won't be long."

"I'd rather stay," he said.

Anne shrugged and turned to Howie. "What is it, Howie?"

Howie looked from Jack to Anne. "What's the story? I mean, why no plea bargaining?"

"Innocent people don't plea bargain, Howie."

"Oh, yeah? Since when? I thought your clients were always innocent?"

"Until proven otherwise, yes. This one, however, happens to be as pure as the driven snow."

"In a pig's eye," said Howie, then turned a sheepish look at Jack. "No aspersions, Professor, you understand," he said. "I have fond recollections of your classroom. I have the utmost respect for you."

Anne laughed out loud, and even Jack grinned.

Howie shrugged and smiled. "Listen, only doing my job." He turned the smile on higher as he looked at Anne.

"Annie, how about dinner tonight? We've got things to talk about."

"In a pig's eye, Porky," she said, then turned and headed out of the courthouse. Behind her she could hear Jack's chuckle. She turned around and said, "We used to call him Porky in school because he was such a pig."

Jack burst out laughing.

"Where are we going?" Jack asked as she headed over the causeway to Miami Beach.

"Shopping," he was told. "But first I want to stop by my place and change my clothes."

"You look fine," he told her, which was an understatement. She looked exquisite. In that outfit he didn't see how she could lose a case. If he were on a jury he wouldn't be able to keep his eyes off her.

"These are my work clothes," she said. "I want to change into my shopping clothes."

He didn't ask for a further explanation. He would never understand women.

In a move that had him hanging on to the door, she picked up her car phone with one hand and punched out a number with the other. Meanwhile, her knees were doing the steering. And all of this at well over the speed limit.

"Bolivia? Want to meet us for lunch? We're heading over to Bal Harbour to outfit Jack.... Today?... Oh, all right— I'll talk to you later." She was punching out another number, and he averted his eyes from her driving. "Hi, Joe, is Sandy around?... Is that today?... Okay, I'll give her a call later."

He waited until her hands were back on the steering wheel where they belonged before he said, "I'm willing to go shopping with you, but I don't need advisers along."

"Oh, they don't like to shop. I just thought they could meet us for lunch."

"I don't mind eating lunch alone with you."

"We need to do some more brainstorming."

"Are you afraid to be alone with me now?"

"Don't be ridiculous. We're talking about lunch. In a mall. At an outdoor table."

She took a sharp left, then another, and then pulled into a metered parking spot on the ocean side of the street. He hadn't been in South Beach in years, and while he'd read about the changes, they were hard to believe. What had once been a stretch of run-down buildings with old people sitting out on porches was now a row of restored art deco buildings with nary a senior citizen in sight.

The park running the length of the beach looked as though it had also been restored. The park itself looked wider, the palm trees taller and the benches newly painted. Tourist season had ended for the moment until it started up again in the summer, and only a few people could be seen on the beach.

Anne got out of the car saying, "I'll just be a minute."

Jack got out of the other side and locked the door. "I'd like to see where you live."

"You really wouldn't," said Anne.

"I really would," he insisted, crossing the street with her. "Is this your building?"

She nodded.

"It looks very nice." Boring, but not bad.

"It's just been redone."

"They did a good job of it."

"I haven't lived here very long."

"Look, if you're not settled in yet, don't worry about it." He pictured cartons still sitting around the floor and pictures, unhung, leaning against the walls. It had taken him a long time to get his house straightened out after he moved in.

"Oh, I'm settled in," she said.

They entered the building and rode the elevator up to the top floor. When Anne opened the door to an apartment and waited for him to go in, he thought she was kidding. He was pretty sure this was an empty apartment and she was playing a joke on him. When she walked in and closed the door after her he wasn't so sure.

"Where's the furniture?" he asked, looking around at a large but completely empty room.

"In the bedroom."

"All of it?"

"All I have, yes." She disappeared into what was no doubt the bedroom, looking back and saying, "I'll just be a minute," before she closed the door.

The walls were white, the floor was white tile, and there was nothing at the windows. He could understand that, though, as there were no buildings tall enough for people to look into her apartment, and the windows afforded a spectacular wraparound view of the ocean. He could see for miles, and he thought pictures on the wall would probably be superfluous when you had a view like that to look at.

He looked into the kitchen. Except for a teakettle on the stove, a dirty mug in the sink and a jar of instant coffee on the counter, there was nothing. She was obviously of the same school of thought as he was: as long as there were restaurants, why not use them?

When she came out of the bedroom she looked like a different person. She was wearing white cotton pants, a navy blue T-shirt, white running shoes and had her hair brushed back into a ponytail. This wasn't the corporate attorney or even the softball player. Now she looked like one of his students.

"You have a great view," he told her.

"Umm. Too bad I never get to see it. At night it's just a large expanse of black."

He could see past her into the bedroom where, beneath a pile of clothes, was a large, unmade bed. She saw where he was looking and quickly closed the door.

"Come on," she said, "we've got shopping to do."

"I don't think I've ever been here," he said as she pulled into the parking lot and took a ticket.

"You live in Miami and you've never been to Bal Harbour?"

"If I have to shop, I usually go to Dadeland."

"You haven't shopped until you've shopped at Bal Harbour."

Jack didn't see what was so impressive about it. Since it was all outdoors, it didn't even have air-conditioning.

She took him into an elegant men's store to look at men's suits. He thought she had in mind one suit. It turned out she had two suits in mind, plus an additional pair of slacks and a sport jacket. He took a look at the price tag on the first suit, a gray silk, and balked. "Their prices are ridiculous," he informed her.

"You get what you pay for."

"Well, I'm not paying for that. It's a total waste of money. I'll never wear it again."

"Look at it as an investment in your future. The jury isn't going to know you're a good, honest man. All they're going to know about you is how you're dressed and how you part your hair."

"I don't part my hair."

"Whatever."

"Anne, I don't even have this kind of money on me."

"I'll put it on my charge card and bill you later," she told him, sending him off to the dressing room with one of the salesmen.

When he came out to show her she nodded in approval and pointed out a few alterations to the salesman. Jack saw that she was holding several white shirts in her arms.

"I have plenty of dress shirts," he said.

"You only have blue ones."

"I like blue."

"That's too bad, because you're getting white."

He decided to shut up and let her have her way. The other alternative was to make a scene, but with his luck it would make the newspapers with headlines such as: Law Professor Indicted for Murder Goes Berserk at Mall.

They walked the length of the mall to another store for ties and socks, and also a pair of soft, leather shoes. There was a white cotton, V-neck sweater Anne had her eyes on and Jack said, "There's no way I'm going to need a sweater. This is for the courtroom, right?"

"This is for me," she said, asking the sales clerk to cut off the tag, then tying the arms of the sweater around her neck. She looked as if she were getting ready to sail off on her yacht.

"What's the matter?" she asked, catching him staring at her.

"I'm just admiring your outfit."

"Well, you have a few of your own to be admired in now."

Jack groaned as she reached for the charge slip, not even wanting to know the amount.

"What now?" he asked as they headed back outside.

She grinned at him. "Relax. Now we have lunch. And it won't cost you anything, because it's business."

They sat outdoors at one of the sidewalk tables, and Jack ordered a beer, which he felt he needed. Spending that much money in so short a time was having a traumatic effect on him. And for clothes, something he'd always felt were way down the list of priorities.

Anne ordered a margarita without the tequila and then made a face when she tasted it. "The food is good here," she said.

It should be, thought Jack, noting the price. Still, their entire lunch wouldn't cost as much as one of the silk ties she had picked out.

She ordered lobster salad; he ordered a steak sandwich and another beer, and he was just starting to feel himself relax when he remembered the arraignment. He couldn't help thinking that here he was, sitting over lunch with a beautiful woman, and another beautiful woman, for no reason on earth that he could fathom, had been responsible for his having to plead not guilty to a charge of criminal homicide. Somehow, somewhere, the world wasn't making sense anymore. His vision of how things should be was now skewed.

"A penny for your thoughts," she said.

"I don't understand it," said Jack. "I don't suppose I've led a totally perfect life, but I can't for the life of me come up with any reason for her to do this to me. I mean, it's a beautiful afternoon, I'm sitting across from a beautiful woman, on the surface everything seems to be perfect. But I've been indicted for murder! This is the worst thing that's ever happened to me, but I can't seem to take it that seriously. It doesn't seem real."

Anne started to chuckle.

"What's so funny?"

"You say it's the worst thing that's ever happened to you. You want to know what the worst thing that ever happened to me was?"

"If you want to tell me."

The chuckle turned to laughter.

"I don't see how it could be so bad if you're laughing about it."

"It was you."

"Me?"

"You. When I had you for Torts. You totally demolished me in class one day. It was so bad it gave me nightmares."

"I gave you nightmares?"

"My dear Professor, I'd be willing to wager that you give all your students nightmares."

"If I demolished you, you couldn't have been properly prepared."

"No, I wasn't. It was probably the only time in all three years of law school that I wasn't."

"Well, I'm not going to apologize. In my opinion, all of you had it exceedingly easy. You don't know the meaning of demolish unless you've been to Harvard Law."

"Your professors there gave you nightmares?"

"No, not nightmares, but that was only because they didn't give us time to sleep at night."

"I don't think I like the idea of teaching through intimidation."

"That's because you've never taught classes of young people who'd rather be getting stoned than study. But I'm sorry about the nightmares. They can be nasty things."

"I don't believe you've ever had nightmares, Jack. You're not the type."

"Only once. And that was back in my college days, but it had nothing to do with a professor."

"Some girl give you a hard time?"

"No. Something a lot more serious than that. It was spring break, and I was driving down to the Keys with some of my friends, and I came within inches of being in a head-on collision." He wondered what had reminded him of it after all this time. Her nightmares, yes. It had been the only time he had ever had nightmares.

"My God, it's lucky you're alive!"

"The man driving the other car isn't. He was drunk, coming at me down the center of the highway, straddling the white line. At the last minute I was able to swerve a little out of the way, but he still hit me, although not head-on. I was able to bring my car to a stop, but his went over the side of the bridge. We dived in after him, but his car was locked, and we couldn't get him out. He was dead by the time the police brought him up."

"No wonder it gave you nightmares."

"It was terrible."

"What an awful thing to have happened."

"We went by to see his wife a few days later. We were all feeling guilty, even though the man was at fault. His wife was okay. She knew the man was a drunk, and it seemed as though she had been expecting something like that to happen. But he had this little girl, around seven, I think. And she screamed at me that I had killed her daddy. It was the little girl, and those screams, that gave me the nightmares."

Anne dropped her fork, and it bounced off the table onto the sidewalk. "Jack."

"What?"

"How many years ago was that?"

"About sixteen."

"And the daughter would now be in her early twenties."

"I suppose so."

''Jack. What if she's Marissa?''

''Oh, come now, that's really reaching for it.''

''Maybe, but it seems to be all we have. And her fear of water would fit right in with her father's having drowned. Just think about it, Jack. She thinks you killed her daddy.''

She started up the car and reached for the phone. She breathed a sigh of relief when Bolivia picked up at the office.

''Bolivia? I think we've got a lead, and I need a favor.''

''What's happening?''

''Jack was in a car accident—'' She turned to him. ''What was the date, do you remember?''

He thought a moment. ''March 28, 1973.''

She repeated the date for Bolivia. ''It happened on one of the bridges in the Keys. A drunk driver on the wrong side of the road, college students on spring break—the man's car went off the bridge, and he was killed. Left a widow and a young daughter.''

''Will you please tell me what this is about?''

''Trust me, Bolivia, this is very, very important. Just go back in the files and see if you can find out anything about the accident.'' She put her hand over the phone. ''What was his name, Jack?''

''I've been trying to remember, but I can't. I seem to have blanked it out.''

''Listen, we're on our way to Jack's house, and I'll wait there to hear from you.... Thanks. Listen, I owe you one.''

She drove out of the parking lot, paid the attendant, and headed for I-95. Suddenly anything was looking possible.

''What if it is Marissa?'' Jack asked her. ''What does that prove?''

''It's motive, Jack. It's a reason for her to set you up. Revenge. Revenge is one of the strongest motives of all.''

"I think you're wrong about this. Why would she wait sixteen years?"

"She was a child. There wasn't anything she could do about it then, but her urge for revenge festered inside of her and then, when she was finally an adult, she went after you."

"I still say you're reaching. I don't think she could have maintained that kind of single-mindedness all those years. And she didn't just become an adult a few months ago."

"I know I'm reaching, but it's the only thing we've come up with. Listen, if some college kids caused my father's death, I'd still be furious."

"Would you frame me for murder?"

"No, I'd probably just kill you straight off."

"You wouldn't, though. It would just be a sad memory by now."

"Look, Jack, I know what you're saying makes more sense than what I'm saying, but it's worth looking into. At the moment we have no motive. At least this gives us something to work with."

"Why are we going to my house?"

"To put away your new clothes."

Jack groaned. "Don't remind me."

They were upstairs in Jack's bedroom, putting his new clothes away, when Bolivia called. Jack picked up the phone, then handed it to her.

"Did you find it?" Anne asked her.

"Bingo," said Bolivia. "Exact date, written up on page three. The man's name was William Jorgensen."

"Is there an address for him?"

"It just says he was from Plantation."

"Thank you, I love you, I'll forever be grateful to you," said Anne, hanging up the phone and calling information for Plantation.

She couldn't believe it when the operator told her there was no listing for a Jorgensen. "Are you sure?" Anne asked.

"There is no listing for a Jorgensen."

"Hell!" said Anne, slamming down the phone.

"It's been a long time," said Jack. "She probably moved."

"There's got to be a way to find her."

"Look, Anne, I doubt very much whether—"

"Have a little faith in my hunches, Jack, okay?" She picked up the phone and called Sandy. Luckily she was back from the stakeout.

"I need a favor, and I need it immediately," said Anne.

"Fine, thank you, and how are you today, Annie?"

"Sorry, but this really is crucial."

"What do you need?"

"I need you to call the police in Plantation and get the address for a William Jorgensen who was killed in a car accident in March of '73."

"You at the office?"

"No, I'm at Jack's house. Get back to me right away, okay?"

She hung up and gave Jack a smug smile. "It helps to have friends in strategic places."

"I can see that."

"If there's anything you need to do before we drive down to Plantation, do it now."

"Why don't I drive this time?"

"Not this time. My car needs a little exercise, and the Turnpike is perfect."

* * *

She saw Jack reach for his seat belt for about the sixth time, making sure it was fastened securely. She didn't know what he was so worried about; there was hardly any traffic on the Turnpike.

"Relax," she said to him.

"I'm waiting for the phone to ring and you to lose total control of the car."

"I've never lost control of it yet." He didn't look convinced, so she took the phone off the hook. "Okay? Is that better?"

"It would be even better if you would slow down."

"How did you get to be such a stodgy old professor?"

"Years of practice."

After stopping for directions at a gas station in Plantation, Anne found Everglades Drive without any problem. It was a quiet neighborhood of small, well-tended houses, and the address she was looking for turned out to have a collection of tricycles in the driveway. She parked in front of the house and got out.

"Unless the daughter has grown up, has children of her own and still lives at home, I don't think we have the right house," said Jack.

"No, but they might know where the Jorgensens moved to."

Anne rang the doorbell and heard chimes sound in the house. A moment later a young woman appeared at the screen door.

"I was wondering if you could help us," said Anne. "We're looking for some people who used to live here by the name of Jorgensen."

"They don't live here," said the woman.

"I know. I was wondering if you knew where they moved?"

"I don't know anything about them," said the woman. "People we bought this house from were named Borchard."

"Well, thank you anyway," said Anne, stepping back off the porch.

The woman opened the screen door and poked her head out, staring at Jack. "Don't I know you?"

"I don't believe so," said Jack.

"You look kinda familiar."

Anne grabbed Jack's hand and pulled him away from the house. "You're getting famous," she told him.

"Great. Just what I always wanted."

"When you get acquitted, you can write a book about it and get on all the talk shows."

"I'll leave that to you," Jack told her. "What now?"

"Now we question the neighbors. You take this side of the street, I'll take the other."

"What if I'm recognized again?"

"If that happens, scare the information out of them."

Anne hit pay dirt at the fifth house, where she found an older woman sitting out on her front porch in a swing. The woman smiled as Anne approached the porch.

"You takin' some kind of survey?" she asked Anne.

"No, ma'am, I'm not."

"Selling something?"

"I'm not selling anything."

"I've already been born again."

"Ma'am, I'm looking for a Mrs. Jorgensen who used to live across the street."

"That would be Sally, moved away seven years ago. Got remarried. Nice man. Something to do with plumbing supplies. It was hurricane season. I remember that, because we were having some of those torrential rains. All her furniture got wet in the moving.''

"Do you know where she moved to?''

"We exchange Christmas cards every year.''

"Would you mind telling me her address?'' And if she did mind, she'd send Sandy to do the job.

"Want me to go in the house and get it for you?''

"If you wouldn't mind.''

"Don't mind at all. Don't have anything better to do.''

When the woman went into the house, Anne looked across the street and saw Jack watching her from the sidewalk. She raised a hand, then pointed to the car. He read her signals, and she watched while he got back into the Jaguar.

"Here you are,'' said the woman, coming out of the door with a piece of paper in her hand. "You going to see Sally?''

"I hope to,'' said Anne.

"Well, tell her I said hello. Joan Murray is the name.''

"I will, Mrs. Murray, and thank you. Thank you very much.''

"We drove all the way to Plantation and she lives in Miami?''

"Quit complaining, Jack. It's a beautiful day for a drive, and you had nothing better to do. Anyway, South Kendall's almost this far away.''

"What did she say about her?''

"That she remarried. Someone in plumbing supplies. Her last name is Johnson now.''

"Not much of a change in last names.''

"Yes, but maybe this one isn't a drunk.''

"What're we going to do after we talk to her?''

"What do you mean?''

"Are we going to have dinner?''

"You just had a steak a couple of hours ago, Jack.''

"I was just wondering what you were doing tonight."

"You sound like you're trying to date me."

"Maybe I am."

"Knock it off, Jack. Do you want articles in the paper about how a certain murder suspect is keeping company with his defense attorney? You think that would help your case?"

"We could stay home."

"Look, I know you're probably bored, with no classes to teach, and I know you're starting to think about me the way people think about their doctors, but I want you to cool it, okay?"

"If I thought it was one-sided, I would."

"It's academic anyway, I have a game tonight. Against South Kendall, actually. If I'd worn my uniform I wouldn't have to go home and change. You could've watched us."

"I hate baseball."

"You *what*?"

"I think it's a mindless, boring, juvenile game."

"Well, I hope the prosecution doesn't find out about that, because the jury would convict you for being un-American."

"I used to play when I was a kid. I think I lost interest in it along about college."

"Well, if I were you, I wouldn't breathe a word about that to Sandy or Bolivia, or they might stop being so helpful."

"What position do you play?"

"Center field. Okay, so it's not a big deal, but I'm one of our best hitters."

"I don't care if you're the female Mickey Mantle, I just hope you're good in court."

Sally Jorgensen Johnson was a small woman, soft-spoken, seemingly eager to please. She wore her graying blond hair in an outdated bouffant, and legs thick with varicose veins stuck out of her shorts. She let them in her house without even asking them their names, then told them to make themselves comfortable on the couch.

When Anne set her briefcase on her lap and opened it, Mrs. Johnson moved her chair closer as though to inspect whatever samples Anne might have inside.

Instead of samples Anne pulled out the picture of Marissa. She handed it to Mrs. Johnson saying, "We were wondering if you recognize her, ma'am."

Mrs. Johnson reached for a pair of reading glasses on a table and put them on, then looked closely at the picture. "I saw this picture in the newspapers," she said. "I have no idea who she is."

"We thought maybe it was your daughter," said Anne.

Mrs. Johnson looked up, the shock on her face genuine. "Monica? You thought that was Monica?"

"We thought it was a possibility," said Anne.

"That's not Monica. She doesn't look anything like Monica." She turned to look at Jack. "I know who you are. I saw your picture in the paper, and your name."

"I'm sorry, Mrs. Johnson," said Jack. "I should have told you straight off. It seems as though I never see you under happy circumstances."

"Wasn't your fault," said the woman. "He was a drunk. It was going to happen sooner or later. I'm happier now than I ever was with Billy. But why in the world would you think that woman was Monica?"

Jack told her about Anne's theory, ending up with, "It was just a wild hunch. I didn't really think anything would come of it. How is Monica? I felt so bad for her at the time."

"Oh, that was a problem for her, all right. She adored her daddy, and he adored her. Used to knock me around when he got drunk, but never in front of Monica. I never told her how he really was, though. Didn't seem no point, with him dead and all.''

"Where is she now?" asked Anne, not ready to give up on her hunch.

"Don't know," said the woman. "She left home at sixteen, and I haven't seen her since. She didn't take to my getting remarried, said she wouldn't live in the same house as Ernie. I thought she'd get over it, but we no sooner moved here than she ran away. Police never did find her.''

Anne leaned toward Mrs. Johnson. "Isn't it conceivable that this could be Monica? After all, seven years is a long time. She could have changed.''

"Not that much," said Mrs. Johnson. She got up and left the room.

Jack looked at Anne, and she shrugged. She was just about to suggest they leave when Mrs. Johnson came back carrying a framed picture. She handed it to Anne.

"That's Monica when she was fifteen. School picture. It's a good likeness.''

Anne looked at the girl in the picture. She had long, straight blond hair, parted in the middle and hanging down to partially shield her face. The face itself was chubby, with light blue eyes behind round glasses. Her mouth was smiling, but her eyes looked sad. She wasn't an attractive teenager, and Anne felt sorry for her. She handed the photograph to Jack.

"I don't see any resemblance," said Jack.

"None at all?" asked Anne.

He shook his head and handed the picture back to Mrs. Johnson. "I'm really sorry we bothered you.''

"I'd almost rather it was Monica," she said. "At least that way I'd know she was all right.''

"I'm sure she's not only all right, Mrs. Johnson," said Anne, "but probably a lot better off than the young woman we're looking for."

"I keep thinking that someday the doorbell will ring, and it will be Monica at the door and we can be friends."

"Did the police try very hard to find her?" Anne asked.

"They said there wasn't much they could do."

"I have a friend on the police department in Miami," said Anne. "If you want, I'll have her give it a try."

"I don't know," said Mrs. Johnson. "It's not as though she's a child anymore. She's an adult now, and if she wanted to see me, I guess she would. I appreciate it, though. It was a nice thought."

Jack was clearly as dejected as she was when they left the house.

"We'll think of something else," Anne told him.

"It's not that. I feel sorry for her. Because of that accident, her whole life changed."

"But she said she was happier now."

"I know she said it."

"Then what's the matter?"

He gave her a wry smile. "Could you be happy living in South Kendall?"

"No way. But I'll be ecstatic if we can beat them tonight."

Chapter 9

Judge Silva looked down at Jack. "Professor Quintana," he said with a nod, "I'm sorry to see you again under such circumstances."

Anne looked over at Jack with surprise. He hadn't mentioned that he knew the judge. The legal community in Miami wasn't that large, though, and it was possible that everyone had at least a nodding acquaintance with everyone else.

This was her first look at the judge. He was an older gentleman, quite distinguished looking, with silver hair and the narrowest of mustaches. He was thin, with strong bones in his face, a face devoid of humor lines if she wasn't mistaken.

They had been summoned to the courthouse by the judge for a status hearing on the case and so that the judge could rule on the requests that had been filed in the defendant's pretrial motions, and also in order to discuss a trial date.

The judge now looked down at Anne, and she introduced herself. Howie, a few minutes late, appeared at her side just in time to hear the judge rule on her motion to disqualify Howie as being a former student of Jack's. Although she felt this was prejudicial to Jack's case, a judge would more likely see it as a conflict of interest.

"Your motion to disqualify Mr. Leonard is not granted," said the judge, and then, with the slightest of smiles for Jack, "I'm afraid if I start disqualifying people for having studied under Professor Quintana, that would ultimately mean disqualifying the entire District Attorney's office. Isn't that right, Mr. Leonard?"

"You've got that right, Your Honor," said Howie, with a smirk at Anne.

"As for defense's motion to set an immediate trial date," the judge continued, "I am in complete agreement, and I'm setting it for two weeks from today."

That was faster than even Anne had hoped for. She saw Howie becoming visibly agitated at her side.

"Do you have a problem with that, Mr. Leonard?" the judge asked Howie.

"My vacation," Howie began, then caught Anne's eye. She stared him down, and he finally cleared his throat, vacillated for a moment and then said, "No, sir, no problem."

"Good," said Judge Silva. "Then all we have left to discuss are the motions for production, all of which are granted."

Outside the courthouse Anne walked Jack to his car. Today he was on his own, as she had some work to clear up for Centricon at the office.

"You didn't tell me you knew the judge," she said to him.

"I don't really know him. He occasionally teaches a semester of Constitutional Law at the university, and I've run into him at different functions, but we've never really talked."

"I liked his attitude," she said. "It looks as though you'll have the court's respect."

"Why wouldn't I have his respect?"

"Oh, you'd be surprised. There are some judges who could have made it very hard on you. I think you lucked out that he isn't young enough to have been your student."

"You're not going to let me forget that, are you?"

Bolivia called another brainstorming session for after their game that night. Jack was induced to go to this game, and while he professed to be pleased by their prowess, he had looked bored silly by the end.

They took pizza back to Jack's house and gathered around the kitchen table.

"I'm getting nowhere with a defense," Anne told them. "The investigators couldn't find anyone who saw Marissa leaving the neighborhood on foot, which seems inconceivable, since two of the neighbors are members of a neighborhood Crime Watch and see everyone who goes into or out of the neighborhood."

"They do a good job, too," said Jack. "I drove home in a loaner once that the garage let me use while my car was being fixed, and one of them came out of the house to make sure it was me."

"We've got to think logically here," said Bolivia. "Who don't people notice?"

"That's a good point," said Jack, "but the thing is, I don't think Marissa was smart enough to have thought of that."

"I think she was a lot smarter than you thought," said Anne. "So far she hasn't made a wrong move."

"Mailmen," said Jack, looking pleased with himself. "I that what they're called today?"

"I think they're called mail carriers," said Sandy.

"But people do notice them," said Bolivia. "People watching for their mail notice them, and one would surely be noticed walking out of Jack's house. Plus she would have had to obtain a uniform."

"Strike mail carriers," said Anne.

"Deliverymen?" asked Jack, not looking so sure of him self this time.

"Again," said Bolivia, "that would require a uniform And a truck. But keep coming up with the ideas. That' what brainstorming is all about."

"Domestics," said Sandy. "A neighborhood like this you must get a lot of cleaning women coming in and out."

"That's a possibility," said Anne. "Except that they wear their own clothes to and from work, and I have a feeling n one would have mistaken Marissa for a domestic."

"Why not?" asked Sandy. "We're already pretty certai she disguised herself."

"Okay, I guess she could have," said Anne. "I'll get on of the investigators to canvass the neighborhood tomorrow with that in mind."

"I'll tell you what's all over my neighborhood," said Sandy, "and that's kids. They all look alike to me. Maris sa's about my size, isn't she?"

"She's very tiny," said Jack. "Five feet, maybe ninety five pounds."

"I think it's a better possibility than a cleaning woman," said Anne.

"I'm always being mistaken for a kid," said Sandy "When I'm in my baseball uniform people are always call ing me kid. And I just thought of something else. If she wa dressed like a kid and rode off on a bike, no one would notice. Kids on bikes are all over the place.''

"I have a bike," said Jack. "I rarely use it, but I have one out in the garage.''

"Is it still there?" Anne asked him.

"I don't know. I'd have to check."

When he came back from the garage he was grinning. "It's gone. I never thought I'd be happy to have my bike stolen, but it's not there. She could've taken it out the back, cut across the neighbor's lawn and appeared down the street.''

"That's great," said Bolivia. "Now we know how she got away, but we still don't know where she is.''

"At least it's a place to start," said Anne. "I'll have the investigators ask about kids tomorrow, too, although it's unlikely anyone would remember after all this time, unless she ran over someone's pet or mowed down their flower garden.''

"Jack, you ought to report it as stolen," said Sandy.

"My bike?"

Sandy nodded. "Just to get it on the record in case Anne needs to use it as evidence.''

"Good thinking," said Anne.

"But I could be making it up," said Jack.

Anne said, "Do you have a bill of sale for it, or do you have it on your home-owner's insurance?''

"Yes to both," said Jack.

"Good," said Anne. "Then get on the phone to the police. If they give you a hard time, tell them you're going to put your attorney on the phone.''

As Jack left the room to make the call Sandy asked Anne, "Marissa had her own car, didn't she?''

Anne nodded.

"Did anyone search it?"

"I don't think so," said Anne. "You want to handle that, Sandy?"

"Where's it parked?" asked Sandy.

"In the garage," said Anne. "You can get into the garage through the kitchen."

As Sandy left the room Bolivia said, "Listen, what I'd do if I were you is go around tomorrow and hit all the bike shops. At least the ones in Coral Gables. And take a picture of Marissa around. You get young guys working in them, and they're sure to remember her if she was ever in. If she was making her getaway on a bike, she might have bought some equipment."

"That's another possibility," said Anne. "You see people wearing all that biking gear these days. Someone might not have recognized her dressed like that. I know I never give a second look to all the joggers around."

Jack came back into the room. "They weren't thrilled with the major crime I reported," said Jack, "but they're sending someone over in the morning to make a report. What's Sandy doing in the garage?"

"Searching Marissa's car," said Anne.

When Sandy came back in she held a business card aloft. "This is all I found, but it might help. I'll tell you something, I've never seen such a clean car."

Anne took the card from Sandy and read it. "A health club? Did she work out, Jack?"

"Not that I know of."

"Well, I'll check it out tomorrow," said Anne.

"We've done pretty well," Bolivia said. "A little while ago we didn't have anything. At least now we're pretty sure how she got away."

"So what do you say?" Anne asked. "Tomorrow night, same time, same place?"

"You play ball tomorrow night?" asked Jack.

"No, we're off," said Anne.

"Then why don't you make it a couple of hours earlier? I'll get in some pizza."

"I never say no to pizza," said Bolivia.

"I'll bring the beer," said Sandy.

"And Coke for me," said Anne.

"And," said Sandy, "if we get any really great news tomorrow, I might make it champagne."

"If the news is that good," said Anne, "I might even drink some."

"Over my dead body," said Bolivia.

"My name's Anne Larkin," said Anne, holding out her hand to the woman.

"Polly Gordon," said the woman, almost breaking Anne's hand when she shook it.

It was a small health club, for women only, and the woman in charge knew who Marissa was even without the picture. "Yes, she worked out here," Polly told Anne, "but I haven't seen her in a couple of weeks."

Anne eyed her muscles, her extremely strong build and wondered if she could recruit her for their softball team. "I wonder if you'd mind answering some questions," she said.

"Are you the cops?" The woman looked too damn healthy to be worrying about cops in Anne's opinion. Although, steroids were against the law.

"No, I'm an attorney," said Anne, getting out her card and handing it to the woman.

"I guess it depends on the questions."

"What kind of working out did she do?"

"All she was interested in were the stationary bikes. She used to ride for an hour and a half almost every morning."

"That's it? None of the machines?"

Polly shook her head. "She'd come in, hop on a bike and then do the whirlpool and the sauna. I tried to get her interested in free weights, but I wasn't successful. She could have used it, too—no muscles on her at all."

"She must at least have built up her leg muscles," said Anne.

"Maybe she would have in time, but she hadn't been coming in here all that long. Joined about two months ago. Oh, wait a minute—one other thing. She used the tanning machine regularly."

It was beyond Anne why someone living in Miami had to use a tanning machine. "I may want to subpoena you as a witness in a case. Would you be willing to testify?"

"You mean just answer what I answered today?"

"Essentially, yes."

"I guess so. Listen, is she in some kind of trouble?"

"She's disappeared, and my client is being accused of murdering her. It's been in the papers."

"All I ever read is the sports page. Yeah, I guess I'd testify."

"One other thing," said Anne. "Did you ever see her when she was in the whirlpool or sauna?"

"Sure."

"The reason I'm asking is that one of her neighbors told the police that my client used to beat her up. What I was wondering is, did you ever see any bruises on her?"

"Never," said the woman. "She had flawless skin."

"Thanks, Polly," said Anne. "You've been very helpful."

"Listen, you could use a little weight lifting yourself. If you're ever interested . . ."

"Maybe when this case is over I'll take you up on it," said Anne.

"That's what they all say," Polly said with a grin.

* * *

Anne had no idea there were so many bike shops in Coral Gables, but the number of them must have been due to the university students. At the fifth one she got lucky. The owner, Peter Deutch, a young man in his twenties with dark curly hair and a gorgeous smile, was looking her over as soon as she walked in the door. If he looked over all his female customers that closely, and if he had ever seen Marissa...

"What can I do for you?" he asked her.

"I'm an attorney," said Anne, handing him her card.

"Oh, hell, am I being sued again?" he asked her. "Hey, you don't look like an attorney."

"You're not being sued," said Anne. She took out a picture of Marissa. "I was wondering if you've ever seen her before."

"Marissa? Sure."

"Is she one of your customers?"

"She's bought a few things here."

"What sort of things?"

"Biking gear, a backpack. I'd have to look it up in the records if you want me to be more specific."

"Would you mind? I'll need the dates of purchase."

"What's this about?"

"She's disappeared."

"So?" asked Peter. "Is disappearing against the law?"

"My client's accused of murdering her."

"Heavy stuff," said Peter, backing away a little. "I guess I ought to read the papers more often."

"Could I possibly get photocopies of the receipts?"

"Hey, I don't think I want to get involved."

"I can always have you subpoenaed as a witness."

"Do your worst, lady, but how about doing it outside my shop?"

"See you in court, Peter," she told him, making her exit.

* * *

"I brought champagne just in case," said Sandy.

Anne took the bottle from Sandy and handed it to Jack. "Start it chilling," she told him. "We'll celebrate when I win the case."

"Hey, I wanted some of that," said Sandy.

"The news is good," said Anne, "but not that good."

"Now that Sandy's here, will you please tell me?" asked Bolivia. "Come on, the suspense is killing me."

"Since you've already heard the news, Jack," Anne said, "how about setting up the pizza?"

Anne told them quickly about the health club and bike shop. "The investigators struck out, however. No one noticed a kid on the bike."

"But that's great news," said Bolivia. "I mean, come on—she was training on a stationary bike, she bought racing gear and Jack's bike is missing."

"Yes, but it doesn't prove he didn't kill her," said Sandy.

"No," agreed Anne, "but we don't have to prove that. I think what it will do is put enough reasonable doubt into the minds of the jurors."

"They'll just say she was planning her escape from me," said Jack.

"Then where's the bike?" asked Sandy.

"I could've thrown that in the canal, too, I suppose. Or hauled it to a dump."

"I think it's strange behavior," said Bolivia. "It would cast doubt in my mind."

"I don't get the tanning machine," said Sandy. "Why would she use a tanning machine when she had a backyard? It's not like she worked all day and didn't have time to get out in the sun."

"She never sunbathed," said Jack.

"Did you wonder where she got her tan?" asked Anne.

"I didn't know she had a tan."

Anne gave him an extremely dubious look. "Come on, Jack, you must've noticed."

"We're assuming this wasn't a platonic relationship," said Sandy.

"She's had the same skin color since the day I met her," said Jack, "and there were no lines from a bathing suit."

"You wouldn't get lines from a tanning machine," said Bolivia.

"Did she have dark skin?" asked Anne.

"About the same shade as mine. But it went with her hair and eyes. And I assumed she was Hispanic, with a name like Jarlan."

"Your skin's not very dark," said Anne.

"Neither was hers. She wasn't pale, but she wasn't dark."

"Maybe she wanted to look dark so Jack would think she was Cuban," said Bolivia.

Anne was doubtful about that. "What would be the point?"

"Maybe she thought he liked Cubans."

"That's really reaching for it," said Sandy.

"Actually, I like blondes," said Jack, and Bolivia and Sandy grinned at Anne.

"Well, at least I have some witnesses," said Anne. "And with the state coming in with such a circumstantial case, I'd say we'll be able to show some reasonable doubt. And you know juries—they just love reasonable doubt."

"I wonder where she went on a bike," said Bolivia.

"We may never find out," said Anne. "Whoever she was, I'd say she was pretty smart and covered her tracks."

"You said she rode for an hour and a half every morning on the bike?" asked Bolivia.

Anne said, "That's what I was told."

"I've got an idea," said Bolivia. "Why don't we all get on a bike, each go a different direction, and see where we end up in an hour and a half."

"That's the stupidest idea I ever heard," said Sandy.

Bolivia said, "I think it sounds like fun."

"Forget the fun and forget the bike riding," said Anne. "What we've got to do is come up with some more ideas."

"But not immediately," said Jack, setting the pizza on the table. "First a little sustenance, then some more brainpower."

After Bolivia and Sandy left Jack and Anne walked down to his dock and sat for a while, their legs dangling over the side. The sky was clouding up, the humidity was rising, and the temperature seemed to climb a few degrees with record speed when Jack put his arm around her.

"You know something?" he said. "I should hate her, but I can't. If it weren't for Marissa, I never would have met you."

Anne turned to look at him. "I don't believe I'm hearing this. You met me when I was in law school. I can't help it if you were too stupid at the time to recognize my potential."

He burst out laughing, the sound seeming to echo over the water. "You're not going to let me get romantic, are you?"

She gently removed his arm from around her. "Nope. And certainly not in such a romantic setting."

"Romantic? This is my backyard."

"Well, maybe your being here makes it romantic."

"In that case, you must have found Torts class romantic."

"Touché, Professor."

"But when this is over..."

"Oh, yes. Then you can get as romantic as you want."

"And you won't stop me?"

"I might even start it."

"One thing does gripe me, though," said Jack.

"And that is?"

"How pleased Guy would be if he could hear us now."

"Mr. Talbot?"

"Your boss, my best friend. He set us up, you know."

"Well, good for him."

"Yes," said Jack, putting his arm back around her. "I guess it is."

Chapter 10

Are you listening to me, Jack?"

"I'm listening," he said. Anne was in her bossy mode, and he knew better than to not listen. "I'm to sit up straight and to make notes on the legal pad if I have any questions, not whisper to you."

"Right. And if somebody says something stupid—and they will, I'll guarantee it—I don't want to see that supercilious smile of yours. No one likes a know-it-all, Jack, and you have a proclivity for that kind of thing."

"That's only in the classroom, and only if the student is being particularly stupid."

"Maybe I'll make one exception. If Howie does or says something stupid, you may smile. But try to make it a smile of wonder, or maybe of disbelief. Just not a superior smile."

"And if you do something stupid?" he asked her.

"You do not smile under any circumstances! If I do something particularly clever, you also don't smile. You might look a little heartened, but that's it."

"Anything else?"

Anne looked down at her list. "Do not flirt with the female jurors."

"I don't flirt," he said.

"You do flirt. You've flirted with me."

"That's different. I'm interested in you. I'm not interested in the jurors, male or female."

"Well, you'd better be interested in them. Your life's in their hands. And they'll flirt with you. They'll smile at you and try to catch your eye. When that happens, look innocent."

"I am innocent."

"Yes, but you don't always look it."

"Anything else?"

"Yes, and this is the most important thing of all. Do not, under any circumstances, look bored. Don't close your eyes, don't stare off into the distance, don't draw pictures on your legal pad. I want you looking alert and interested every moment of the proceedings. Look properly concerned."

"I don't think that'll be a problem, Anne. I don't think there's anyone more interested in these proceedings than I am."

"I'm aware of that. I also want the jury to be aware of it. And while I'm picking the jury, I don't want you showing your like or dislike for any of them. If there's someone you'd particularly dislike having on the jury, you can tell me or write me a note, but don't signal that dislike to anyone else."

"Do I look all right?"

"I know you're being facetious, but I'll tell you, Jack, you look marvelous. No one who's guilty could possibly be dressed so elegantly."

"Am I dressed *too* well?"

"There's no such thing as being dressed too well. There's nothing wrong with wearing a beautifully tailored suit and a silk tie. You're not a drugstore clerk, after all. You're a distinguished law professor and legal scholar, and now you look it. The haircut is wonderful, too, and not too short."

"It's not called a haircut where you sent me. It's called a style."

"You could've gone a little lighter on the after-shave, though."

"You don't like it?"

"It's just a little overpowering, and I'm the one who has to sit next to you."

"I got it to drown out the smell of your perfume."

"You don't like my perfume?"

"Not in close quarters."

She grinned at him. "Okay, no more scents on either of us after today, agreed?"

He shook her hand on it.

Anne began to unload her briefcase, shoving a legal pad and a pen over to him in the process. He lined it up in front of him and then looked around the courtroom. It was already packed with spectators. There were two rows filled with members of the press, three sketch artists, whom Anne had pointed out to him, and what looked like most of his students from the university. He couldn't be sure whether they were there to support him or to cheer on the prosecution. He also wondered whether they were ditching school or had been given permission to come. Perhaps the dean had thought it would be a learning experience for them.

He saw Bolivia seated with the press, and she winked at him.

"Your friend's flirting with me," Jack told Anne.

Anne turned around and waved to Bolivia. "Ignore her. I think she has a crush on you."

"On me?" asked Jack, feeling unaccountably pleased.

"She thinks you look like a pirate."

"Is that good?" asked Jack.

"With Bolivia it is."

He was surprised when he saw Guy come through the door. He walked straight up to the front, and Jack stood and shook his hand.

"My God, Jack, that's a beautiful suit," said Guy. "You look good enough to work for our firm."

"I hope I look good enough to get acquitted," said Jack.

"People versus Jack Quintana. For trial!" yelled the docket clerk into the packed courtroom, and Guy left to find a seat. Jack looked over at the prosecution table and saw that Howie was now flanked by two younger attorneys. He had a feeling that Anne could hold her own against any number of assistant district attorneys.

He saw that there were armed bailiffs positioned at the corners of the judge's bench. The judge entered, and everyone in the courtroom came to their feet.

Anne stood beside him, and he thought she looked fantastic. She was wearing a suit of some thick, silky looking material in a light shade of khaki, a white silk shirt blouse, a very narrow red tie, red heels, no jewelry except for a stainless steel watch that looked like a man's, and she currently had red reading glasses perched on her nose. Her hair was somewhat subdued by the two silver combs that were holding it back from her face.

The docket clerk called out, "Oyez, oyez. The Superior Court for the County of Dade is now in session, the Honorable Thomas Silva, Judge, Presiding." He banged the gavel. "Call Case Number 96-1433 for trial."

The judge took his seat. "Are we ready to call for a jury?"

"The prosecution is ready, Your Honor," said one of Howie's minions.

"The defense is ready, Your Honor," said Anne in a clear, confident voice.

They entered then, seventy-five people, twelve of whom would serve as his jury. The clerk called for sixteen to sit in the jury box and directed the remainder to the first four rows on the prosecution side of the courtroom, from which the bailiffs had dismissed the spectators and sent them to stand out in the hall.

The judge then went into a little speech about what the case was all about. He instructed them that the defendant was presumed innocent. When he said this some of the prospective jurors looked over at Jack. Jack was sure he looked properly concerned because he *was* properly concerned.

The judge went on to expound on the state's burden to prove guilt beyond a reasonable doubt and the defendant's constitutional right to remain silent. Jack knew that it was his right to remain silent, and also knew that if Anne got her way he would never take the witness stand in his own defense, but despite this, he shared the attitude that he was sure most of the jury would share, which was that he didn't trust a defendant who refused to testify on his own behalf. It was irrational but there it was. He was determined to take the stand despite Anne's objections.

The judge questioned the prospective jurors about what they had read or seen on television about the case. All admitted to having heard something about it, although one man—and it took all Jack's self-control not to laugh at this—said that he found stuff like that boring and usually only read the sports page. A few spectators did laugh, and the judge even managed a small smile.

In no uncertain terms the judge told them that anything they had seen or heard was completely worthless because it wasn't evidence, and evidence was the only thing they were supposed to listen to.

Jack was finding everything about it fascinating. It had been years since he had been in a courtroom, not since he had been a clerk for a State Supreme Court judge his first year out of law school. He had forgotten how engrossing it was to watch each case slowly unfold. He wouldn't give up teaching to go into litigation, but he could understand the fascination it held for many lawyers. He had always found it more fascinating to mold the minds of the future lawyers and to research obscure rules of law for his papers.

The judge finally wound down and they moved into the *voir dire*, where the jurors were questioned about their backgrounds. Jack could tell that they were already impressed with the judge, and that most of the prospective female members were impressed by Anne's clothes. None of them seemed to be impressed so far by anything about Howie. He was one of the few law students Jack had a clear memory of, however, and most of that memory had to do with the man's very quick mind. He might not look impressive, but dig beneath the facade and what was beneath had been enough to impress most of the faculty.

Jack listened as Anne, Howie and the judge took turns questioning the prospective jurors. They were asked everything from what TV shows they regularly watched to what newspapers they read to their educational backgrounds and even whether any family members had ever been in trouble with the law. The defense was allowed to excuse ten jurors without any explanation; those dismissals were called peremptories. The prosecution was only allowed six. Jack, who had always thought the law was loaded in favor of the criminal, was now glad of the difference.

A breakdown of the jury pool was much like a breakdown of the city of Miami. More than fifty percent were

Hispanic, and most of the Hispanics were Cuban; of the rest, more were black than white. A large percentage of the whites were senior citizens and Jewish, and they seemed, of all the groups, to be the most interested in serving. Jack supposed that at their age it beat watching game shows on TV.

By the time the judge called a lunch recess, Anne and Howie had only agreed on five jurors. Guy took Anne and Jack to lunch some distance from the courthouse so they wouldn't run into any reporters or prosecution attorneys. As usual, with Guy, the restaurant had both excellent food and high prices.

Jack found that he was starved.

Guy said, "I've been trying to figure out what it is exactly that you're looking for in a jury, Anne."

Anne was hoping to just be able to eat and not do a lot of talking, but she saw that wasn't going to be possible. "Well, I'll tell you," she said, putting down her fork. "What the prosecution seems to be going for is older people, ones who might think it sinful for Jack to have been living with a woman. The kind who would think, 'Poor little thing,' when they saw a picture of Marissa. They're also going to go for blue-collar workers who believe professional people get off too easy."

"You should've let me wear my blue shirt," said Jack.

Anne decided to ignore him. "What I want, primarily, are educated people who won't resent Jack's education. You can bet Howie's going to make a big deal of Jack's having gone to Harvard."

"Is there something wrong with Harvard?" asked Guy.

"Not if you can afford it," said Anne. "I also want intelligent people, educated or not, who will understand the law and not convict out of suspicion."

"I would think you'd go for Cubans," said Jack.

"You're only half-Cuban," said Guy.

"The jurors don't have to know that," said Jack.

"I'd like to get some Cubans on the jury," said Anne, "but I can't tell them apart from the rest of the Hispanics, and some of the other groups resent the Cubans because they've been so successful here."

"Just look at me," said Jack, "and if I touch my tie, it means the person is Cuban."

"I also don't want any religious nuts," said Anne, "but it's sometimes hard to find that out about them before it's too late. They might forgive certain behavior in their television evangelists, but they won't forgive it in Jack. That's another reason for going for educated people."

"I wouldn't count out younger men, despite their education," said Guy. "I'm sure they're going to find you very attractive."

"That could backfire," said Anne. "They might find me attractive, but some of them are also going to find me threatening. There are a lot of men who don't like to see women in positions of power, and from where they're sitting, I have a lot of power. I will, however, choose women whom I think find Jack attractive."

"Don't do me any favors," said Jack, and Guy burst out laughing.

"I do believe you're managing to lighten up my friend," said Guy, smiling at Anne.

"Oh, he's coming along," said Anne.

"I was impressed with the judge," said Guy.

Anne nodded. "So was I. And it looks as though he's going to bend over backwards in order to ensure a fair trial. They don't all do that."

"Thank God my students aren't old enough to be judges yet," said Jack.

"No," said Anne, "but the prosecutor was."

"I always got along fine with him," said Jack.

"You did?" asked Anne. "How is it that you got along fine with the man prosecuting you, and here I am defending you, and you scared the hell out of me?"

"I guess I favored the male students."

"I ought to get even with you for that," she said, "and rig the jury."

"I think we should all have some dessert," said Guy, in an obvious effort to keep the peace.

By four-thirty the jury had been chosen, and Judge Silva recessed the court until the following morning, when the trial would begin.

Driving Jack home, Anne professed herself satisfied with the jury. They were predominantly young. There were five Hispanics, four of whom Jack had signaled to her were Cuban, and three blacks. Five of the jurors were married, four were divorced, and three were single. There were seven men and five women.

The oldest member of the jury was Sarah Brown at seventy. She was black, married and a retired schoolteacher. Anne was hoping she'd be sympathetic to a fellow teacher. She had also liked the woman's quiet, reasoned manner.

There was Maria Cruz, twenty-five, an assistant manager at a hotel in Coconut Grove. She had graduated from the International University in Miami in hotel management. She was also Cuban, and Anne had detected the fact that the woman hadn't appreciated some of Howie's questions.

Christine Larson was white, twenty-seven, divorced and worked as a word processor for one of the airlines. She answered the questions put to her intelligently, but didn't seem eager to serve. This was all right with Anne, who wondered about people who did want to spend time on a jury.

Anna Rodriguez was thirty-two, married and a housewife. Anne wasn't crazy about her as a choice because the woman had seemed bored by the proceedings. She hoped that Mrs. Rodriguez would show more interest in the trial when it got started.

Lisa Krunk was white, twenty-nine, divorced, and was a dress buyer for one of the big chains. If nothing else, Ms. Krunk had seemed to admire Anne's clothes. Anne had also admired Ms. Krunk's clothes, which had been just slightly outrageous for a courtroom. Howie had seemed to hang on her every word.

Roy Jackson, black, thirty and married, worked at the Metro Zoo in maintenance. Anne had liked the fact that he played on a local softball team. She had asked him what position he played, and he had looked pleased when he told her that he was a pitcher.

George Morris, black, fifty and divorced, was a librarian of the branch library in the Little River section of Miami. Of all of them, he seemed the most intelligent.

Julio Bustamante, twenty-six, single, Peruvian, was another hotel employee. Anne had not liked him but had used up her peremptories. What she had mainly not liked about him was the way his eyes were on her chest when he answered her questions.

Raul Velez, thirty-two, married, was a cabdriver. He seemed to have a good sense of humor, which she thought might be valuable on a jury.

Luis Delgado, forty, married, was a laboratory technician and had gone to school at U of M. Anne was hoping he'd feel some loyalty to his alma mater.

Michael Levitt, thirty-six, divorced, was a car salesman. He seemed a little too slick to Anne, but she let Howie have his way with this one. Mr. Levitt did not seem at all happy at having been picked, and she was hoping he'd blame Howie for it.

Samuel Gross, sixty-seven and a widower, was a retired garment worker from New York. Anne was hoping a New Yorker might be more apt to look benignly on the fact that Jack had lived with a young woman. Despite his age, Mr. Gross still seemed to have an eye for the ladies.

"What're you doing tonight?" asked Jack. "Practicing your opening address to the jury?"

"I don't practice them," said Anne.

"Does that mean you don't know what you're going to say?"

"No, it means I speak better extemporaneously than I do when I write it down first and then rehearse it."

"You do know what you're going to say, don't you?"

"It's not that important what I say."

"To me it is."

"Look, we don't have to prove you're not guilty. You heard the judge. They have to prove you're guilty."

"I'd like to hear what you're going to say."

"You'll hear me tomorrow. Unless Howie goes on and on all day, which I hope he does, because he'll bore the jury to death."

"So what're you doing tonight?"

"Relaxing."

"How can you relax the night before the trial?"

"I couldn't if I stayed home and worried about it. I'm going to go to a club and hear some music."

"I'm going to be home pacing the floors, and you're going out?"

"You can come along if you want."

"What kind of music?"

"Well, it's not classical."

"That's what I figured."

"I hate classical music."

Jack seemed to go into a state of sustained shock for several moments. "How can you possibly hate classical music? It's one of the finest heritages left to us by civilized man."

"You sound like a music professor."

"I'm serious."

"I know you are. You're a serious person. I, on the other hand, am a frivolous person, and I don't happen to appreciate classical music. Especially after having been forced to take piano lessons as a child."

"You're a pianist?"

"Hardly. Jack, let's not argue about this. Why don't I pick you up around eight? You might not like the music, but at least it will keep you from pacing the floor."

"Do I have to wear this suit?"

"No. And I don't want to see one of your blue shirts, either."

"That's all I have."

"Wrong. You have a perfectly suitable T-shirt from Austin. Wear it with jeans."

"I only wear jeans to do yard work."

"Tonight you'll wear them to go out."

He had been sure he would hate the music, and he did. He also didn't like the way Anne was dressed, which he thought was too sexy by far. Once again she looked like a completely different person. She was wearing an extremely short skirt that didn't even try to reach her knees, a skimpy cotton sweater that didn't quite cover her midriff, and, if he wasn't mistaken, she had left her bra at home. She was wearing silver eye shadow that appeared to be metallic and wouldn't surprise him if it lit up in the dark. And her hair was not just curly, it had been brushed out into a mass of frizz that made her head appear four times larger. And despite all of the above, she looked sexy as hell, like some kind of temptress right out of a Greek myth.

The club was dark, but not too dark for Jack to see that he was probably the oldest person there. He had felt ridiculous going out in jeans and a T-shirt, but now he was glad he had worn them. At least his clothes fitted in, even if his face didn't.

He ordered a beer and hoped it would do something to relieve the headache that was already starting as a result of the loud music. If it could be called music. To Jack it sounded like a lot of jarring sounds all competing to see which would prevail. The musicians were very young, and he felt they could have used several years of music lessons before going out into public with their act.

Anne seemed to be in her element. Her face was fixed raptly on the group, her body was moving with the music, and most of the people in the club seemed to know her. Every other second someone—always male—was stopping by their table to say hello to her. She didn't bother introducing him to them, which was all right with him. They barely seemed old enough to even be his students.

He was feeling slightly put out that she had come here the night before the trial began in earnest. Surely she could have taken him to a more soothing place. Ideally, she could have come to his house and soothed him in private. He briefly thought of what it would be like to make love to her, but when he found that the image he was getting wasn't in the least soothing, that instead it was stimulating to a degree he didn't want to try to deal with in public, he tried to think of something else.

"What to dance?" Anne asked him.

"What?"

"Dance. Let's dance. Come on, I feel like dancing."

"I don't think I'm up for dancing to this," said Jack, trying to find the beat in the music and not succeeding. He had never been much of a dancer, not even in college. Now, if it was a slow tune he might give it a try, but this group didn't seem to know the meaning of slow.

"Please, Jack, dancing always relaxes me."

"Feel free to dance with someone else," he told her, certain that she would ignore him. Instead, she gave him a quick smile, then got up and asked one of the young guys at the next table to dance.

He was a little ticked off that she would do such a thing. He was more annoyed when he saw the way she was dancing. Her entire body moved. Her breasts were bouncing around under the sweater, which was being pulled up to expose her entire midsection every time she raised her arms; her hips were gyrating, and occasionally her skirt would move up when she did some sort of shimmy where her knees almost touched the floor. He saw that half the guys in the place were watching her, and his only consolation was that they were all much too young to interest her.

Jack quickly downed his beer and ordered another. Maybe the second one would relax him.

Anne didn't return to the table until the group finally took a break. Jack was glad that he finally had her to himself. Now, without the distraction of the loud music, maybe they'd be able to talk.

"You seem to enjoy dancing," he said to her. She seemed hyper and excited and almost unable to sit still.

"Good music always puts me in a good mood," she said.

"Good music? You consider this good?" He was appalled when she nodded.

"They're an up-and-coming group," she said. "You're going to hear about them one of these days."

"Not if I can help it," murmured Jack, too low for her to hear.

Suddenly their table was surrounded, and the young men in the group were pulling chairs up and sitting down. The drummer, a particularly pretty boy with long, golden curls, moved his chair very close to Anne.

"Annie," the boy said, giving her a kiss that made Jack think they were more than casual acquaintances.

"You guys are great tonight, Scotty," said Anne. "Hey, guys, this is Jack," she said, then told him their names too quickly for him to remember anything more than that they all ended in "y" or "ie," which made them sound even more like children.

Jack tried to overhear what the drummer was whispering to Anne, but it was drowned out by the chatter of the rest of the group. He found himself slowly starting to burn. This had been a mistake. He should have stayed home. He was losing all confidence in his defense attorney, who had no business being chummy with a drummer in a teenage rock group. Why wasn't this gorgeous woman paying attention to him, discussing his case, allaying his fears? Why was she acting like a teenager on a Saturday night?

Finally, almost too furious to speak, Jack stood. "I'm going to get a cab home, Anne, if you don't mind," he said to her.

"See you around, mate," said Scotty, and Anne merely raised a questioning brow at him. Since he wasn't going to be begged to stay, he quickly left the table and headed out of the club.

He waited outside for a few minutes, sure that she would join him. When she didn't, he was forced to find a public phone and call a taxi. When the taxi arrived twenty minutes later she still hadn't left the club. By that time he recognized his rage for what it was—pure, unadulterated jealousy.

The first thing he did upon arriving home was to take a long, cold shower.

"I wonder where Jack went?" Anne said to Scotty, realizing that he had been gone an awfully long time.

"He said he was splitting," said Scotty.

"Splitting? I thought he was going to the men's room."

"I'm sure he said something about getting a cab," said Scotty. "Why don't you stick around, though, and go out with us later?"

"I'd love to," said Anne, "but I have to be in court in the morning. Big trial."

"That was the defendant, wasn't it?" asked Scotty.

"How'd you know that?"

"Saw his picture."

"I didn't know musicians read newspapers."

Scotty laughed. "We don't, but we watch television. So how about the weekend?"

"You're not going to believe this, Scotty, but I've got a bet with my friends that I can lay off booze and men for three months."

"I don't believe it."

"Well, it's true."

"It doesn't look that way to me," said Scotty. "You looked pretty cozy with Jack. It didn't look like all business between the two of you."

"Well, you're wrong, it's strictly business," said Anne, realizing as she said it that it was a lie. Jack was already making her see these musicians as the excuse she had used not to get really serious with a man. But the way she was feeling, that she could get really serious about Jack, was scaring her.

"Well, if it isn't the other two-thirds of the Three Mouseketeers," said Scotty, looking up.

Anne followed his glance and saw Bolivia and Sandy by the table. "What are you guys doing here?" she asked.

Two of the musicians were pulling up chairs for them. "Just checking up on you," said Sandy.

"I knew it," said Bolivia. "We let you out of our sight for one night, and you're drinking and taking up with musicians again."

"You owe us some money," said Sandy.

"You're wrong," said Anne. "Tell them, Scotty. Tell them that I told you I wasn't dating for three months."

Scotty crossed his heart with one finger. "I have to admit it, she turned me down."

"What about this?" asked Bolivia, picking up Anne's glass.

"Taste it," said Anne.

Instead Bolivia sniffed the drink, which was a straight Coke. "All right, but who knows what would've happened if we hadn't shown up when we did."

The musicians went back up to play another set, and Sandy asked where Jack was tonight.

"He was here, but at some point he walked out," Anne told them.

"Was there a reason for that?" asked Bolivia.

"It was my fault," said Anne, "I shouldn't have brought him here. He didn't like the music, and he wouldn't dance, so I danced with some other guys, and I think he got mad."

"I would say justifiably so," said Sandy.

"We're not dating," said Anne. "He's my client."

"We should've been here," said Bolivia. "I would have gotten him to dance. But then, I'm not attracted to kids the way you are."

"They're just friends of mine."

"You used to date Scotty," said Sandy.

"Yes, but we're friends now."

"Well," said Bolivia, "if you aren't interested in Jack, I'd still like permission to go after him."

Anne felt herself stiffen. "Well, you don't have it."

"What is this?" asked Bolivia. "Is there something going on here that we don't know about?"

"It's been obvious since the beginning," said Sandy. "They're perfect for each other."

"Well, it wasn't obvious to me," said Anne.

"You're seriously interested in him?" asked Bolivia.

"I think so."

"I think it's great," said Sandy. "It's about time you got interested in a grown man."

"Just one thing, though," said Bolivia. "You'd better make sure you get him off, unless you want to end up being a pen pal with a convict."

Anne threw off her clothes, leaving them in a pile on the floor, then took a cold shower. Now that she had time to think about it, she didn't appreciate Jack walking out on her like that. It was childish behavior on his part and not at all professional. Not that she wouldn't have walked out if he had been dancing with all the women in the club, but that was different. He had given her permission to dance with other people, and she wouldn't have given it to him.

Now things were going to be strained between them in court in the morning, and that would probably throw her off and make her give a bad opening statement. And if she didn't sound confident when she spoke, the jury would take it as a sign that she wasn't confident about his innocence.

She got into bed and called him. At least he sounded wide-awake when he answered.

"Listen, Jack, I think we have to talk."

"I thought so several hours ago."

"Walking out like that, you were acting like some jealous boyfriend. I think you'd better start acting like a client who's been charged with murder."

She expected him to be angry at her words, but instead she heard him chuckle. "You're right, I did act like a jealous boyfriend."

"Well, don't let it happen again."

"Don't make me jealous again."

"You were really jealous?"

"I know it sounds stupid, particularly since they were only kids...."

"They're not *that* young. They're over twenty-one."

"You mean you like young guys?"

"I did before."

"Before what?"

She was silent for a moment, wishing she hadn't gotten into this particular subject. "I guess before you."

"This is crazy behavior on our parts, I guess."

"Very crazy."

"I guess we should cool it until the trial is over."

"I guess so."

"Anne, if you can't sound more decisive than that, there's no way I'm going to cool it."

"This is crazy. I used to hate you more than anyone in the world."

"And I didn't even know you existed."

"That makes me mad, too, you know. Here I was, with this mad crush on you in law school, and you didn't even notice me."

"You had a crush on me?"

"All the girls had a crush on you. It helped alleviate the boredom of your classes."

"You ought to try teaching. I bet you wouldn't bore your classes."

"Not me, I hate school."

"How could you go to school so long if you hated it?"

"Because I wanted to be a lawyer."

"You realize we have nothing in common, don't you?"

"I keep thinking we'll find something."

"I have a feeling we will."

"If you're talking about what I think you're talking about—"

"You know exactly what I'm talking about."

"Let's not talk about that until after the trial."

"Fine."

Anne sighed. "Let's not even think about it."

"I don't know about you, but it's pretty hard to monitor my thoughts all the time."

"Damn it, Jack, it's going to be impossible to sleep tonight."

"Do what I did."

"What's that?"

"Take a cold shower."

Anne started to chuckle.

"What's so funny?"

"I already did."

Chapter 11

The jury filed in from the waiting room where eventually they would deliberate. Anne saw Christine Larson, the airline employee, cast a smile in Jack's direction. Several of the male jurors were looking at her, and she nodded, almost imperceptibly, in their direction. It was as though she and Jack were on stage now. They would be the major focus of the jury's attention from now on, and they had to play their parts with just the right amount of friendliness and reserve.

Anne dressed with care for trials, because she'd found that when she looked good, it gave her the self-confidence she needed to get on with the job at hand. She didn't have to worry that they were staring at her because her hem wasn't straight or her slip was showing; she knew that they were staring at her out of interest in the entire court process, or because she was doing a good job and they were paying attention.

Today she was wearing a faded blue, unstructured silk suit with a white silk blouse. Her hat, which she had removed, was sitting on the defense table, and she had her hair on top of her head in a knot with a few loose strands curling down. Jack was looking extremely handsome in one of his new suits, his white shirt immaculate, his silk tie in a perfect knot. He looked far too sophisticated and elegant to ever have stabbed a woman and thrown her body in a canal.

In a moment the judge would call on Howie to make his opening address. This would be a forecast of the state's evidence, not an argument, although Howie was known to try to get an argument in on occasion. If he did, she would let it go by. She had found the jury resented having speeches interrupted. Howie would set forth the inferences that he thought arose from the proof. In a circumstantial case—and this one was definitely that—a prosecutor needed some way at the outset to make the jury see how it all fit together.

Judge Silva said, "Mr. Howard Leonard," and Howie stood. Anne thought he looked like a balding bulldog, although his suit, for a change, looked as though it had just come back from the cleaners. His tie was still straight, although she knew from experience that by the end of his opening statement it would be somewhat loosened and greatly askew.

Howie began, "May it please the court, the evidence will show that the defendant, Mr. Jack Quintana, and the deceased, Ms. Marissa Jarlan, lived together, without the benefit of marriage, for several months before the murder. During this time, he was physically abusive to her to the point where she feared for her life and was planning on leaving him."

He had the jury's full attention now. Howie might make a bad appearance, but he had a hard-hitting style that usually impressed a jury. Since Anne also employed a hard-hitting style, she began to think that in order to strike a contrast with Howie, she might be smart to lighten up and

show that she was amused by his efforts, as though his behavior was childish and his case a farce. This was something Howie wouldn't even think of doing, as he lacked any
sense of humor at all.

And so, while Howie was describing the knife and bloody
clothes, Anne leaned over to Jack, smiled and whispered,
"Don't you smile, but once in a while look up at Howie and
put a little serious doubt in your eyes."

Jack looked at *her* with a little serious doubt, but he did
what she said.

As Howie drove home point after point, over and over,
Anne thought how she'd do things differently. Howie tended
to overkill, repeating things several times that the jury had
gotten with no effort the first time, thus managing to bore
them almost immediately. The jury on a whole struck her as
being intelligent; she was sure that if she told them something once, it would stick. She would also make her opening address short, in contrast to Howie's, which was
threatening to take up most of the morning. She was cog-
nizant of the fact, though, that he had a lot more to say than
she did.

Howie was moving into motive now, which was a defi-
nite weakness in the state's case. He was playing with the
ideas of jealousy and possessiveness, but Anne knew that he
couldn't prove either and had only hearsay evidence from a
couple of neighbors as evidence.

Howie, who was almost shouting into the jury's faces by
the end, closed with, "The prosecution will prove, beyond
a reasonable doubt, that the defendant did indeed kill Marissa Jarlan and that he threw her body in the canal for the
alligators to devour."

There were a few gasps at the word "alligators," and
Anne had to control her urge to laugh out loud. Howie was
really overdoing it at that point.

Anne moved to the podium. Before beginning her opening address she said, "I feel I must state for the record that had alligators devoured the body, as Mr. Leonard would have you believe, there would be no body."

There was a little laughter at this, and the judge banged his gavel for silence, although she could see that he was trying not to smile.

"May it please the court," said Anne, "ladies and gentlemen of the jury. What can I say when a distinguished law professor from the University of Miami, perhaps the most noted authority on Maritime Law in the country, is put on trial on the basis of circumstantial evidence that, as any average first-year law student would be able to determine, does not approach the standards of reasonable doubt?

"Reasonable doubt—remember that term. The judge has already explained reasonable doubt to you, and you will be hearing it mentioned again and again in this case. The prosecution must prove its case *beyond a reasonable doubt*."

She looked over at Jack and saw that the jury was following her eyes. Jack looked attentive and not the least bit guilty.

"The defendant, Professor Quintana, has devoted his life to the training of lawyers, one of whom is in the courtroom in the person of the senior prosecutor, Mr. Leonard. Professor Quintana has given his life to teaching the law. He has never broken that law.

"Like many of you on the jury and in this courtroom, Professor Quintana's family fled Castro's Cuba in search of freedom. Did he find that freedom only to have it snatched away from him in a miscarriage of justice?" She paused for a moment and made the mistake of catching Jack's eye. He was giving her a quizzical look, and she wondered what she had said wrong. She hoped that his father hadn't been one of Batista's men and had fled before being executed.

"Let me tell you the story of the relationship between Jack Quintana and Marissa Jarlan. Jack met her at his tennis club, when she appeared to accidentally trip over his racket. She was a beautiful young woman, and he fell in love with her. She moved in with him. Things began to go wrong between them almost immediately. Jack had never lived with a woman, and thus had nothing with which to compare this relationship. There were arguments, there was erratic behavior on her part, and, not knowing any better, he thought he must be at fault. Never once did he lift a hand to her. He is of a tradition that honors women, that seeks to put them on pedestals, not knock them to the floor. He treated Marissa with the same respect with which he treated his mother, with the same respect he treated all female members of his family.

"And then one day he came home from work and found her gone. The car he had bought her was there, but she was not. And so he did what any concerned person would do, he reported her missing to the police.

"Now we come to the mystery, which the prosecution has not addressed. Our investigators have been unable to turn up any evidence of Marissa having existed. She claimed to be from Austin, Texas, but there are no records in Austin of anyone by that name. She had no driver's license or identification under that name, with the exception of charge cards that Professor Quintana got for her. There is no record anywhere of her fingerprints. It's as though she didn't exist, at least as Marissa Jarlan, before the time she conveniently tripped over his tennis racket."

She could see that the jury was becoming intrigued. Here was an additional mystery for them to try to solve. There was also a stirring among the members of the press as one of them made his way to the back of the courtroom, no doubt heading for a phone.

"What does all this mean?" asked Anne. "The truth of the matter is, we don't know. We do know that a body was fished out of the canal approximately a mile from the professor's house. The body cannot be positively identified and is not recognizable. We do know that bodies turning up in canals are a common occurrence in Miami."

She saw members of the jury nod at this.

"So, we have a mystery here. Who was Marissa Jarlan? There was obviously a real woman involved—we don't deny that. The professor lived with her, the neighbors saw her and talked with her, but who was she really? And, perhaps more importantly, what did she want?"

She let that sink in a little as she went to the defense table and took a sip of water. Jack looked at her with what she thought was approval.

"We have been able to find out very little about Marissa Jarlan. We know she joined a health club in Coral Gables and worked out regularly on the stationary bicycles there. We know she made purchases in a local bicycle shop, including racing gear and a backpack. And we know that when she disappeared, Professor Quintana's ten-speed bike also disappeared. We know that this woman, who appeared so abruptly in Jack Quintana's life, disappeared equally abruptly."

Anne turned back to the jury. "And now for motive. What would have been the professor's motive in killing Marissa Jarlan? If he had wanted to end the relationship, all he had to do was ask her to leave. They weren't married, so neither would benefit financially if one of them died. And it wasn't jealousy, as neither the prosecution nor the defense has been able to come up with another man in Marissa's life.

"So we have a double mystery here: who was this woman, and what would his motive be in killing her?

"I'm sure, when you think about this, you will have no trouble coming to the conclusion that reasonable doubt exists." She stood there for a moment in front of the jury, looking into their faces, showing her own skepticism at the state's evidence and hoping they agreed with her. Then she turned and went back to the defense table.

Jack slid his legal pad over in front of her. On it he had printed, I'm impressed. She would have liked to put her hand over his for a moment, but resisted the impulse.

The judge called a recess for lunch.

Anne piled Moo Shu pork into a pancake, folded it over and managed to get a large portion of it into her mouth.

Jack, ignoring his own food, stared at her. "How can you eat at a time like this?"

"I'm starving," said Anne.

"I'm too nervous to eat."

"I eat when I'm nervous," she told him. "I must have gained fifteen pounds when I was working for the Public Defender's office, strictly from eating out of stress."

"I don't know how you do it."

"Well, I do, and if you want me to perform well in court, keep quiet and let me eat. We'll discuss how it's going when I'm finished."

The evidence cart was wheeled into the courtroom, and the prosecution called its first witness. This was Detective Betancourt, and he looked over at Jack and nodded after taking his seat in the witness stand.

He was a good witness, intelligent and precise in his answers, and the jury seemed to like him. Or maybe they had just enjoyed their lunch; it was sometimes hard to tell.

He described the knife being found and Jack's identification of it. The knife was then placed into evidence. He also described how he had watched the evidence technicians seal the evidence in a baggie and how Jack had acted unconcerned during all of this. He ended his testimony at the point where he had read Jack his rights.

Anne stood up for cross-examination and smiled at the detective. He was a good witness, and both sides usually benefited by a good witness.

"Detective Betancourt, could you tell the court what type blood was found on the knife?"

"Type A."

"And what type was Marissa Jarlan?"

"We don't know."

"If you don't know Ms. Jarlan's blood type, then is it not true that the blood on the knife was not necessarily hers?"

"That's right."

"In your experience, Detective, doesn't a murderer usually wash the blood off a murder weapon and put it away or get rid of it altogether?"

"If they're intelligent."

"Just answer the question, please, for the record."

"Yes."

"Detective Betancourt, would you consider Professor Quintana intelligent?"

"Objection, Your Honor," Howie called out. "Calling for an opinion."

"Sustained."

"No further questions," said Anne.

The next witness was Jack's neighbor to the north, Judith Zimmerman. She was dressed inappropriately for court in a backless sundress, her hair teased into a platinum beehive. She smiled at the judge and at Howie and generally acted as though she were appearing on stage. Anne disliked her immediately.

Her testimony, however, was quite convincing. She told how her young neighbor, Marissa, came to her on many occasions in tears, confiding in her that Jack beat her and that she could never seem to do anything to please him. She said that when, more than once, she'd tried to convince Marissa to leave him, the young woman had said that he'd threatened to kill her if she tried. She'd said she feared for her life.

Although the witness wasn't likable, her testimony was believable, and Anne saw that several of the jury members were now looking at Jack with little sympathy.

On cross-examination Anne asked, "Mrs. Zimmerman, did you ever see any evidence of these beatings?"

"What do you mean?"

"I mean, did Marissa ever come to you with a black eye, or with injuries?"

"No."

"With bruises?"

"She could've been bruised. She always wore things with long sleeves."

"But you never actually saw any evidence of beatings having taken place?"

"No."

"Mrs. Zimmerman, were you friends with Marissa?"

"Not what I'd call friends."

"Did you ever go shopping with her, maybe to the movies?"

"We didn't socialize."

"So the only times you saw Marissa were when she'd come to you in tears and accuse Professor Quintana of beating her?"

"That's right."

"Thank you," said Anne, going back to the defense table. She hoped it sounded as strange to the jury as it had to her. She couldn't imagine herself going to a total stranger and complaining of being beaten. Of course, Anne wouldn't go to anyone and complain, unless it was the police. Nor would she stick around long enough for a second beating.

The prosecution's third witness was a woman who lived across the street from Jack and who testified to the fact that loud arguments were often heard coming from Jack's house. Since loud arguments were not a crime, and since Jack had admitted to them himself, Anne didn't cross-examine the witness.

The next witness was Albert Kronstadt, a neighbor to the south of Jack who testified to having seen Jack dumping the contents of a trash bag into the canal. Anne had to admit that it was suspicious behavior.

When her turn came to question him, Anne asked, "Mr. Kronstadt, have you ever dumped trash in the canal?"

"Sure, but only biodegradable stuff."

"But you have dumped trash in the canal."

"Yes, ma'am, but not in the middle of the night."

"The witness will limit himself to a yes or no answer," cautioned Judge Silva.

"Yes," said Mr. Kronstadt.

"On the night in question," said Anne, "there was a blackout in your neighborhood due to a severe electrical storm, am I correct?"

"That's right. Yes."

"In addition to the lights in your house being out, the streetlights were also out, am I correct?"

"Everything was out," said Mr. Kronstadt.

"Was it overcast because of the storm?"

"Yes."

"And yet you were able to see Professor Quintana?"

"Yeah, I saw him. He was in his pajamas. So was I, for that matter."

"Were you able to see what it was he was dumping out of the bag?"

"No, it was too dark. It made a loud splash, though."

"So it could have been anything."

"Anything heavy."

"It could have been a twenty-pound turkey."

"Sure."

"Thank you, Mr. Kronstadt."

From the prosecution table Howie asked, "Mr. Kronstadt, to your knowledge, have you ever seen anyone dump a turkey in the canal?"

"No, but I never seen anyone dump a body, either."

The next witness was Michael Flynn, a young man who worked at the gas station near Jack's house in Coral Gables. He said he was familiar with Marissa because she often brought her car to his station to have it serviced, and they sometimes talked. He testified, in the most damaging testimony yet, that Marissa had told him that she was leaving the man she was living with because she was afraid he'd kill her. Since this went directly to motive, Anne was hoping she could counteract it.

"Mr. Flynn," said Anne, "did you usually have conversations of a personal nature with Ms. Jarlan?"

"No. Usually we just talked about the weather."

"So, before the day Ms. Jarlan confided in you that she was leaving Professor Quintana, she had never confided in you before?"

"That's right. She didn't call him professor, either. She just said she was splitting from the guy she was living with."

"Did it strike you as strange that she would suddenly tell you something so personal?"

"Nah, I just thought she was coming on to me."

"Did you believe that she was really afraid for her life?"

"Yeah. She was acting pretty frightened."

Having expected a no, Anne was angry with herself for asking that question of him. She looked over and saw Howie's grin and knew she had almost handed him his case.

"Thank you," said Anne, going back to the table.

"What was that all about?" asked Jack.

"It sounds like such a setup," she told him. "I only hope it sounds that way to the jury."

"How do you think it's going?"

"Not well. It's all circumstantial, and it sounds like a conspiracy, but the witnesses are all believable."

She had to do something or the prosecution was going to wind up their case and she wasn't going to have anything to counter it with. She could always put Jack on the stand, but she didn't want to do that unless she was truly desperate. He would impress a group of lawyers, but she had a feeling he would intimidate the jury.

The next witness was Steve Goodhue, the hair dresser who had wanted to do something with Anne's hair. He looked a little less like an aging beachboy today in slacks and a dark sport shirt. He went all out in his testimony trying to please Howie. He was persuasive when he told of Marissa confiding in him, partially because so many women confided in their hairdressers. Marissa had also told him about being beaten and, what was more believable, how Jack had verbally abused her and made her feel stupid. This was something Anne could believe of him.

It was damaging testimony, and she didn't know what to do to counteract it. She almost decided not to cross-examine him at all, but was afraid that doing so would add credence to his testimony.

Then she had her first good hunch. The only thing they had ever had going for them was the possibility of Marissa's being Monica Jorgensen. And if it didn't work out, she had nothing to lose.

So, on cross-examination, the first thing she asked Steve was, "Did you dye Marissa's hair?"

Steve looked surprised at the question, as though wondering how she knew. "Yes," he said.

She looked over at Jack and saw the beginnings of a smile on his face.

"What color was her hair naturally?"

"She was a natural blonde," said Steve, "which is what was so crazy. I mean, I never got a customer before who wanted to go darker."

"Was she blond when she first came to you?"

"No, it was dyed a dark brown. I begged her to let me lighten it for her, at least a few streaks, but she wanted it dark."

"Did you dye anything else for her?"

"Since you mention it, yeah. I dyed her eyelashes so that she didn't always have to wear mascara, and I even dyed her eyebrows. That was a first for me."

"Did she ever tell you why she wanted dark hair?"

"She said her boyfriend liked brunettes."

"Thank you. Thank you very much," said Anne, feeling a tremendous surge of excitement. She saw Howie looking questioningly at her, but she was pretty sure he thought she was just grabbing at straws. Well, she *was* grabbing at straws, but this just might be the right straw.

The prosecution only had one more witness, Dr. Siegel, who had performed the autopsy on the body that had been taken out of the canal. He was ponderously slow, and Anne couldn't wait for him to finish so that she could begin investigating Marissa once again.

Photographs of the body were passed among the jury. They were grisly pictures. One had to look closely to detect that the body was even human, and she knew that these pictures, even though there was no proof they were of Marissa, would be more damaging to the case than anything the coroner might have to say.

Anne asked only six questions.

"Dr. Siegel, were you able to get fingerprints from the body?"

"No."

"Was the victim's hair analyzed for dye?"

"No, we weren't asked to do that."

"Could you tell us the color of the victim's eyes?"

"I'm afraid not. They'd been plucked out."

"What about the teeth?"

Dr. Siegel shook his head. "We had no dental records from Ms. Jarlan with which to compare them."

"So, Doctor, all you are going by is the fact that both the victim and Marissa Jarlan were female and had dark hair?"

"That is correct."

"Tell me, Doctor, how many autopsies have you done this year on bodies that have been fished out of canals?"

"Probably two dozen."

"Thank you, Doctor." She allowed herself to smile at Jack as she walked back to the table.

"The prosecution rests, Your Honor," said Howie.

Anne stood and made a motion for a directed verdict of acquittal—a request that the judge terminate the trial, declaring that there was not enough evidence for a reasonable jury to convict.

The request was denied, as she knew it would be, and the judge asked her, since it was almost four o'clock, whether she'd prefer to adjourn for the day and begin the defense in the morning. Anne said yes, and court was adjourned.

She signaled to Bolivia, calling her up to the front of the courtroom.

"That was great about the hair," said Bolivia.

"It was just a hunch. Listen, get hold of Sandy, and both of you meet us at Jack's house. I've got about ten million things that have to be done before tomorrow morning."

"Hey, I've got to file my story."

"This is more important than your story," said Anne. "Stick with me and you'll have a better story."

Bolivia looked at Jack. "Do I get an exclusive interview with you when this is over?"

"Don't bother him now, Bolivia," said Anne.

"It's all right," said Jack. "Yes, you'll get an exclusive interview," he told her. "It would be a pleasure."

"I'll call her right away," said Bolivia.

Anne turned to Jack. "Call Guy and ask him to send the investigators over, too. We're going to need all the help we can get."

Jack was already heading for the phones when Howie walked over to her. "What's this with the hair?" he asked her. "You gonna try to say that he was justified in killing her because she was a natural blonde and she deprived him of that?"

"You'll see tomorrow, Howie."

"I can't wait. Face it, Annie, you don't have a defense. It's not too late to do a little plea bargaining, you know. Not that I don't think I can win, but out of deference to the professor. He was my favorite teacher."

"You're kidding!"

"Not at all. I thought he was great."

Which only went to reinforce her notion that something was definitely wrong with Howie.

"Marissa Jarlan has got to be Monica Jorgensen," said Anne. "A completely changed Monica who even her mother wouldn't recognize. I just realized—even the initials are the same."

"That was brilliant," said Bolivia, "asking the hairdresser if he ever dyed her hair. How did you think of that?"

"I don't know," said Anne. "It was just a hunch. It came to me. I really expected him to answer no, but I was desperate to try anything at that point. The dumb part is, I should've thought of it before."

"It wasn't dumb," said Jack. "Her mother was emphatic that the picture wasn't her daughter. How do you argue with a mother? If she doesn't recognize her, who could? Anyway, you're forgetting one minor detail. Marissa has brown eyes, and as far as I know, you can't dye eyes."

"No, but you can get tinted contacts," said Bolivia. "Although I never heard of anyone getting them in brown."

Anne nodded to Ted, one of the investigators. "Ted, would you mind calling around to different opticians? Find out if they carry brown contacts."

Ted was about to leave the room when Sandy said, "You've got to start thinking like a cop, Annie. Don't just have him ask if they carry them. If they don't carry them, find out if they can be specially ordered, and, if so, if anyone has done so."

Ted grinned at her. "I would've asked that anyway."

"We're going to need the mother's testimony," said Anne. "It's crucial. And we're going to have to get it before tomorrow."

"Could you get a delay?" asked Bolivia.

Anne shook her head. "I doubt it. Anyway, with a little luck, maybe we can wrap this up tonight."

"If you want the mother's testimony," said Sandy, "I have an idea. Why don't I get the police sketch artist over here? He can draw a picture from Marissa's photo and give her blond hair and blue eyes. Maybe glasses. Then, if she still doesn't recognize her, I'd say we're following the wrong leads."

"I know they're one and the same," said Anne. "It all fits. Even the tanning machine. I think I can understand the mother not recognizing her. If I changed my skin color and hair color and the color of my eyes, maybe cut off my hair. I'm not sure my mother would recognize me if she hadn't seen me in a few years. Particularly in a photograph. And for all we know, that photo might have been touched up."

"It wasn't touched up," said Jack. "It looked just like her."

"Well, so she got better looking as she grew up," said Anne. "Lost some weight, got rid of the glasses ... But the most convincing thing is that she's the only one with a motive, unless Jack has a past he's not sharing with us."

"You mean, was I Jack the Ripper?" he asked.

"Something like that," said Anne with a grin. It was all coming together now, and she was feeling great. If—and this was a big if—they could pull it off in time. "Sandy, get Ted off the phone and call the sketch artist. You think he'll be willing to help?"

"If he won't, I won't buy him doughnuts anymore," said Sandy, already on her way out of the room.

"So what we'll do," Anne said to Jack, "is drive down to South Kendall with the sketch and see if her mother recognizes it."

"You're forgetting one important thing," said Jack. "Even if we prove it's Monica, that doesn't mean I didn't kill her."

"We need her dental charts," said Anne. "If we can prove they don't match those of the body they're claiming is her, then I think we've proved it. They'd have no body and we'd have the motive—revenge on Monica's part.

There's no way I could lose the case with all that evidence, especially not with a jury as smart as this one seems to be."

"You know what I wonder about?" asked Jack. "Here's this young woman with this consuming hate for me. A hatred that has pretty much structured her life. What's she going to do if she doesn't succeed in getting her revenge on me?"

"Maybe just having you arrested for her murder and tried will be enough," said Anne. "It's a pretty humiliating experience for a law professor to have to go through."

"Maybe you're right," said Jack. "But what if you're not? What if she does a better job of it next time?"

Looking into his face, Anne felt the ebullience of just a moment ago fade away. Jack was right. Anyone who geared her whole life to that kind of revenge had to be a little crazy.

And she was still out there. Somewhere.

Chapter 12

It was another nightmare, though Anne would have thought that with less than two hours to devote to sleep, she wouldn't have had time for a nightmare.

The jury had reached a verdict. She and Jack rushed back to the courtroom and were seated just in time to see the jury file in. She looked over at the jury box in an effort to read the verdict on their faces, but for some reason the jurors were all in shadow. She squinted, she leaned her head forward, she even stood to get a better look, but, while she could see their bodies quite clearly, their faces seemed to be invisible.

She began to panic, turning to Jack to ask if he could see them, and she saw something even more frightening. Where Jack's face should have been there was, in its place, a skeletal head. There was no hair, no flesh, no discernible features and only cavernous holes where there should have been eyes.

She started to scream then, and she was still screaming when she turned once again to look at the jury and clearly saw their faces this time. And each face, every single one, was the face of Marissa.

The shock brought her fully awake, and the horror of the dream lasted until she looked at her clock radio and saw, with even greater horror than the dream had provoked, that it was due to go off in a scant ten minutes, and it seemed as though she had only just gone to bed.

She sat up, because if she didn't, she was in danger of going back to sleep again and sleeping right through the rock music that was due to burst forth from the radio any minute. As far as she was concerned, she had just gone to bed. Two hours constituted a nap, not a night's sleep. It was going to be one of the most important days in one of the most important trials of her life, and she felt very close to the edge of death.

A quick trip to the bathroom told her that she also looked on the edge of death. Wearing her makeup to bed was always a good way of ensuring that the face that looked back at her from the bathroom mirror the next morning would not be the first, or even the second, thing she would want to see.

She gave her face a good washing, her teeth a good brushing and then got into the shower for a long, hot ten minutes of soaking. Then, one towel around her waist and another around her head, she went out to the kitchen and downed three successive cups of coffee and hoped that the caffeine plus the loud rock music that was now blaring forth would succeed in reviving her.

Poor Jack. He deserved better than a hung-over lawyer today. From sleep, not from booze, but hung-over nonetheless. Of course, if Jack had had his way, she'd now be waking up in his bed, which would have been even worse, because in that case she would have gotten no sleep. But oh, how she'd been tempted.

She rubbed her head with the towel, then let her hair fall down to dry naturally. She wasn't going to put it up today, and she wasn't going to pull it back. Falling free was her best look anyway, and today she wanted to look her best. If that was possible.

She patted on a little foundation beneath her eyes to try to hide the circles. She loaded on the mascara and the eyeliner in an effort to make her eyes look fully open. She brushed on some blush and added a little pink lip gloss, and a more human face now looked back at her from the mirror.

She'd saved her best outfit for today. She knew the women on the jury enjoyed the way she dressed, and the press had always loved it. And anything she used in order to help her own self-esteem was a bonus when she had to be in the spotlight. And today she was definitely going to be in the spotlight.

She put on sheer panty hose and a silk teddy, then lifted off the plastic covering from her tan linen dress. It was sleeveless and simply cut and hit her right above the knees. She fastened a brown leather belt with a silver buckle at the waist, then took out her necklace made of large chunks of unpolished turquoise and hung it around her neck. Three silver and turquoise rings, a chunky silver watch and silver earrings completed her accessories, and she slipped into her brown leather shoes and got her turquoise jacket out of the closet. The jacket was a blazer, cut extra long, with enormous shoulder pads, so that even if she got tired and started to droop, it wasn't discernible. She debated adding one of her hats to the outfit, but decided enough was enough.

She was either going to look very well dressed for victory tonight on the news, or very well dressed for defeat. And it had damn well better be for victory, or she was going to be very sorry she hadn't taken Jack up on his offer of the night before.

There were reporters in front of Jack's house when she pulled up. She got out, posed for a couple of pictures, then hurried up the front walk. He opened the door immediately.

He looked great. He was obviously capable of surviving with less sleep than she was.

He started to step out, but she pushed him back inside and closed the door behind him.

"I'm ready," he said.

"In a minute," said Anne, throwing her arms around him and burying her head beneath his chin.

"Hey, what's this?"

"I just want to hold you for a minute, that's all."

His arms went around her, and his lips found her hair. "I have total confidence in you."

"Do you?"

"Don't you know that?"

"It's a miracle I'm going in there with any kind of a defense today."

"I had confidence even before that. If I hadn't, I would've fired you and gotten a real criminal lawyer."

She pushed herself away from his chest and looked up at him. "A *real* criminal lawyer? What's that supposed to mean?"

He started to smile. "I knew that would get a reaction. Come on, let's get going. Any more of this hugging and I'm going to drag you upstairs and the hell with the trial."

Anne straightened her jacket. "Okay, now there are reporters out there."

"They've been there for over an hour."

"I know I told you not to talk to them, but today I want you to exude confidence."

"I am confident."

"Smile at them. If they ask you how you think it's going, tell them it couldn't be going better. Look the way you want to appear in the paper tomorrow morning."

"I want to look free is how I want to look."

"And you will be."

They got to the courthouse early, and already the courtroom was packed. The TV cameras outside the building had videotaped their arrival, and inside the courtroom sketch artists went to work the minute they appeared. Anne was glad to see that Howie, who had probably gotten eight hours more sleep than she had, looked as if he had slept in the courtroom. As far as she could tell, he hadn't even changed his tie.

"Lookin' good, Annie," he said, as she walked by the prosecution table.

"I'm feeling good, too," she told him with a big smile, thinking what a talented liar she was. If lawyers weren't talented liars, though, their clients would be in even bigger trouble.

Anne hadn't seen Bolivia outside, but now she appeared and leaned over the table to whisper to Anne, "Have you heard from Sandy?"

"I hardly expect to hear from her this soon. Dentists' hours aren't that long."

"Some are," said Bolivia. "Some take you in before you go to work."

"Still, she had to go all the way down to Plantation."

"What if she doesn't get them?"

"I still think we have a dynamite defense. After all, the prosecution hasn't proved the body is Marissa."

"Still, it would be nice to have that last bit of evidence so there aren't any lingering doubts about Jack's innocence."

"I can live with a few lingering doubts," said Jack, "as long as I'm not living in a prison cell."

"I did a series on prisons once," said Bolivia. "Did you know—"

"I don't want to hear about it," said Jack.

The clerk started to call the court to order and Bolivia said, "Well, listen, good luck to both of you. And, Annie, you look absolutely smashing."

When Judge Silva asked if the defense was ready to begin, Anne stood up and told him yes. Despite the fact that she still didn't feel wide-awake, she could feel the adrenaline begin to surge. She was prepared to get Jack acquitted today or die trying. Because if she didn't get him acquitted, then the unimaginable was going to happen, and they were never going to get together. And the longer she knew him, the more she could see that they were perfect together.

Anne said, "Your Honor, I call Mitchell Quarry to the stand."

The young man winked at her as he took the stand and was sworn in.

"State your name, please," said Anne.

"Mitchell Stanton Quarry."

"And your occupation, Mr. Quarry?"

"I'm employed by the Miami Police Department as a sketch artist."

"And what—" Anne began.

Howie called from the prosecution table, "We will stipulate to Mr. Quarry's qualifications."

Anne walked to the defense table and returned to the witness with a photograph in her hand. "Mr. Quarry, have you ever seen this photograph before?"

"Yes. You showed it to me last night."

"Do you know who is pictured in the photograph?"

"Marissa Jarlan."

Anne asked that the photograph be placed into evidence, then said to Quarry, "Would you please tell the jury what we asked you to do with that photograph?"

"You asked me to draw a picture of the woman in the photograph, but changing her hair to blond and her eyes to blue, and drawing glasses on her."

"And did you do so?"

"Yes."

Anne walked back to the defense table and picked up the sketch. "Is this the sketch you made?"

"Yes," said Quarry.

Anne asked that the sketch be placed into evidence, and then turned the witness over to Howie for cross-examination.

"Not at this time, Your Honor," said Howie, "but I reserve the right to have the witness called back."

Anne looked over at the jury. They were looking confused, as well they might. There had been talk of pictures, but so far they hadn't been given a look at them. *Bear with me for a while,* Anne vowed to them silently, *and I'll soon have you coming out of your seats.* One of the female jurors was taking a good look at Anne's outfit, then caught Anne's eye and smiled.

Anne called Sally Johnson, and the woman took the stand looking years older than she had looked the first time Anne had met her. She had probably gotten even less sleep than Anne had. When they had left her, she had still been in tears but, despite her despair over her daughter, she was willing to testify in order, as she said, to right a wrong done by Monica.

"Will you state your name, please?"

"Sally Jorgensen Johnson."

"Will you tell the jury, Mrs. Johnson, about the fatal accident your first husband was involved in a little over sixteen years ago?" She backed away from the witness stand so that the jury would have a clear look at the witness.

The woman turned haunted eyes to the jury. "My husband was a heavy drinker. He would always drink and then drive, and I worried that someday he would get into a bad accident. The night in question, he was returning home, drunk, hit another car and plunged off one of the bridges in the Keys. He drowned before they could get him out of the car. The police reports showed that he was driving on the wrong side of the road and was responsible for the accident."

Anne looked around. The jury, Howie and even the judge were looking mystified.

"Mrs. Johnson, who was driving the other car in the accident?"

"Jack Quintana."

"Would you point him out for us?"

"The professor, over there," said the woman, pointing to Jack at the defense table.

"Was Jack Quintana in any way at fault?" asked Anne.

"No. In fact the police said the accident would have been much worse had he not swerved at the last minute to avoid a head-on collision."

Anne looked at the judge. "I have copies of the police reports regarding the accident, Your Honor, that I would like to place into evidence." Thanks to Sandy, who also hadn't gotten much sleep the night before.

She handed the reports to Howie, who immediately began reading them.

"Mrs. Johnson, would you tell us about your daughter?"

"Monica was seven at the time. She thought her daddy was perfect. She didn't know about his drinking."

"Did your daughter blame Jack Quintana for the accident?"

Mrs. Johnson nodded. She seemed unable to speak for a minute.

"Would you answer yes or no for the record?" Anne prompted her.

"Yes, she did. He came to visit us, he and his college friends, to tell me how sorry he was about the accident. I told him it wasn't his fault, but Monica didn't see it that way. She always blamed him for killing her daddy. She adored that man. I don't think she ever got over it."

"Did you have problems with Monica after that?"

"Yes. Nothing but problems. Problems in school, problems trying to discipline her at home. She wouldn't listen to me. She'd always preferred her daddy, and now she wouldn't listen to me."

"What happened when you remarried several years later?"

"That was when Monica was sixteen. She was furious. She thought my husband was trying to take her daddy's place. I couldn't reason with her, and she finally ran away from home. I haven't heard from her or seen her since."

"Mrs. Johnson, did Professor Quintana and I visit you and show you a picture of Marissa Jarlan?"

"Yes, you did."

"Did you recognize her as Monica?"

"No. Monica had blond hair and blue eyes. The picture you showed me didn't look at all like Monica."

"Mrs. Johnson, would you tell the jury whether you recognized the sketch we showed you last night?"

Mrs. Johnson nodded. "With the hair different, the coloring and all, and the glasses, it looked a lot like Monica. It looks like Monica would probably look now at twenty-three. I'm glad she turned out so pretty.''

Anne held up the sketch. ''Is this the sketch we showed you last night?''

''Yes.''

''Only a couple more questions, Mrs. Johnson. Did Monica wear prescription glasses?''

''Yes. She was farsighted.''

''Mrs. Johnson, did your daughter hate Professor Quintana?''

''Oh, yes. She hated him so much it was scary.''

''Did she hate him enough to plot revenge against him?''

''Objection,'' yelled Howie.

Anne decided to let it go. ''Thank you, Mrs. Johnson. We're very grateful for your testimony today.''

The judge looked at Howie who said, ''No questions.''

Anne called the manager of Vision Land to the stand. They had been lucky last night. Vision Land was located in a mall and had still been open when they called. Mr. Baum had been kind enough to agree to testify on such short notice and also to bring along the order form and a copy of the receipt.

''Mr. Baum,'' she began when the witness was sworn in, ''do you recognize this woman?'' She handed him the picture of Marissa.

''Yes. She is one of our customers.''

''Why is it that you specifically recognize her?''

''She is the only person who has ever specially ordered brown contact lenses from us.''

''And were the contact lenses prescription?''

''Yes. For farsightedness.''

Anne placed the new evidence into the record, and again Howie declined to cross-examine. In fact, he was beginning to look rather stunned.

Half the courtroom looked stunned when Polly Gordon in a sleeveless blouse that showed off her muscles, took the stand. She smiled around at the courtroom and then grinned at Anne. "Hi," she said to her.

Anne grinned back. "Would you state your name please."

"Polly Gordon."

"Your occupation, Ms. Gordon?"

"I work at the New Silhouette Health Club, specifically as a weight trainer." She flexed her right arm, and Anne could hear a little laughter.

"And could you identify this woman for us?" asked Anne, holding up the photograph of Marissa.

"Yes, that's Marissa Jarlan. She's one of our members."

"Did Marissa Jarlan train with weights?"

"No."

"Did she use the Nautilus equipment?"

"No."

"What equipment did she use, Ms. Gordon?"

"Mostly just the stationary bikes. She was a fanatic on those bikes, though."

"Did she use any other equipment?"

"She sure should have," said Polly. "I could've shown her how to really build up those muscles."

There was more laughter from the courtroom, and even the judge was smiling.

"Did she use any of the club's other facilities?"

"Oh, yeah. She used the tanning machine regularly, and she also used the sauna and whirlpool."

"Tell me, Ms. Gordon, did you ever see Marissa Jarlan in the nude?"

"Oh, sure, all the time. The health club's for women only so we're not too modest around there. I saw her in the locker room, the showers, sometimes in the sauna. Nice body, and she wasn't ashamed of it. Not much muscle tone, though, if you ask me.''

After a great burst of laughter, Judge Silva banged his gavel for order and requested that the witness try to limit her answers to a simple yes or no.

Anne continued. ''Did you ever see any bruises or other marks on Marissa Jarlan's body?''

''Never. I mean no.''

''No signs whatsoever that she might have been physically abused?''

''Her? No way. Her skin was flawless.''

Anne walked away from the witness, Howie shook his head, and amidst some general laughter, the judge called a lunch recess until one-thirty.

''You're not spelling it out for them,'' argued Jack. ''I think I ought to take the stand.''

''I'll spell it out for them in my closing address,'' said Anne. ''Anyway, the jury's smart—you've seen their faces—they don't need anything spelled out for them. And if Sandy manages to get the dental records here in time, I don't think there'll be any question in anyone's mind that you've been framed for this.''

''This whole process is scary,'' said Jack. ''What if you hadn't had that hunch yesterday, and what if we hadn't come up with all that stuff last night? You'd be up there today with no defense at all.''

''Well, this is certainly more conclusive,'' said Anne, ''but the state never had a very good case.''

''I'll bet there have been people convicted on less.''

''It works most of the time.''

"How can you eat? How can you sit there eating black-forest cake at a time like this? And with whipped cream piled on top of it, too."

"Jack, this is something you're going to have to get used to. I work hard, I play hard, I use up a lot of energy, and it consumes a lot of calories. And, as a result, I have to eat to keep up my strength."

"Are you telling me black-forest cake keeps up your strength?"

"No, but it gives me an immediate surge of energy, which I'm going to need to go back into court and end the defense with a bang."

"By bang, do you mean the dental records?"

"That's what I'm hoping."

"So what did you mean when you said I'd have to get used to it?"

"You know what I mean."

"You sure that after the case is over you're still going to be interested in me?"

"I could ask the same of you. A lot of defendants form a bond with their attorneys, but it usually doesn't last once the case is over."

"I'm forming a bond, all right."

"It's happened before, Jack."

"Not with me."

"For all you know, a relationship with me could turn out to be as unsatisfactory as the one you had with Marissa."

"Well, if that happens, I can always kill you and throw you in the canal."

"We shouldn't laugh about that."

"Why not? I'm sure she's laughing along about now."

"I wonder where she is."

"She could be in the courtroom right now in one of her disguises, and we wouldn't even know it."

That sounded even creepier to Anne than her nightmare had been.

Sandy still hadn't shown up by the time the trial had resumed for the afternoon session, so Anne called Peter Deutch to the stand. He wasn't a friendly witness, and he wouldn't say much of consequence, but she had to do something while she waited for Sandy.

He had dressed up for the occasion, and his looks were not in question, but Anne could tell from the surly set of his mouth that he wasn't going to forget he was there under duress. Which made it even more propitious when, as Peter was being sworn in, Anne saw the door at the back of the courtroom open and Sandy walk in.

She wasn't alone. With her was the coroner, and from the look on Sandy's face, Anne was about to wrap up the case in style.

"Excuse me, Your Honor," Anne said, "but I've decided I don't really want to call this witness."

"Objection," yelled out Howie.

Anne turned to look at him, surprised by the outburst.

"And your grounds for objecting?" the judge prompted him.

"I take that back," mumbled Howie. "No objection. No objection at all."

More from her sudden good mood than at any good feeling toward Howie, Anne smiled at him and was surprised to see an answering smile.

She walked back to the defense table, where Sandy was now handing something to Jack. "I guess you got it," said Anne, then held her breath in anticipation.

"You bet I got it," said Sandy, "and I've already checked it out with Dr. Siegel."

The doctor held out his hand to Anne saying, "I'd be quite willing to testify immediately and put an end to this nonsense. Hell, my daughter had the professor in law school. Got an A, too."

"Thank God for that," murmured Jack.

"Your Honor," said Anne, "I'd like to recall Dr. Siegel to the witness stand."

"You're still under oath, Doctor," the judge advised him.

"I have here," said Anne, "the dental records of Monica Jorgensen, also known as Marissa Jarlan. Would you please look at them, Doctor, and tell me whether they match the dental records of the victim in the morgue, pictures of whom have already been offered into testimony?"

The doctor took an interminable length of time perusing the dental charts. Finally, in an academic tone, he began to speak, but only the occasional word made any sense to Anne.

She looked over and saw that she was losing the jury, which didn't surprise her. Finally interrupting him she said, "Doctor, could you just try to tell us, in the simplest terms possible, whether the dental charts in any way match?"

"Absolutely not," said Dr. Siegel. "And for the court record, that means no."

Anne looked up at the judge and smiled. "Your honor, the defense rests."

As she turned back to the table several reporters were already running for the door. She saw the members of the jury smiling at her in approval and Howie conferring with the other attorneys for the prosecution.

By the time she reached her table, Howie was already on his feet and approaching the bench.

"Your Honor," said Howie, "I'd like to move to dismiss this case."

"I would think so," the judge was heard to say, motioning for Anne to approach the bench.

Sotto voce, the judge said to Howie, "In my years on the bench, I have seldom seen a more ill-managed prosecution. At best the case was purely circumstantial, at worst it publicly humiliated one of the best legal minds in common law. I only hope for your sake, Mr. Leonard, that Professor Quintana does not choose to bring a civil suit against the police department, the office of the District Attorney, et al."

The courtroom was now buzzing, and the judge banged his gavel several times. "A motion to dismiss the case has been heard and accepted. I thereby dismiss this case."

There was a sudden uproar with a lot of cheering from the law students, the noisier segment of the courtroom.

"Professor Quintana," said the judge, "it is my pleasure to tell you that you are officially discharged. Case dismissed."

As the judge rose to leave, Anne flew into Jack's arms. Then, remembering that they were, after all, in a public courtroom, she changed the personal hug to a more businesslike one, then stood aside while he was congratulated by several of his students.

Howie came over to her and said, "Don't even tell me, I know what a travesty this was. And our investigators are sure as hell going to hear about all this evidence they failed to turn up." He turned to Jack. "Professor, I really apologize. You sure didn't deserve this from me."

Anne and Bolivia and Sandy flanked Jack as they made their way out of the courthouse to the reporters waiting on the steps. They smiled for the evening news, and Jack fielded their questions with a great deal of confidence. But then, why not? He had certainly been a pro at handling students' questions.

When they were finally allowed to leave Bolivia said, "Where are we going to go to celebrate?"

Anne opened her briefcase and took out her wallet. Removing two one-hundred-dollar bills, she handed one to Bolivia and the other to Sandy.

"Hey, I don't want to get paid," said Sandy. "I wanted to help."

"This is really an insult," said Bolivia.

"It's not pay," said Anne. "You both won the bet."

"Oh, come on, we'll let you have a little champagne," said Bolivia.

"We wouldn't think of celebrating with champagne and leaving you stuck on the wagon," said Sandy.

Anne smiled sweetly. "It's not the booze I have in mind," she told them. "It's the other part—the part where I'm off men for three months. Sorry, guys, all bets are off!"

Bolivia and Sandy exchanged glances, shrugged and each gave Jack a quick hug.

"You guys have fun," said Bolivia.

"Don't worry," said Anne. "We will."

Chapter 13

When Anne pulled up into his driveway and they got out of her car, neighbors came out of some of the houses, and there was the sound of scattered applause.

"Hypocrites," muttered Jack, not even nodding to them but instead heading directly for the house.

"Maybe just concerned citizens," said Anne. Not that she would have felt any differently than he did if they had been her neighbors.

"I've lived here six years. Marissa only lived here three months, and yet they rushed to accuse me."

Seeking to lighten things Anne said, "And I'll bet in that six years you never once invited your neighbors over for a friendly drink."

Jack gave her a rueful smile. "Is that what you're supposed to do?"

"Out here in suburbia? I would imagine so."

"Maybe I'll move out of suburbia."

She didn't believe him for a minute. Not after putting all his time and work into making himself such a beautiful home. And the old Spanish splendor of the house suited him, suited the kind of scholarly, semireclusive life-style she pictured him living. Of course, that would have to change; Anne was anything but reclusive.

She headed for the kitchen as soon as Jack opened the front door. The bottle of champagne was still there, nicely chilled. She opened cupboard doors, looking for wine glasses, but all she found were a set of thick beer mugs and some small glasses suitable for orange juice. She heard the central air-conditioning kick in, and when she got to the living room, mugs and bottle in hand, she found Jack on his knees in front of the fireplace.

"What're you doing?"

"Building a fire."

"It's warm in here already."

He turned his head and smiled. "It won't be in a few minutes. I set the thermostat at sixty."

"What a lovely idea," said Anne.

"I have champagne glasses in the dining room."

"These will do."

"No, let's do it right."

Anne went into the dining room and found a large, glass-doored cabinet filled with every conceivable kind of stemware. She carried two long-stemmed crystal flutes back to the living room.

While Jack built the fire she took off her jacket and hung it on the back of a chair, then kicked off her heels. Her feet were killing her from having to stand up in court all day.

She sat down on a soft suede couch and carefully opened the bottle of champagne. By the time the cork hit the ceiling, the fire was taking hold and Jack was closing the screen in front of it.

He sat down beside her on the couch. "This seems almost criminal," he said.

"What does?"

"Most people are just getting home from work, and here we are, prepared to indulge excessively."

"I'm not planning on getting smashed."

"That isn't what I meant."

"Good," said Anne, pouring them each some champagne. "Indulging excessively in other areas is permitted, then?"

"Not only permitted, but encouraged." He raised his glass and said, "To my brilliant defense lawyer."

"Well, maybe a little brilliant," said Anne, taking a sip of champagne. It gave her an instant jolt before the warmth began to spread through her body.

"You can't be a 'little brilliant,'" Jack said.

"Let's not get into semantics."

"What shall we get into?"

"For one thing, a more comfortable position," said Anne, moving closer to him and settling in the space his arm made when it moved around her shoulders.

She finished off her champagne and was about to pour herself more when he took her glass from her and set it down on the table. She moved into the kiss with her mouth already parted, her tongue tasting his lips and her hand going to the back of his head to draw him close. She moved so that her breasts were brushing against the front of his suit jacket, hoping he would drop the "staid professor" act and start being the passionate man she was certain he was capable of being.

It seemed a little sudden for him, and he backed off. "You do know I love you," he said, being of the school of thought, she supposed, that said declarations of love were in order about now. But his eyes, which had once seemed so cold, were burning as warmly as the fire, and he didn't move away from her.

"I know you're playing with the idea," she murmured.

"Playing with the idea? Are you accusing me of toying with your affections?"

And where did he get those antiquated phrases? "You can toy with me all you want," she challenged him, moving so that she was now across his lap, the hem of her dress riding up over her thighs. *Come on, Professor,* she silently urged him. *Show me some of that passion you usually reserve for the teaching of torts.*

"Just let me say—" he began, but she silenced him with her mouth and brought up her knees so that the edge of her silk underwear was exposed. Hot breath was expelled into her mouth, and then she felt his hand on her thigh. She wiggled a little, causing his hand to move higher, then a little higher still, then paused for a moment, the flesh of his hand feeling like fire to her skin.

And then, abruptly, he removed both his hand and his mouth. "Why don't you get out of that dress before we ruin it?"

Gladly, thought Anne, as she turned a bit so that he could get at the zipper in the back. "Why don't you help me?"

His hands moved to the zipper, tugging at it for a moment before sliding it down. She reached down and pulled it over her head, revealing the silk teddy, which was all she was wearing besides panty hose. He must have been prepared for several more layers and could only stare at the spot where lace barely covered skin.

He said, "Did anyone ever tell you that you have an incredible body?"

Anne didn't think he really wanted to hear the answer to that. "Why don't you get out of that six-hundred-dollar suit?" she suggested.

"Which was five hundred too much."

"A small price to pay for your freedom."

"You'd have gotten me off even if I'd been wearing my old clothes. I don't think the way I was dressed was ever a factor."

"Are we going to sit around here arguing about the price of clothes?"

"Absolutely not!"

She moved off his lap to allow him to get up. He stripped down to his shorts, the old-fashioned, baggy kind, which came as no surprise to her. But there was nothing old-fashioned or baggy about his lean, smooth body, looking golden in the light the fire was throwing out.

He stood there uncertainly for a moment until, with a smile, she pushed the straps of her teddy off her shoulders, so that the silky, lacy, altogether frivolous concoction seemed to collapse in a heap somewhere around her waist. And then, as he moved to her, she stood up and let the teddy fall to her feet before stepping out of it. She wished she hadn't worn panty hose. It seemed anticlimactic to now have to roll them down and remove them, but the activity didn't seem to be boring him.

She held her arms out to him, but for one long moment his eyes drank in the sight of her body, before he moved with the speed of a heat-seeking missile to embrace her with a passion that had them both trembling. They sank to their knees on the rug in front of the fire, his hands moving to her breasts, her hands on his smooth chest and back, tracing patterns on his silky skin. Their lips met and locked, and all the built-up frustration threatened to explode in that moment, leaving Anne to wonder where all their previous self-discipline had come from. She closed her eyes and rolled back on the rug, reaching to pull him on top of her.

* * *

Anne fully clothed hadn't prepared him for Anne in the flesh. Her breasts were larger, her waist smaller, her thighs firmer and more muscular than he had imagined. And he had imagined her like this on more than one occasion. She was tan almost all over, and against the off-white rug, with the firelight playing patterns on her skin, she looked like a Renaissance painter's dream. Her mass of golden curls spread out from her head and there, between her legs, was a miniature mass, the same golden color, curly and slightly damp and eminently inviting. He had loved her mind before, but now he found he also adored her body.

"Tell me," he said, his voice sounding a little hoarse to his ears.

"Yes?" she murmured, smiling up at him, one hand reaching to wipe the sweat off his upper lip. She was pure temptress in that moment, and an overpowering surge of desire swept over him.

"Tell me you love me."

"I love you," she said, moving her hand behind his head and pulling his mouth down to one erect nipple. "I love you," she repeated, her other hand moving to the opening in his shorts, then seeking entrance. And as his hand moved to her golden triangle, pushing her legs apart and then invading her warm, moist, incredibly soft opening she said, "I love you, I love you, I love you, I love you...."

"Jack," she said, several minutes later. Or it could have been several hours; he'd lost track of time.

"Yes?"

"Take off those shorts. And while you're at it, bring the bottle of champagne over here."

"You want to *drink*?"

"Not exactly. I had in mind pouring it on your body and then licking it off."

Something like that would never have occurred to him, and he wondered why. She smiled at him as he stood and removed his shorts, her smile widening by the moment.

"You're pretty impressive for a law professor," she noted, blatantly staring at him. And then, in a move that had him momentarily reeling, she got up on her knees and kissed the tip of his aroused manhood.

She looked up at him, and her eyes were full of mischief. "Come on," she said, her voice hinting at laughter, "bang my gavel."

He knew he was looking shocked, even as he started to laugh. "Bang your *gavel*?"

She was laughing now, too, and reaching for him, pulled him down on top of her again.

Some Puritan streak that he hadn't even known about told him it shouldn't be this good, this utterly enjoyable. It shouldn't be pure pleasure. And yet he knew that if he spoke those thoughts aloud, she would laugh and call them nonsense.

And damned if they weren't nonsense. Why shouldn't it be this good? Why shouldn't it be the way he'd always thought it would be?

And then all thought was suspended as he lost himself in her, and from then on everything was pure sensation.

She was on her back on the rug, and he was propped on one elbow beside her.

"Do you always—" he began, but she put her fingers on his lips and shook her head.

"No critiquing, Jack. No analysis, no tearing apart, no delving deeply into it for the rule of law. If you enjoyed it, nothing else matters."

"I was just going to—"

"You're not in a classroom now."

"What do you do afterward, discuss the weather?"

"Only if it's hurricane season."

"Well I—" he began, and then a movement on the other side of the French doors caught her eye. She looked over Jack's body and there, pressed to the glass, was Marissa's face. For one shocked moment she froze, sure she was hallucinating, but then the face changed expression. She quickly looked back at Jack, trying to make it appear as though she hadn't seen the woman.

"What's the matter?" he asked.

"Don't look around and don't move, but I just saw Marissa looking in the door."

"My God, are you sure?"

"Very sure, and for all I know she's been watching us for some time. Now listen, get up slowly and don't look toward the door. Put on your pants and go out in the yard and see if you can catch her. I'm going to go out the front. We ought to be able to stop her before she can get away."

"I don't want her anywhere near you."

"Don't worry about me. I can take care of myself."

Anne got up, keeping her back to the door, and reached for Jack's jacket. It was the fastest thing to put on and would probably cover her all the way to her knees. The urge to look around to see if they were still being watched was almost overwhelming, but instead she headed slowly for the front door. Jack already had his pants on and was going to the kitchen to exit from the other back door.

When she heard his door close she opened the front door and stepped outside. Even with the fire going, it was a good ten degrees hotter outside than it had been in the air-conditioned house.

It was dusk, light enough to see, but not light enough to see clearly. She stepped onto the lawn and started to cross it, thinking she would look in the shrubbery that bordered

Jack's house to the south. If Marissa was hiding, it was the logical place.

She was almost to the shrubs and looking over them, scanning the yards of the houses between Jack's and the corner, when she saw a woman emerge from a yard farther down the street. At this distance Anne couldn't tell whether it was Marissa or not. She started running when she saw the woman get into a car parked at the curb.

Hoping no one would see her running bare legged and clad only in a man's suit jacket, Anne burst through the shrubbery and sprinted across the next two lawns. By the time she had reached the third yard, the car had started up and was already at the corner. Anne picked up speed, but by the time she got to the corner, the car had vanished.

When she got back to Jack's house, he was coming around the side. "I couldn't find her," he said.

"She drove off. I only missed her by seconds."

"Did you get the license number?"

Anne shook her head. "In this light, I couldn't even swear to the make."

"Do you think we ought to call the police?"

"I don't know. I don't think they'd get too excited about the report of a female trespasser."

"My God, I can't believe I'm at that woman's mercy. There must be something we can do." He put his arm around her and drew her back into the house. "If she'd go as far as getting me accused of murder, she'd probably go further. She might go after you."

"I wonder if she knows who I am," Anne mused.

"I'm sure she does. I'm sure she's seen pictures of us on the news. And now she knows it's more than an attorney-client relationship."

"She was watching us, Jack. I feel invaded."

"So do I. I should've pulled the shades down. I should've known better. I wasn't thinking."

Anne pressed her head to his chest. "Hey, it wasn't your fault. I don't remember giving you much time to think."

"What should we do?"

"Come home with me tonight."

"I'm not running away from this, Anne."

"Jack, we beat her today, and that must make her furious. Now I'm going to call the police and tell them to keep a watch on your house, and then we're going to get dressed and drive to my place. I think we deserve tonight together—without Marissa—and if we stay here we're going to spend the whole night waiting to see what she'll do next."

"I'll drive."

"What's the point of that?"

"If she sees your car here, she won't know we've left."

"You know," she said, "I've never seen you drive."

"Well, don't expect an adventure, the way it is when you drive. But at least you won't have to listen to any ringing phones."

"I could use something to eat."

"So could I. We'll stop on the way."

There was nowhere to sit around and talk, maybe have a cup of coffee. And so they were propped up in her bed, their desire for lovemaking shattered, because even now, in Anne's place, safe from Marissa's peeping eyes, she was still between them.

"I'm sorry about tonight," he said.

"You don't have to be sorry," she said. "I should've thought of this. Obviously, if she failed in her attempt to get you convicted for murder, her revenge isn't going to be satisfied. And now you can add jealousy to revenge. She was probably furious when she saw me with you."

"I don't think she's jealous. You don't get jealous of someone you never loved."

"I suppose not."

"Are you sure it was her?"

"She looked exactly like her picture."

"So she's still got dark hair?"

Anne nodded. "We should probably try to sleep."

"I don't think I could."

"I don't think I could, either, but why don't we turn the light out and at least give it a try. We didn't get much sleep last night, either."

She switched off the bedside lamp and snuggled down under the covers. Jack wrapped his arms around her and pulled her against his chest, his body curving naturally around hers.

"I don't usually go to bed this early," he said.

"Neither do I, but I'm making an exception for you."

"I could get used to this."

She was already getting used to it, and she wanted to tell him that, but the lack of sleep from the night before was catching up with her, and she found it took too much effort to even open her mouth. She could feel herself starting to drift off, aware of his hands now moving to cover her breasts, aware of his lips against the back of her neck, aware that any second she was going to be asleep.

The ringing of the phone shattered the silence, and he felt Anne come awake beside him. He hadn't been able to get to sleep yet, but he was sorry hers had been disturbed.

"Do you want me to answer it?" he asked her.

She mumbled something incoherent and then said, "Ignore it."

The phone kept ringing.

"It's probably one of your friends."

"In the middle of the night?"

Jack chuckled. "It's not even midnight yet."

Anne sat up and turned on the light. "It couldn't possibly be Bolivia or Sandy. In the first place, they know I'm not home, and in the second, they'd never let it ring this many times."

She picked it up on about the thirtieth ring saying "Hello" in a way to discourage future calls. She frowned at whatever she was hearing and then said, "Who is this?"

She put her hand over the receiver and looked at him. "I think it's Marissa."

Jack was about to say, "Hang up," but that wouldn't solve anything. If she knew where he was, she'd call again.

He took the phone from her and said, "What do you want, Marissa?"

"I want to talk to you, Jack."

"Go ahead."

"I need to see you in person."

"Fine. You can meet with me and my attorney tomorrow."

"Tonight."

"No, Marissa, I have no intention of meeting with you tonight."

"If you won't meet me now, I'm going to kill myself."

"Is that supposed to be a threat?"

"I mean it."

"Then go ahead," he said, thinking to call her bluff.

The sound of a shot being fired reverberated through the phone, paralyzing him for a moment.

"My God, Jack, what was that?" asked Anne, her eyes getting big.

"Marissa," Jack said.

There was silence at the other end, but he hadn't heard the phone drop.

"Marissa, listen to me. Put the gun down and don't do anything stupid. This isn't worth dying over."

He heard the sound of crying then. "You killed my daddy." It was the voice of a child.

"I didn't kill him, Marissa. He was drunk, and he caused the accident."

"My name is Monica, and the next one is aimed at my temple."

"Don't do it, Monica. Put the gun down and listen to me."

"Meet me, Jack, and tell me the truth about the accident. If you do, I'll never bother you again. I swear."

"Where are you?"

"Meet me in Islamorada."

"I'm not driving all the way down there in the middle of the night."

"If you don't, I'll be dead."

He heard her hang up.

"She's got a gun?" asked Anne.

"I'm afraid so. And crazy as she is, she'll probably use it."

"Where does she want you to meet her?"

"Islamorada. It's down—"

"I know where it is," said Anne. "Why there?"

"Why anywhere?"

"She probably intends to use the gun on you."

"I'm aware of that."

Anne reached for the phone. "I'll call Sandy and Bolivia. If we get the police down there, and some reporters, she won't get a chance to do anything to us."

"Us?"

"You don't think I'm letting you drive down there alone, do you?"

"Maybe we should just unplug the phone and forget about it. I don't think she has any intention of killing herself."

"Let's get it over with. As long as she's still trying to get revenge on you, she's going to keep making chaos out of your life. Damn it, I wish I had my car."

"Forget it. The last thing I need is a death-defying drive down to the Keys."

Traffic was almost nonexistent once they got on US-1. Jack drove a little slower than she would have preferred, but he was a skilled driver and didn't get annoyed at her attempts to raise her status from passenger to copilot.

She'd been fully awake ever since hearing the gunshot and still couldn't get that sound out of her mind. She would have been devastated had she been on the receiving end of it, but Jack had remained calm throughout.

"How did you know she hadn't killed herself?" she asked him.

"It's me she's after. Killing herself wouldn't have accomplished that."

"But she's acted crazy all along. How could you be sure?"

"I just had a feeling she was there on the phone listening for my reaction. I could have been wrong, but I'm glad I wasn't."

"Poor thing. I hate what she's done to you, but what she's done to herself is so much worse. Imagine making revenge the focus of your whole life."

"I hope something can be resolved tonight. I hope she hasn't gotten us down here on some wild-goose chase, while all the time she could be back at my place, maybe burning it down."

"I wonder why Islamorada? It seems strange she'd drive all the way down there."

"Everything she's done seems strange."

The first sign that anyone else was still up were the lights in Key Largo. A couple of cars joined them on the highway there, but soon turned off, leaving them the lone car on the road again.

"Maybe we should've called her mother," said Anne.

"What for? The last thing that woman needs is more grief."

Anne opened the window on her side and turned off the air-conditioning. There was the smell of salt water and fish, and the darker smell of rotting mangroves. They passed through Tavernier, heading for Plantation Key, and after that would be Islamorada. It seemed strange that the last time she'd been there she had just given up men, and now here she was with a man.

"I love you, Jack," she said.

"Why are you telling me that now?"

"Just in case."

"Nothing's going to happen, Anne. The police may have spotted my car already."

"I haven't seen any police."

"That doesn't mean they're not there."

"You've got more confidence in them than I do."

"Even if they're not, Islamorada is always full of people. We'll head right for the bar, and if she's not willing to see us there, that's too bad. Anyway, she said she wanted to talk."

"It's hard to trust people who say they want to talk and then bring along a gun."

"I wonder where she got it."

"Are you kidding? All she had to do was walk into any store."

"Do you have a gun?"

"Are you crazy? Why, do you?"

"Of course not, but right now maybe it wouldn't be a bad idea."

"It's never a good idea."

"Not for me—but if anything happened to you . . ."

"Nothing's going to, Jack," she said, and then found herself squinting at the bright light that hit her eyes. Someone was coming from the other direction with their brights on.

It didn't seem to be bothering Jack. "It's strange," he was saying, "but this is the very spot where Marissa's father—"

"Jack, watch out!" The car was now moving into their lane, heading right for them. They were on a bridge with nowhere to turn off, and Anne found herself instinctively covering her face with her arms, certain they were seconds away from a head-on collision.

She felt Jack turn the wheel and waited for the crash. Instead, the car screeched to a stop.

Anne uncovered her face. "What happened?"

He was already opening the door. "Stay here. Her car went over the bridge, and I'm going in after her."

"No, Jack!"

"I've got to. She's terrified of the water."

She fumbled to unfasten the seat belt, then wasted a few more seconds trying to find the door handle. By the time she was out, he was already diving off the bridge, and Anne looked down in time to see a car slowly sinking beneath the water.

He was a better person than she was. If someone had just tried to kill her in a head-on collision, she would have let the person drown. And if Jack wasn't okay, she'd personally dive down there and make sure Marissa was dead.

She heard a siren in the distance. Moments later, a Monroe County Sheriff's car was pulling up beside theirs. Anne didn't go to meet it, too intent on watching for Jack to reappear.

When he did, holding Marissa's head above the water, she sank against the railing in relief. She looked around and saw the cops standing beside Jack's car.

"Hey," she yelled at them, "will you get over here? There're two people in the water, and they need some help!"

The story made all the papers, with an exclusive by Bolivia. Marissa/Monica had gone over the edge into insanity by the time the police had gotten them safely out of the water. By then Marissa was calling Jack "Daddy" and clinging to him, and the police had to use force to restrain her.

Jack hadn't pressed any charges. What she needed was psychiatric help, and with the help of her mother and stepfather, she was going to get it.

Jack was back teaching and was something of a hero on campus. Bolivia had gotten a raise as a result of her exclusive. Sandy hadn't been promoted, but she was dating the police sketch artist.

As for Anne, she finally furnished her apartment. Not because she felt any need of furniture, but because she wanted to rent it out. And, fully furnished, she had not only rented it immediately, but she was making a nice profit.

As Jack had said, "We don't need two places, you're moving in with me."

He hadn't gotten an argument from her over that.

* * * * *

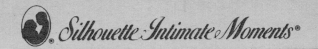
Silhouette Intimate Moments®

COMING
NEXT MONTH

#329 BETRAYED—Beverly Sommers

Journalist Bolivia Smith, assigned to investigate strange goings-on in the jungle outside Miami, is taken prisoner by a mysterious war-gamer named Tooley. Determined to get the exclusive story, Bolivia is willing to risk her life—but is she also willing to jeopardize their love?

#330 NEVER SAY GOODBYE—
Suzanne Carey

What begins as a marriage of convenience for the American Katya Dane and KGB agent Nikolai Dvorov becomes a union of love. Four years later, after a forced separation, they are reunited amidst a brewing controversy to find their passion as powerful as ever. Will loyalty to their countries again divide them, or will love prevail—now that they have a son?

#331 EMMA'S WAR—Lucy Hamilton

Lady Emma Campbell is assigned to work with cynical State Department agent Tyler Davis, to help a Romanian diplomat defect. Caught in a web of suspicion and deceit, they must fight not only for the diplomat's freedom, but to save themselves—and their growing love.

#332 DANGER IN PARADISE—
Barbara Faith

Troubleshooter Matt McKay was almost certain that beautiful Ariel Winston would lead him straight to her stepfather and the missing millions. But others were after the money, too, and soon their Mexican paradise became a jungle of danger...and desire.

AVAILABLE THIS MONTH:

A celebration of motherhood by three of your favorite authors!

Birds Bees and Babies

JENNIFER GREENE
KAREN KEAST
EMILIE RICHARDS

This May, expect something wonderful from Silhouette Books — BIRDS, BEES AND BABIES — a collection of three heartwarming stories bundled into one very special book.

It's a lullaby of love . . . dedicated to the romance of motherhood.

Look for BIRDS, BEES AND BABIES in May at your favorite retail outlet.

BBB-1

You'll flip . . . your pages won't!
Read paperbacks *hands-free* with

Book Mate・I

The perfect "mate" for all your romance paperbacks

**Traveling • Vacationing • At Work • In Bed • Studying
• Cooking • Eating**

Perfect size for all standard paperbacks, this wonderful invention makes reading a pure pleasure! Ingenious design holds paperback books OPEN and FLAT so even wind can't ruffle pages — leaves your hands free to do other things. Reinforced, wipe-clean vinyl-covered holder flexes to let you turn pages without undoing the strap . . . supports paperbacks so well, they have the strength of hardcovers!

Pages turn WITHOUT opening the strap.

SEE-THROUGH STRAP

Reinforced back stays flat.

Built in bookmark

BOOK MARK

BACK COVER HOLDING STRIP

10" x 7¼", opened.
Snaps closed for easy carrying, too.